"Wait." He clambered to unsteady feet. Courage and fear were so carefully balanced in her now that he could crush her in an instant. He didn't want that much power over her. He wondered what she would do if she realized how much power she wielded over him. Hesitantly he placed a hand on her shoulder, searching for words to bridge the chasm he had opened between them. "Diana."

She gazed up at him, her beautiful eyes shimmering with tears. Sunlight washed over her face and lit her hair to fire. And he knew, there were no words, and bent his head to touch his lips to hers. . . .

By Lynn Kerstan
Published by Fawcett Books:

FRANCESCA'S RAKE
A MIDNIGHT CLEAR
CELIA'S GRAND PASSION
LUCY IN DISGUISE
MARRY IN HASTE

MARRY IN HASTE

Lynn Kerstan

FAWCETT CREST • NEW YORK

A Fawcett Crest Book
Published by The Ballantine Publishing Group
Copyright © 1998 by Lynn Kerstan Horobetz

http://www.randomhouse.com

Library of Congress Catalog Card Number: 98-92934

ISBN 0-449-00185-7

Manufactured in the United States of America

First Edition: October 1998

10 9 8 7 6 5 4 3 2 1

For Marian Jones, teacher and friend

Chapter 1

Diana dreamed of a spider made of glass.

She tossed in a restless half sleep, tears burning her eyes as she watched it creep toward her.

She had dreamed this dream before, and the ending was always the same. The spider—

A crack of thunder made her shoot upright on the bed. Heart pounding, she pushed away the lingering nightmare and drew in a long, steadying breath.

All around her, the old house shuddered against the fierce spring storm. Wind moaned over the chimney pots and howled past the windows, most of them badly fitted in their casements. As Lord Kendal had informed her, Lakeview was in a sorry state.

But it would do for now. She sank back against the pillows and pulled the thick goose-down coverlet over her head. For a few more hours she could conceal herself and pretend she was someone else, doing all the things she had once thought Diana Evangeline Whitney would do.

A thudding noise, louder than all the others, penetrated even the thick coverlet. She sat up again, attending closely.

It came one more time, from the direction of the front door. Could someone be knocking for admittance?

Springing from the bed, she dug her feet into a pair of fleece-lined slippers and pulled a dressing gown over her night rail. In the drafty room, the taper on her night table had gone dead. She relit it from the sputtering hearth fire and sped into the passageway.

As she approached the bedchamber nearest the stairs, she heard Miss Wigglesworth's rumbling snore. Ought she to rouse her? But an elderly woman would be of little help, she decided, continuing past the room and down the stairs to the entrance hall.

Windblown snow blasted over her when she opened the door, immediately snuffing her candle. There was no one there. She took a step outside and looked around.

"Hullo?" she called. "Where are you?"

No answer. Well, she had to have a look, didn't she? She tussled with the door, fighting the wind to pull it closed, and finally stood shivering in the dark foyer with her arms clutched around her waist.

For a time she considered making herself a cup of chocolate before returning to bed. But she didn't know how to brew chocolate, and Mrs. Cleese would be displeased if she made a mess in the kitchen. The cook would not return before late afternoon, though, giving her plenty of time to put the kitchen to rights again. And she did know how to make tea, which would be a much safer proposition than chocolate.

But the uneasy feeling of being virtually alone in the house persuaded her that a hot drink would be more trouble than it was worth. Carefully picking her way across the dark entrance hall, she found the splintery banister and started up the stairs.

Thud.

She froze. There was no mistaking *that.*

It came from the kitchen, she thought, or thereabouts. Sound was distorted by Lakeview's stone walls and high ceilings, so the noise may have been the one she'd heard before—a tree slapping against the house, perhaps, or a wooden shutter come loose. The footman had done his best to repair the kitchen shutters after Mrs. Cleese complained about them, but he was no better a carpenter than Diana, who had insisted on helping him. It would be little wonder if the shutters had failed to hold.

At least she now knew where to find a hammer and nails, and she would certainly get no more sleep this night. Tea and carpentry, she resolved, turning back in the direction of the kitchen. As she came near the end of the passageway, it occurred to her that a loose shutter really ought to be banging with more . . . well, consistency. But then, what did she know of such things? Still, she proceeded cautiously to the kitchen door and stole a look inside.

The banked fire cast an eerie glow over the room. Across the way, the door to the garden was closed and barred. Wind rattled the shutters at the three windows, but they appeared to be intact. She moved to them for a closer examination, aware that her knees were trembling. Strange sounds in a strange house, that was all. Noises were to be expected in a gusty storm.

And of late, there was no denying, she took fright at the least little thing. A bird suddenly erupting from a tree caused her to jump. A stranger pausing on the road to look up at the house set her heart to thumping. One afternoon while she was walking in the hills above Lakeview, a sheep came up behind her and nuzzled at her skirts. She had actually screamed, sending the poor ewe scampering away in terror.

Feeling foolish for chasing stray sounds all over the house, she went to the hearth and held out her hands to warm them. If she really wanted tea, she would have to fire up the stove, which she had seen done. Or she could unbank the hearth fire and hang the kettle over it. Or—she could simply go back to bed. More and more, that seemed the better choice.

With a sigh, she looked at the pots and pans suspended from hooks on either side of the fireplace. She couldn't have said what half of them were used for. In all her life she had never so much as boiled an egg, and if she wanted an egg at this moment, she had no idea where they were kept. She ought to—

A noise, one she could never mistake, sent her to her knees on the flagstones.

Splintering glass. From close by. The next room over. Someone was breaking into the house!

Jumping to her feet, she seized a cast-iron skillet from the wall and crept to the door that led from the kitchen to the breakfast room. Little light reached from the hearth, and she was able to distinguish only the outlines of chairs, the dining table, and a bulky sideboard.

She looked to her left, to the window at the far end of the room, and saw a large shape loom up against the background of falling snow. With only seconds to make a decision, she wavered between flight and attack. Every instinct clamored for her to run, but where could she hide? Who would protect Miss Wigglesworth? And what if it was only a refugee from the storm in search of shelter?

Even as the questions roiled in her head, she edged in the direction of the window until she was standing with her back against the wall, skillet raised to strike.

The intruder swiped at shards of glass protruding from the windowpane, using something that looked very much like a rifle butt. It might have been only a length of wood, but she was taking no chances.

Well, perhaps *one* chance. How could she assault someone who might be perfectly harmless? She was about to demand that the man identify himself when he lunged inside.

Of its own accord, her arm swung the skillet at his head.

He must have sensed the attack coming, but he spun away too late. The skillet struck a glancing blow, and he dropped at her feet like a stone.

For a long moment, she stood frozen in horror at what she had done. The man lay on his stomach, arms bent at the elbow and stretched over his head. A dark greatcoat was twisted around his body and legs. The muzzle of his rifle had landed atop her right foot.

She sucked in several deep breaths before gathering sufficient wits to pick up the gun. Darting back into the kitchen, she hid the rifle in the pantry and lit one of the storm lanterns set alongside the hearth. Skillet in one hand and lantern in the other, she stole again to the morning room and lowered herself to one knee beside the fallen man.

A knit woolen cap had been knocked askew by her blow, revealing strands of overlong black hair. His face was shadowed by a dark beard about half an inch long. She had never before seen a ruffian, but she supposed this was how a ruffian would look. He was very large, at least six feet tall if he were standing, and the leg protruding from his greatcoat was heavily muscled.

Heart racing, she set down the lantern and pressed her fingers to his throat. His flesh was cold, and she detected no pulse. Had she *killed* him?

The skillet fell from her hand, clattering against the oakwood floor.

At the sound, he stirred. The one eye she could see flickered open as he raised his head to look at her. "Who the devil are you?" he asked blearily.

She slid her hand under his chin just before it fell again. Alive, thank heavens. Now unconscious—possibly. He might be dissembling.

Despite the icy wind whistling through the broken window, perspiration streaked her brow and the back of her neck. Lucy would know what to do, of course, but Lucy wasn't here.

The man's bristled cheek lay against her hand, warming from the heat of her body. She pulled off the knit cap and ran the fingers of her other hand across his forehead until she encountered a swollen lump. Blood trickled down his temple. Gently she lowered his head to the floor and stood, gazing down at him while panic swept over her.

She held her ground until it subsided. And when the panic was gone, she was left cold and oddly detached. He seemed a long distance away now, less a man than a problem to be dealt with. All to the good. So long as she felt nothing, she found herself able to think.

Miss Wigglesworth first. With a last look at the prone, motionless figure on the floor, she turned and sped out of the breakfast room and down the passageway and up the stairs.

Wilberta Wigglesworth slept like the dead. Diana had to shake her to get any response, and then the elderly woman jolted up with a start and gazed around in confusion. When her eyes focused on Diana's face, she came immediately alert. "What is it, my dear?"

"Come with me," Diana said, tugging a blanket from the bed. "Wrap this over your shoulders. I'll tell you what happened on the way."

The man was sitting up when they came into the breakfast room, clutching his arms around his sides against the cold.

He looked dazed, Diana thought, but no less dangerous. He was large, clearly strong, and he had been carrying a gun. She mustn't forget that in her relief to see him still alive and capable of pulling himself this far from the floor.

Miss Wigglesworth made a clucking sound and hurried to

drape her blanket over him. "Lost in the storm, were you? Bad night to be out. You should have known better."

He raised his head, blood already thickly caked on his cheek. "What hit me?"

Diana stepped forward. "I did."

He put a hand against the lump above his temple. "A *child* brought me down?"

"A frying pan, sir. Why were you breaking into our house?"

He swayed forward.

Miss Wigglesworth dropped to her knees and held him up. "Water and a towel, Diana."

When she returned with a basin of cold water and several clean towels, the man was stretched on his back with his head on Miss Wigglesworth's lap.

He gave Diana an unfocused look. "If you want me alive, Madam Fury, why the deuce did you try to kill me?"

She knelt beside him and began to dab a wet cloth at the blood on his cheek. "I'm not altogether sure I want you alive, sir. You are proving to be a dratted nuisance. And I never tried to kill you. I meant only to stop you." She turned worried eyes to Miss Wigglesworth.

"Scalp wounds bleed more than most," Miss Wigglesworth assured her. "You can't have hit him terribly hard, or he'd not be awake and talking nonsense."

His teeth began to chatter, and soon he was shivering uncontrollably.

"I believe we should see him warm before tending to his head," Diana said, setting aside the towel. "Are you able to crawl into the kitchen, sir? It's only a short distance."

"C-crawl?" His eyes flashed. "I think not. Help me to my feet."

"It would be best," Miss Wigglesworth said, "to get him upstairs. The kitchen fire can be built up, of course, but the stone floor is prodigiously cold."

"I'll make a pallet on the table," Diana suggested. "He can climb up there."

"Stop t-talking about me as if I wasn't here!" He sat up, reached for one of the wooden chairs, and used it to pull himself

6

to his knees. A few moments later, he managed to stagger to his feet. "Where the devil are we going?"

Even in the flickering lantern light, his face was ominously white. He swayed, and looked about to topple over.

Diana rose swiftly and slipped her arm around his waist. "If you care to try, sir, I'll help you to one of the bedchambers. Or you can—"

"Let's get on with it then." He steadied, one hand propped on the chairback for support. "Don't attempt to support my weight, madam. Should I fall, I'd bring you down with me."

"I won't let you fall," she told him, not at all sure she could keep that promise. "And it would be no more than I deserve if you were to land atop me."

"A not unpleasant prospect," he said with a flash of white teeth.

"Come along," Miss Wigglesworth said briskly, taking the lantern and leading them into the passageway.

Diana kept hold of his waist, more to secure his balance than to keep him upright. He was wet clear through to the skin, and cold as a block of ice. She sensed the effort it was costing him to continue moving, step by slow step, but he never faltered. He was definitely weakening, though, and she began to wonder if he could make it up the long flight of stairs.

He did, using the banister to pull himself up. Once his foot caught on a step and he nearly tumbled over backward. She held on to him with all her strength until he righted himself, and then they went on.

"In here," Miss Wigglesworth said when they reached the landing. "We'll put him in my bed."

"It's far too small," Diana objected. "His feet would hang over the end."

"Never mind his feet. Your room is at the far end of the house. He won't make it."

"Dammit," he swore, breathing heavily. "This is one hell of a time for a debate."

"Come, sir." Diana towed him along the passageway.

He made it to her bedchamber, but not by much, and fell onto the bed face-first with a groan. At least he had stopped shivering, Diana thought. The exertion had gone a long way to warming him up. But his strength had run out, and it was all she could do to strip off his soaked greatcoat while Miss Wigglesworth helped her lift his arms and roll him from side to side. There was no point trying to remove his boots, she decided. He was virtually a deadweight now, and would simply have to stay in his wet clothes.

After a considerable struggle, they got him onto his back with his head on the pillows and piled blankets and the down coverlet on top of him. By then he was unconscious or asleep—she didn't know which—but his pulse was strong and he was breathing easily. She allowed herself to hope he would survive the attack, even if he had come to the house bent on robbing it and murdering the inhabitants.

While Miss Wigglesworth built the fire to a roaring blaze, Diana examined the wound on his head. It had stopped bleeding, thank heavens, but dried blood covered the right side of his face. Fearing that she would reopen the cut if she tried to clean him up, she left him be.

"You have got wet from holding him," Miss Wigglesworth said, touching her on the arm. "Change into dry nightclothes, my dear, and go to bed in my room. I'll sit up with him."

"I will change," Diana agreed, "but it would be impossible to sleep. Could I persuade you to make some tea, Miss Wigglesworth? I'm feeling a bit shaky at the moment. Then you can return to your bed."

"I'll bring up the tea, yes, and we'll keep watch together." On her way out of the room, Miss Wigglesworth paused for a moment to study the man's face. "He has a familiar look about him, although I am quite certain I have never seen him before. I wonder who he could be."

Chapter 2

Pale light crept over the sky as Diana made her way down the sweeping hill to the road. Like the countryside, it was still covered with pristine, ankle-deep snow. No one had passed this way since the storm, which had blown out three hours earlier. A light breeze ruffled the fur lining of her hood.

Just beyond the road, Coniston Water lay smooth as glass, its color a deep pewter gray. On the hills behind the house, bare tree branches were mantled with snow. Everything was still. Hushed. The vapor of her breath wafted like white smoke in the cold air.

Mr. Beadle would be along soon. Whatever the weather, he never failed to pass by shortly after dawn. She had met him soon after taking up residence at Lakeview. Word of her arrival had spread quickly, and visitors avid to meet the new tenants soon began to call. Mrs. Alcorn, wife of the local squire, had fluttered and clucked to see the shabby condition of the parlor.

"Is all the house in such decay, Miss Whitney? I declare, two gentlewomen such as yourself and Miss Wigglesworth must not be permitted to live in such a fashion!"

Helpless under the assault of so formidable a woman, Diana found herself giving Mrs. Alcorn a tour from attics to cellar. There was no hiding the smoky chimneys, the peeling wall coverings, the drafty windows.

"Mr. Beadle is the man you need," Mrs. Alcorn had declared with authority. "He is a man of many trades, and whatever you require, he will provide it for a remarkably small fee. Mind you, he does not speak. Some say he cannot speak, but I heard from Mrs. Corbel, whose uncle was at school with him, that he'd a terrible stammer as a boy and was so bedeviled for it that one day he simply stopped speaking and has never spoken since. I shall have him call on you first thing tomorrow."

And so he had done. Diana, expecting a strapping young fellow, was surprised to see on her doorstep a short, narrow-faced man of at least threescore years. Everything about him was scruffy, from his worn boots to his droopy felt hat. She soon discovered he invariably wore that hat, indoors and out.

Mr. Beadle handed her a piece of paper where he had inscribed his offer and the terms. He would spend two entire days on the most urgent repairs, and thereafter come by three afternoons a week until his services were no longer needed. He asked a painfully small fee, reimbursement for supplies, freedom to keep any leftover materials, and one meal a day.

Unable to imagine what such an unimposing little man could accomplish, she had agreed to employ him. And she very quickly learned that Mr. Beadle's small body concealed wiry strength and remarkable endurance. He was, moreover, a gentle, comforting presence around the house. She felt less lonely simply knowing he was there.

Diana stomped about in the snow to stay warm. If not for the townsfolk who continued to drop in uninvited, she might have considered staying at Lakeview until her birthday. But Lord Kendal would never permit it, she supposed. He was displeased with her as it was, and would sweep her back to his estate when his houseguests took their leave.

A dark splotch appeared in the distance, moving slowly along the road, and soon Diana could make out the familiar shape of Mr. Beadle's pony cart. When he reined the gray nag to a halt directly in front of her, she rushed to his side.

"Good morning, Mr. Beadle. Forgive me for being abrupt, but I must beg a favor of you. A stranger became lost in the storm last night and sought refuge at the house. He has sustained an injury to his head. Will you stop by Mr. Crackett's house and ask him to come here as soon as may be?"

Mr. Beadle's weathered face scrunched into a worried frown. He sketched a question mark in the air with a knit-gloved forefinger.

She had learned to read some of his own peculiar language, made up of posture, facial expressions, and hand gestures. "The gentleman does not appear badly hurt," Diana assured him with more confidence than she felt. "But Mr. Crackett will be a better judge."

Mr. Beadle nodded and made a sign that meant *quickly.*

"Yes. Thank you. And I brought you some bread and ham." She handed him the small parcel. "The gentleman arrived on horseback, but we've no hay. Will you secure some, and oats as well, and deliver them here on your way back? Here's money for the purchase."

He accepted the coins and raised a brow.

"No, nothing more. Unless you think of something I've forgot. And do tell Mr. Crackett to hurry."

Touching the brim of his hat in a salute, Mr. Beadle snapped the reins against Old Molly's backside. The nag swerved her head to give him a look of astonishment before proceeding with unaccustomed briskness along the snowy road to Coniston.

Thank heavens for Mr. Beadle, Diana thought as she made her way back up the hill. He asked no useless questions and simply did what had to be done. She had not been altogether honest with him, but there was no reason to mention that the gentleman had tossed and turned in bed, mumbling indistinguishable words in the throes of what she expected were terrible nightmares. She had sat with him until shortly before dawn, when she left to dress herself and come down to the road.

Guilt continued to rake at her conscience. Had he not jerked away in time, he'd have required a coroner instead of an apothecary. What had possessed her to attack him in such a way? In general, she could not bring herself to swat a fly.

She still didn't know if the stranger was a housebreaker or a perfectly innocent man caught by the storm. She had studied his face while she sat beside the bed, the shadows marking out the hollows in his cheeks and the small lines at the corners of his eyes.

In his restless sleep, he appeared more exhausted than wicked. His nightmares had roused her sympathy, for she rarely passed a night without bad dreams. And then his startling good looks, which she had scarcely noticed until her toes started to curl for no apparent reason, drew her attention and held it for longer than was proper.

Even handsome men can be villains, she reminded herself.

She felt his presence the moment she stepped into the house. And sure enough, she soon spotted his tall straight figure at the head of the stairs, his hand wrapped around the newel post.

"Sir! You should be in your bed."

"Nonsense." He set out, not rapidly, down the steps. "And you needn't dash for cover, madam. I am perfectly harmless."

She forced herself to hold her ground. "Where is Miss Wigglesworth?"

"When I left, asleep in a chair. She snores like a sailor." He stopped a short distance away, towering a head above her, his shaggy hair and whiskers giving him a decidedly menacing appearance. "Is there coffee to be had?"

"Only tea, I'm afraid." Her voice squeaked perceptibly. "Do you mind taking it in the kitchen?"

He followed her down the passageway, going directly to the trestle table when they reached the kitchen. Atop it was a large cast-iron skillet. He eyed it sharply. "Is this what you clubbed me with last night?"

She nodded.

Hefting it in his hand, he whistled softly.

She turned her back to him, concealing her trembling hands, and removed her cloak. "I am most frightfully sorry, sir."

"And well you should be. When you take up a weapon, madam, have the bottom to use it properly. I might have been a cutthroat."

"I supposed that you were." She glanced over her shoulder. "And how do I know that you are not?"

"You don't. Two more muttonheaded females I have yet to meet. One thinks nothing of taking a snooze when she is supposed to be standing the watch, and the other waltzes me into the kitchen and all but puts her own weapon of choice into my hands."

Flushing hotly, Diana went to the stove. "If you mean to throttle me, sir, please get on about it. Otherwise, I shall brew the tea." She heard a sharp crack of laughter and looked up in time to see him wince.

"I've the devil of a headache," he confessed, "and a lump the

12

size of a pineapple. Providentially, the men in my family have skulls of steel."

"I'm sorry for striking you," she said, misery knotting her stomach. "I ought to have asked beforehand why you were breaking into the house."

"Oh, by all means. Do clarify whether a housebreaker is bent on robbing you, ravishing you, or murdering you in your bed before deciding whether or not to bludgeon him. You require a keeper, madam. Is there no man in residence?"

"Only you, at the moment."

"Excellent." He scowled. "Reassure me that I can get on about my nefarious business unimpeded. Are you an absolute goose-wit, young woman?"

"It would seem so." She went to the pantry and returned with a canister, rather expecting him to renew his lecture. But he sat quietly, one elbow propped on the table and his chin buried in his hand, watching her every move.

Unnerved by his steady gaze, she fumbled with the spoon and dropped as many tea leaves on the floor as made it into the pot. Then she lost count and was forced to dump the leaves back into the canister and begin measuring again. One. Two. Three. The pulse pounded in her ears.

He appeared at her shoulder, holding the steaming kettle. "You're shaking," he said. "Stand aside." He poured hot water into the teapot and returned the kettle to the stove.

For such a large man, he moved like fog. "Th-thank you," she said.

He made a noise that sounded like disgust and went back to sit at the table.

She tried to pretend he wasn't there, but she could as easily have ignored a panther. He terrified her, but she didn't precisely fear him. If he meant to do her harm, he would surely have got on about it by now. She laid out cups, saucers, spoons, and a cone of sugar while he continued to stare at her, so intently he might as well have been touching her.

He was, of course, looking at the scar. What else could hold his attention to such a degree?

The scar was the only thing people ever looked at, before turning their eyes away and deliberately *not* looking at it. But their gazes inevitably strayed back. He at least had the grace to regard her openly. Not once had his eyes shifted, as others' eyes so often did, vacillating between curiosity and repugnance.

"Before coming through the window," he said, "I pounded on the front door."

"That was what brought me downstairs. But there was no one there, so I decided I had been mistaken. Then I heard glass breaking, so I grabbed up the skillet and . . . well, you know the rest. I'm sorry."

"If you say that to me one more time, madam, I may yet throttle you. There will be no more apologies. Understood?"

"Yes, sir." She busied herself straining tea into the cups.

"At the time," he said, scraping sugar from the cone, "I thought this to be *my* house. Last I heard, it was standing empty. But I haven't set foot in this area for half a dozen years, and with snow blinding me, I could not be certain. Still, there were no lights at any of the windows, and when no one came to the door, I was sure I had the right place."

"I see. Well, as to the dark windows, we keep fires only in the kitchen and in our bedchambers." She brought a tin of almond biscuits to the table. "This house is in need of repair, I'm afraid. Most of the rooms are drafty, so we purchased exceptionally heavy curtains for the few rooms we are using."

He waved a hand. "Do sit, madam, and drink your tea."

She perched on the edge of the bench across from him, wishing he would stop looking at her in such a way. If only she'd thought to put on one of her veiled bonnets before going outside, she would be wearing it now.

"I left a horse in the stable," he said after an eternally long silence.

"Yes." She felt relief to have something to say. "We'll see he is cared for."

"Unfortunate nag. A job horse I hired in Liverpool, not at all suited for this terrain. He must be wondering how he got himself assigned to the Forlorn Hope."

"Whatever is that?"

"The name given to troops at the head of a charge, or the first to be thrown at the wall of a city under attack. Most all of them die."

"Oh." She tasted the words on her tongue without speaking them aloud. *Forlorn Hope.*

"Earlier," he said, "I told you I had come to the wrong house. That was, indeed, my first impression. But this one is laid out just as I remember."

She dropped the spoon she had been holding. Oh, please, don't let it be *him!*

"Why does that trouble you?" He leaned forward, frowning. "Are you not supposed to be here?"

Heart in her throat, she had to push the words out. "C-Colonel Valliant?"

His dark eyebrows flew up. "The same. So this *is* my house. Well, I have retained a few of my wits, it seems. Are you a new tenant?"

"Oh dear."

"Young woman, I assure you this changes nothing, except that I won't be forced to wander about Coniston Water this morning in search of my residence. And if you are concerned that I mean to evict you, rest easy. I came here for no very good reason and can as swiftly remove myself. The terms of your lease will be honored."

Diana was barely heeding his words. The horror of what she'd done, or nearly done, assailed her. Paralyzed with remorse, she could only gaze helplessly at her teacup.

"Well? Have you gone mute?"

"I almost killed you," she murmured.

"That subject, I believe, was closed several minutes ago. For the last time, you did what you had to do, and you did it badly."

"Thank God. If I'd d-done it better, you would be dead."

"People have been trying to kill me for years, madam. I do not take it as a personal offense. May I know your name?"

"Diana Whitney. My companion is Miss Wilberta Wigglesworth. And we are not, strictly speaking, tenants. It was our intention to stay here only a few weeks. Naturally we shall make immediate arrangements to depart."

"That won't be necessary." He reached for a biscuit. "I planned to go directly to Candale, but when I chanced to learn that my brother had a houseful of guests, I thought to wait here until they departed."

In hiding from those very same guests, she wondered why Colonel Valliant wished to avoid them as well. But she dared not ask, of course, nor could she have located the words. She felt numb from her scalp to her toenails.

"I have been long gone from England, Miss Whitney. Let me see. I was seventeen when I bought a commission in the army, and I am rising five-and-thirty now. In all that time, I came home perhaps six or seven times, never for long. So you see how it is. When I meet my brothers again after so many years, I'd prefer we not be surrounded by strangers."

Her gaze lifted to meet his. "They will take their leave within a fortnight, sir. The strangers, I mean."

"Ah." He drained his teacup and pushed it toward her for a refill. "I had been thinking you'd moved into an unoccupied house to avoid paying rent. Apparently that was a misapprehension."

She took her time straining tea into his cup. "I cannot pay rent, for at present I have no money. But Miss Wigglesworth and I are not squatters. We are here with Lord Kendal's approval, and I mean to repay him every penny spent on my behalf while I remain under his protection."

The colonel's eyes narrowed. "Under his *protection*? I had thought him to be recently married."

"Nearly three years ago, in fact. Before I made his acquaintance."

Colonel Valliant looked so disapproving that her composure fled again. What had Lord Kendal's marriage to do with her presence in this house?

"I appear to have stumbled into murky territory," he said, mauling his hair with one hand. "It's none of my business."

She had no idea what he was talking about.

"Don't tell Kendal," he said. "However innocent the circumstances, I expect he won't like to know I slept in your bed last night. That *was* your bed, I presume?"

"Such a question, young man!" Wilberta Wigglesworth bustled into the room, shaking a finger in his direction. "Mind your manners when addressing a lady."

Cheeks burning, Diana lifted a worried gaze to Colonel Valliant's face. He looked amused.

"Yes, ma'am," he said humbly.

Miss Wigglesworth advanced on him. "And the next time you exit a room where a lady is present, you will first have the kindness to wake her up and inform her of your intentions."

His lips were twitching, as if he wanted to laugh. "My most profound apologies, ma'am. I ought to have done so."

"Well, and I ought not to have dozed off when I was charged with your care. But I am six-and-seventy, so there is some excuse for me. I would have expected more sense from a man of your age. You ought to have known better than to leave your bed at all. You are pale as candle wax. And far too thin for one of your height, I am persuaded."

"Sea travel does not agree with me," he said. "I was too many months on ship from Lima to Liverpool."

"You have come all the way from Peru?" Miss Wigglesworth looked impressed. "Such an adventure. I declare myself envious."

"Unless you've a taste for weevil-ridden hardtack, I cannot think why you would."

Diana took hold of Miss Wigglesworth's sleeve. "This is Colonel Alexander Valliant, you should know. Lord Kendal's brother."

"Ah!" Miss Wigglesworth examined him more closely. "Yes, there is a resemblance. But your eyes are much darker."

"I am darker in every way, ma'am. Hair. Skin. Eyes." There was a short pause. "Temperament."

"Well, if you are who you say you are, it's as well Diana failed to dispatch you. That would have been difficult to explain. Mind you, had I been wielding the skillet, you would be presenting yourself at the Pearly Gates."

"I've no doubt of that," he agreed amiably. "But I'm fairly sure they'd not have opened for me."

"Then it seems you've been given a second chance to redeem yourself." Miss Wigglesworth glanced at Diana, who was frozen in place. "I shall deal with you later, missie. For now, Colonel Valliant, I suggest you take yourself upstairs and have a restorative sleep while we brew up a hearty soup for your luncheon."

Diana expected him to object, but he only nodded. He *did*

look ashen, despite his sun-bronzed skin, and there was pain in his eyes.

"As you say, ma'am." He stood, propping both hands on the table for several moments before letting go the support. "Damn. My head is spinning like a misfired rocket. Will one of you show me the way?"

Miss Wigglesworth looked a question at Diana.

"I'll make the soup," she said in a plaintive voice.

The fact that Diana could not so much as toast bread was not lost on Miss Wigglesworth. Clicking her tongue, she took Colonel Valliant's arm and led him from the kitchen.

When he was gone, air filled the room again. Diana felt exactly as she did after falling from her horse, all the breath knocked out of her.

Forlorn Hope.

The phrase curled in her mind like a serpent.

The least she could do was peel potatoes for the soup, she thought, rousing herself to invade the pantry. By the time Miss Wigglesworth returned, she had produced a bowl of tiny peeled potatoes and a large pile of skins with most of the potato still attached.

"Interesting man," Miss Wigglesworth said briskly. "I shouldn't like to cross him. And what did you think of him, Diana?"

She sucked at the cuts on her thumb and forefinger. "How can I say? He is . . . forceful."

"To be sure. He was uninclined to go off to sleep and quizzed me quite unmercifully. Well, no surprise he wished to know about his brothers. He'd not heard that Kit was married, or that Lord Kendal's wife is expecting her second babe." Miss Wigglesworth filled the soup kettle with water. "He was exceptionally curious about you, I must say."

Diana's heart sank. "And what did you tell him?"

"Nothing of significance. Better he get his answers from the source."

As if she could untangle her tongue to speak with him directly. The very thought he might put questions to her made her shiver. "I've got the potatoes ready," she said. "What shall I do next?"

Before Miss Wigglesworth could respond, a loud knocking at the front door sent Diana hurrying into the passageway. Oh, heavens! It could only be Mr. Crackett. She'd forgot all about him.

Chapter 3

Mr. Crackett, tight-lipped and scarlet-faced, descended the
stairs very shortly after ascending them. He set his case on the
vestibule floor and extended his hand, palm up.

"Colonel Valliant refused to see you?" Diana guessed.

"Oh, aye. Swore at me, he did, and sounded right healthy
while he were about it. I'll be paid anyway, Miss Whitney, for
m'trouble."

"Yes, of course. I do apologize for the unpleasantness, which
was entirely my fault. I neglected to inform the colonel that I
had summoned an apothecary, you see, and I expect your
sudden appearance startled him from a deep sleep."

"Happen it did." Mr. Crackett thawed sufficiently to pick up
his case and proceed to the door. "I'll not charge you this one
time, Miss Whitney. But if there is need to call me back on the
gentleman's behalf, I'll be asking double."

"Certainly you will be paid for coming here through the
snow," she insisted, following him outside. "Won't you stay for
a cup of tea while I persuade the colonel to let himself be examined? I am certain that he ought to be, for he took a fearful blow
to the head."

"Yes, yes, you have told me all that. But I know a lost cause
when it bites me, Miss Whitney. He won't have me look at the
wound. And if he's gone addled, there be nothing I can do for
him anyway."

Helplessly she watched the offended apothecary shuffle
down the hill, untether his horse, and climb into the gig. He was
well on his way before she directed her leaden feet to the
kitchen.

Miss Wigglesworth, just tossing a pinch of something into

20

the soup pot, looked up with a frown. "That took an exceptionally brief time."

"Mr. Crackett's services were refused, I'm afraid. He is quite displeased. And by his report, Colonel Valliant is in a frightful temper."

"I expect he does not take well to being an invalid. You must not worry over him, my dear. Sit yourself down and let us discuss how next to proceed."

Diana sank gratefully onto the trestle bench. "Do you realize how very odd this is? Only . . ." She counted on her fingers. "Only eight months ago, I met Kit Valliant in remarkably similar fashion. He had been shot, and when Lucy came upon him, we found ourselves in a remote place with a wounded man to care for. There were all the same problems as well. Ought we send for a physician? How could either of us tend to his personal needs? Of course, you and I needn't disguise ourselves, or worry that our patient will betray us. But the coincidence is most strange, don't you think?"

"To a degree." Miss Wigglesworth stirred the soup with exceptional vigor. "The Valliant men appear to have a knack for getting themselves into trouble, and it has been your fortune— or your misfortune—to be on hand for two such incidents. But the business with Kit worked itself out to advantage, did it not? I believe that will be the case here as well, so long as you have a bit of faith."

Diana sipped the remains of the long-cold tea in her cup, thinking of how the colonel had looked an hour earlier, sitting across from her at this very table. "Faith in *what*, Miss Wigglesworth?"

"Destiny. There is providence in the fall of a sparrow, you know, and what appears to be purely chance is the manifestation of a greater plan." She waved the dripping spoon. "You may fancy I am speaking rubbish, child, but I've lived nigh four years to your one. And I *wish* you would cease addressing me as Miss Wigglesworth. It is a dreadful mouthful of a name. Call me Bertie, will you? Or Wilberta, if you must."

It wasn't the first time she'd asked, but Diana had been taught the proper way to address her seniors. Moreover, there was a kind of safety in polite manners. "If you insist, Miss—Wilberta," she murmured uneasily. "But however can we plan what to do with Colonel Valliant? Unless I very much mistake his character, he will assuredly decide for himself."

"In which case, my dear, fretting will gain you nothing. Most likely he will take himself off as soon as he can mount his horse. We have only to go about our business."

But I have no business to go about, Diana thought immediately. The one decision she had taken for herself—sending for the apothecary—had resulted in a mild disaster.

"We shall let him sleep for so long as he can," Miss Wigglesworth said. "Then we'll feed him some soup. In the meantime, I suggest you light a fire in the parlor. We'll soon be having guests, I shouldn't wonder, what with word gone out that we are harboring Colonel Valliant."

"Mr. Crackett would spread gossip about a patient he was summoned to attend? Oh, surely not."

"Do you not recognize an old busybody when you meet one? He'll give the tale to Mrs. Crackett, who will swan through every parlor in Coniston with the news. Very shortly, I promise you, the ladies will descend upon us with noses to the wind, sniffing for scandal."

"But . . ." Diana's voice faded off as she began to understand. She had been so concerned for Colonel Valliant's health that she had failed to heed the consequences of his presence in this house. In her bedchamber. In her very bed.

But why must there be any such complications? Once the circumstances were explained, no rational person could fail to understand. "There has been no scandal," she protested. "You have been here all along as chaperone. Besides, he had been knocked senseless. What harm could he possibly do?"

"Fact and perception are quite different things, as I suspect you are about to learn." Miss Wigglesworth tasted the soup and added a sprinkle of salt. "Perhaps I am wrong. I hope that is the case. But prepare yourself, young woman."

Before the morning was out, half a dozen female members of the local gentry had appeared at the door, come to inquire after the health of the unfortunate gentleman. Diana had little choice but to invite them in, and once they were settled in the parlor, they could not be budged. She feared they meant to take root there until they had clapped eyes on Colonel Valliant.

Clustered around the fireplace, they drank tea and nibbled at the biscuits Miss Wigglesworth provided, all the while casting speculative looks in Diana's direction. For her part, Diana fended off their tart questions with vague replies. Only the habit of good manners held her temper in check. Until this particular ordeal, she hadn't realized that she *possessed* a temper, but it was at full boil beneath her polite demeanor.

Unfortunately, she had not thought to put on her veiled bonnet. Well, she had, but it was in the room where Colonel Valliant lay sleeping, and the last thing she wanted to do was wake him up. Perhaps it was just as well. The tabbies had only to look at her face to realize that no man would engage in improper behavior with the likes of her.

"Perhaps you should tell us more about your Miss Wigglesworth," Mrs. Alcorn said when she had run short of questions about the colonel. "She is your . . . er, companion, is she not? Who are her people?"

"Naturally," Miss Alice Yoodle put in, "we are certain she is everything she ought to be."

Miss Gladys Yoodle fluttered her fan. "But of course she is. How could she be otherwise?"

Diana turned her attention from the sharp-faced squire's wife to the Yoodle spinsters. Lilac powder, applied in liberal doses, puffed in little clouds from their clothing whenever they moved.

"Take no offense at my questions," Mrs. Alcorn said sharply. She did not like to be interrupted. "But standards do differ from one place to another. What is regarded as acceptable in, shall we say, Westmoreland might well be disapproved of here in Lancashire."

"Then there can be no misunderstandings among us," Diana said with a forced smile. "Miss Wigglesworth and I are Lancashire born and bred."

"You are not from Westmoreland?" Mrs. Alcorn's eyebrows rose to her scalp. "But I had understood you to be the ward of the Earl of Kendal."

Reluctant to confide in this meddlesome woman, Diana merely nodded.

She should have remembered that nothing would deter Mrs. Alcorn, who had the tenacity of a barnacle.

"How did that come about, Miss Whitney? You will pardon me if I ask what all of us are most eager to learn. Now that you have become part of our small community, we naturally wish to become better acquainted."

"And who the devil are *you*?" said a deep voice.

Like the others, Diana looked over to see Colonel Valliant standing in the doorway, one shoulder propped negligently against the jamb. Black-bearded, scruffy-haired, and altogether menacing, he gazed back at them from cold blue eyes.

"Are you speaking to me?" Mrs. Alcorn said, puffing her chest.

"Not particularly. I only wondered why the lot of you are here. If it is to inquire after my health, you can see for yourselves that I am fully recovered."

"We are so very glad of it," Alice Yoodle simpered.

Gladys Yoodle emitted a giggle. "Oh yes. So very glad."

The colonel rolled his eyes.

"Nevertheless," Mrs. Alcorn said sternly, "our primary concern is for the welfare of Miss Whitney. I am certain you take my meaning, sir."

"Are you?" He spoke in chips of ice. "You are quite wrong, madam. I cannot think what you could possibly mean."

Sensing disaster, Diana scraped up the courage to stand. "Our guests were just about to take their leave, Colonel. How fortunate that you were able to assure them of your recovery before they departed. And now, if you will excuse me, I shall help the ladies gather their cloaks and return to their carriages."

"Do that," he said curtly, striding off in the direction of the kitchen.

It took several minutes for Diana to rid the house of six decidedly reluctant ladies, even with the help of Wilberta Wigglesworth. Colonel Valliant must have sent her to the rescue, because she appeared shortly after his departure.

Just before mounting the steps into her coach, Mrs. Alcorn

fired a parting shot. "I much fear for you, Miss Whitney," she said with a knowing smile. "Truly I do."

"What do you suppose she meant by that?" Diana asked Miss Wigglesworth as they returned to the house. "It sounded rather like a threat."

"Of course it was a threat. She resents you, my dear. What is a mere squire's wife when compared with the daughter of a baron, especially one who also happens to be the ward of an earl? She is accustomed to playing the grand lady hereabouts, and now you have come to steal her thunder."

"But that is purest nonsense. I wish only to live quietly, as well you know. Mrs. Alcorn is welcome to queen it as she has always done."

"I expect she is not convinced of that," Miss Wigglesworth said dryly. "Take yourself off to the kitchen, my dear. The colonel wishes to speak privately with you."

Worse and worse, Diana brooded as she made her way slowly down the passageway. After her ordeal with the Coniston Inquisition, a private conversation with the intimidating Colonel Valliant was the very last thing she felt up to confronting. And to think that she had come to this out-of-the-way lakeside house for a few weeks of quiet reflection!

Colonel Valliant was at the stove, ladling soup into a bowl. "My third helping, I'm afraid. If you expect to have soup for lunch, I suggest you claim a portion before I devour the entire potful."

"You are most welcome to it, sir." She edged into the room. "I'm not the least bit hungry."

"That tangle of vipers would put a saint off her appetite," he said in a remarkably pleasant tone of voice.

Too pleasant. More than ever on her guard, she went to a tall three-legged stool and perched atop it, welcoming the additional height. The colonel filled every room he entered, she could not help but notice, and even the large kitchen felt crowded with only the two of them present.

Instead of taking a seat at the trestle table, he went to the hearth and stood with his back to the fire, fixing her with his gaze as he spooned soup into his mouth.

She looked at her hands, tightly folded on her lap, and willed

25

them to stop trembling. He didn't speak, and she could think of nothing to say. After a while, the longcase clock in the passageway chimed twelve times. Only noon? It seemed much later to her.

Finally he put his soup bowl on the mantelpiece. She heard the sound and looked up briefly. He was standing tall and straight, his legs slightly apart as if he were planting himself against attack. From behind, the firelight outlined the shape of him, the taut muscles and rigid stance, casting shadows on his cheeks and glazing his dark hair with a reddish halo.

"I suppose we may as well go about the thing properly," he said. "Will you, Miss Whitney, do me the honor of becoming my wife?"

Stunned, Diana was distantly aware that her mouth had dropped open.

"Come now," he said. "You must have been expecting this. In point of fact, I'm not altogether sure you didn't set out to arrange it. But I can assure you that if you did, you will soon be very sorry for it."

She made herself look directly into his eyes. It was a mistake. She could read nothing there, but he met her gaze and held it with such force that she could not look away again. From a dry mouth, she summoned the only words that she could put together. "I don't know what you mean, sir."

"No? Well, perhaps I have misjudged you. But when that quack showed up, followed not long after by a flock of hens, I assumed you to be responsible for bringing them here."

"I did send for the apothecary, sir. And I apologize for not mentioning it to you this morning, but I plainly forgot. You may be sure I did not mean him to inform the entire population of Coniston that you were here, although he appears to have made a good start at it within a very short time."

"And the battle-ax with the pointed chin will doubtless cry the news from here to Hawkshead. But never mind how it came about. The deed is done, and we must deal with the consequences. Your reputation has been compromised, through my own fault, and I stand ready to salvage it as best I can. Mind you, marrying a man of my less-than-sterling character will not stand to your credit, but you've little choice in the matter now."

That skillet upside his head must have done more damage than any of them realized, she thought. "But of course I do. How can the misjudgment of a few old gossips signify? I assure you, they mean nothing to me."

"But then, yours is not the only reputation to be considered."

"Oh. I hadn't thought of that." She studied his face. "Do you put store in their opinion of you, sir?"

"By no means. I refer to my family, of course. You are, I have been informed, my brother's ward. As such, the regard in which you are held must reflect on him."

She lowered her head. "I would not have it so."

"Nevertheless, that is the way the world goes, madam. And in this particular situation, Kendal has brought trouble upon himself by permitting you to live in this remote house with only an elderly woman for company. He has clearly neglected his responsibilities."

Outraged, Diana sprang immediately to Lord Kendal's defense. "He has done nothing of the sort. Coming here was entirely my idea, and you may be sure he disliked the plan enormously. You should know, sir, that the role of guardian was all but thrust upon him several months ago. He had never even met me. And when we did meet, he promised that I would be his ward for legal purposes only. Mind you, I'm not at all sure this arrangement *is* legal. But he said that he would not be meddlesome, and that I could do as I wished. So when I wished to spend a few weeks in the country, he could hardly go back on his word."

Frowning, Colonel Valliant lowered himself onto the settle and rested his elbows on his knees. "If he'd dreamed you might do something so bird-witted, I expect he'd not have given his word in the first place."

"To be sure. But as I said, he does not know me well."

He quelled her with a stern look. "However much you wish to absolve him of responsibility, the fact remains that Lord Kendal's ward has been caught in a compromising situation with his brother. There is no walking away from *that*, madam."

"I've no intention of walking away," she informed him woodenly. "Nor will I be stampeded into Parson's Mousetrap." She hesitated. "Unless Lord Kendal insists, of course."

27

The colonel gave a bark of mirthless laughter. "You would marry me on my brother's command?"

"I am greatly indebted to him, sir."

"But not so much that you would oblige him by remaining at Candale, out of harm's way."

"No. Well, yes." She took a steadying breath. "The thing is, who could have imagined any harm would come to me here? Two servants are generally in residence with us, but the footman has gone to care for his father, who is ill, and the housekeeper always stays with her family on Wednesday nights. She will return this evening."

"I chose a particularly awkward time to break into the house," he said wryly.

"Yes indeed." She sighed. "In all our planning, sir, we did not allow for you."

He laced his fingers behind his head and leaned back against the settle, regarding her with a rueful expression. "Nothing is ever simple, is it? So what are we to do next, Miss Whitney? I take it that my proposal of marriage has been rejected."

He didn't sound the least bit sorry for it. "Yes, sir. Lord Kendal is regrettably saddled with me for another year, but I'll not subject his brother to a lifetime tenure."

His laugh sounded almost genuine. "You are trying to *protect* me, madam?"

"I expect you can take good care of yourself," she fired back, astonished at her own temerity. But really, men found amusement in the oddest things. "As it happens, I first went into hiding to escape a marriage my uncle had arranged for me. I'll not be forced into *any* marriage, sir, unless compelled to pay the debt of honor I owe to Lord Kendal."

"He would not call in such a debt. Of that, you may be sure. Much has changed since I saw him last, but his character cannot have greatly altered."

"No indeed. He is a man of uncommon integrity. I am persuaded, Colonel Valliant, that you ought to go home and reacquaint yourself with your brother."

"I mean to. Had I gone there directly, you'd not be embroiled in a scandal." He rubbed the bridge of his nose. "Under the circumstances you will, of course, depart for Candale immediately."

"No." Diana rose and straightened her skirts. "I am done with running away, and it is past time I stopped relying on others to take care of me. Soon enough I shall be entirely on my own, and no matter where I decide to live, there will be the likes of Mrs. Alcorn and her comrades to deal with. I mean to face them down. Or ignore them, or perhaps win them over. Coping with this predicament is certain to be . . . educational."

He smiled then, the first true smile she had seen from him. White teeth flashed, and the tiny lines at his temples and the corners of his mouth crinkled.

It was, she quickly discovered, a breathtaking smile. Feeling suddenly dizzy, she reached behind her and held on to the stool for support.

"As you wish, Miss Whitney." The smile vanished. "But you might as well spare yourself further trouble and come with me now. When he hears of this, Kendal will almost certainly pluck you back to Candale."

"Must he? Hear of it, I mean. He never comes to Lakeview, and even if he did, he'd not mingle with Mrs. Alcorn's set." Her nails dug into the wooden stool. "Unless you tell him, sir, he needn't ever know."

The colonel raised a dark brow. "You would have me lie to him?"

"Not . . . precisely. It is more a matter of withholding the truth, which is not at all the same thing as telling a direct lie. And what is the point, really, of calling this incident to Lord Kendal's attention? It is over and done with."

"You astonish me, madam. I'd have pegged you as a female of strict conscience, but you are squirming around the truth like a politician."

"Yes. I am ashamed of it. I shall do penance for it." She studied the toes of her slippers. "Nonetheless, Colonel Valliant, I beg you to keep silent about what happened here."

"And so I shall. Unless I am compelled to do otherwise, of course, for gossip is rarely contained for very long. The story may reach Candale before I do. But we can hope, Miss Whitney. It's worth a try."

"You are very good, sir."

"I am nothing of the sort. I am abandoning a young woman to the jackals instead of wedding her, which is clearly my duty. I am not even trying to persuade her to accept my offer. What's more, I am about to deceive my brother, whom I've not set eyes on these last several years. And his wife, whom I've never met."

"You heap coals of fire upon my head," she murmured. "Tell him, then. I'll not spoil your homecoming any more than I already have."

"You have certainly made it interesting," he said, crossing to where she stood. "Buck up, my dear. We'll muddle through. And now, I must be on my way if I am to reach Candale before dark."

She regarded his haggard face with concern. "Do you feel up to traveling, sir?"

"Oddly enough, Wellington never asked me that when we were marching through Spain." He put his hands on her shoulders. "I'm an old trooper, you know. And I'm not about to admit that a wisp of a female brought me down with a frying pan. So yes, I am perfectly well enough to ride."

Even through the heavy kerseymere dress, his touch burned into her shoulders. And this close to him, she saw that his eyes were so deep a blue as to be almost violet. The stool she was still clinging to suddenly toppled over, hitting the floor with a loud thump.

He released her immediately. "Will you mind retrieving my coat and gloves while I saddle the horse?"

"Certainly, sir. And your rifle as well."

"Keep it," he said shortly. "And learn how to use it, in case someone else decides to come through your window one of these nights."

And then he was gone, out the kitchen door.

She stood for several moments, willing her heart to start beating again, before rushing upstairs.

Miss Wigglesworth met her in the passageway. "He is leaving, I gather."

"Yes. And so far as Lord Kendal is to know, he has never been here." It occurred to her that Miss Wigglesworth would be caught up in the deception as well. Oh dear. What a tangled web she had set out to weave. "Do you mind very much?"

"Not in the least, child. If you did not look quite so miserable, I would enjoy being part of a conspiracy. Simply tell me what story we are giving out, lest I trip you up."

"Thank you." Bless Wilberta Wigglesworth! "When the colonel is gone, we shall get ourselves in order."

By the time Diana arrived at the stable, her arms full of coat and hat and gloves, he was leading his mount into the courtyard.

Unaccountably reluctant to see the last of him, she watched him shrug into his coat and pull on his gloves. "What shall I tell Mrs. Alcorn about your departure?" she asked, if only to prolong his stay. "She is bound to quiz me."

"Whatever you like," he said curtly. "But I advise you to stick to the truth. The bare bones of it, mind you. Offer no details, and explain nothing. I came to my house, thinking it to be empty. Lacking a key, I broke in through a window. You heard noises, assumed I was a burglar, and ambushed me. When you learned my identity, you put me in one of the two rooms that had a fire and sent for the apothecary. It's simple enough."

He swung into the saddle. "One lie only. You were never alone in my company. Not for a moment. Miss Wigglesworth was with us beginning to end."

She gave him the knitted cap and stepped out of the way. "I understand, sir. And I wish you a happy reunion with your family."

"Naturally, I cannot give them your regards." His lips curved. "May I say, Miss Whitney, that except for the blow to my head, I am glad to have made your acquaintance. We shall meet again, of course, and pretend it is for the first time. But for now, Godspeed."

Touching his forehead in a salute, he turned his horse and made his way down the snow-covered hill to the road.

Diana waited until he was out of sight before trudging back to the house.

I could have *married* him, she thought.

He would have despised her for it, to be sure. He would have been legshackled to a bride he never wanted, and all on account of a stupid coincidence. An accident.

But still, what if she'd said yes to his offer? What would it have been like to be his wife?

Well, she would never know. And it would not do to refine on what would never be.

Kicking a pebble out of her path, she resolved to put him from her mind altogether.

Chapter 4

Two days had passed since Colonel Valliant's departure, and Diana had nearly succeeded in putting him from her mind. But when he was gone from her thoughts, she had nothing of interest to think about. Nothing, in any event, that did not lower her spirits.

The swarm of Coniston ladies had diminished, although Mrs. Alcorn buzzed in every morning with a few of her cronies to make her disapproval excruciatingly clear. A gentleman would have done the decent thing, she declared. And if he failed to offer marriage, a decent woman would have found a way to compel him.

Diana painted on a smile and recited the lines Colonel Valliant had given her to say. As much as she disliked their visits, the Coniston Cats allowed her to play hostess, one of the few things she did well. Above all things, she required something to *do*. Reading, embroidering, and walking occupied too few hours of the day. Miss Wigglesworth had begun restoring the kitchen garden, which had been devoured by weeds after the previous tenants moved away, and Diana enjoyed giving her a hand. But although Miss Wigglesworth would never have said so, Diana knew that she was more of a nuisance than a help.

Resolving to find new ways to occupy her time, she decided to take inventory of her talents and skills. As soon as Mrs. Alcorn had taken regal leave, she closed herself in her bedchamber and seated herself at her writing desk.

It would not be a difficult task, she was persuaded. After nearly a score of years on this earth, she had surely accumulated a considerable number of skills. And not a one of them must be excluded, however unsuitable they might be for the life she would be leading in the future.

At first the words flowed swiftly. *Embroider. Paint with watercolors. Fluent in French, passable in Italian. Converse politely in society. Dance. Excellent penmanship. Well versed in all forms of proper correspondence. Preside over a tea tray. Play the pianoforte and sing.*

She scratched out *sing*. Her voice was melodious, but too soft for drawing-room entertainment.

Turning to household matters, she began with the general heading *Manage a Gracious House* and listed everything from planning menus to cataloging the silver and linens. When she was done she examined the entries, which had carried her to a second sheet of paper, with considerable pride. Unlike the frivolous accomplishments that headed her tally, some of these would prove useful when she set up her own household. The residence of a reclusive spinster would not be precisely "gracious," but neither did she intend to live beneath her station.

Unaccountably, tears welled into her eyes. Rubbing them away with the back of her hand, she set even more fiercely to work.

Thus far she had discovered only what she already knew. Miss Diana Whitney, bred to marry well and be a charming ornament to society, was well suited to the kind of life that had been snatched from her and wholly unsuited for any other.

Spanking rider! she wrote in capital letters. *Perhaps raise horses?* she added in parentheses.

Mr. Beadle was teaching her the rudiments of carpentry—sawing, hammering, planing, and the like. She listed those with a question mark after each one.

Mrs. Cleese, the cook, was reluctantly allowing Diana to help prepare the meals. "Peeling, chopping, measuring, and stirring" got written down.

Her inscriptions grew more labored, more infrequent, and more humdrum. Recalling the short time she'd spent on a pig farm, she noted mucking out sties, feeding poultry, gathering eggs, and churning.

She remembered that she could skate. Drive a gig. Arrange flowers.

Although she'd no prior experience with infants, Lady Kendal had trusted her to hold Master Christopher Alexander. But she discounted that and did not write it down. Everyone at Candale had gone to great lengths to make her feel useful and important, when she was nothing of the sort.

The ghost of Colonel Valliant rose up again, and she ordered him to go away. Once met, he was not a man easily dismissed from one's mind.

Sharpening her pen, she tried desperately to think of something else to write. She'd have done better to list all the skills that she lacked. Years could be spent on such a list as that.

After long consideration she wrote in a shaky hand, *Won't give up.*

It wasn't precisely a skill, but at the end of the day, it was perhaps her greatest asset. Not that it came easily to her. She surrendered constantly. She collapsed under the slightest pressure. But she always scrambled up again. She pulled herself erect and continued forward.

What she needed now was somewhere to go.

Her next task was to find a goal. Discouragement washed through her as she read over her list from top to bottom. So little there. So few things she could do. No hint of anything she *wanted* to do, except for that notion of breeding horses sometime in the future.

"Diana?" Miss Wigglesworth stepped into the room. "Forgive me for disturbing you, my dear. I did knock, but you failed to respond."

"I beg your pardon." Gathering up the sheets of paper, Diana shoved them into the drawer. "I was wool-gathering."

"Thomas Carver has arrived from Candale and brought with him a maidservant. I expect you'll wish to speak with him."

The Candale underbutler, no more than five years her senior, was waiting in the entrance hall beside a pert, curly-haired girl. He bowed, his freckled cheeks flushed red under a thatch of carrot-colored hair.

"Good morning, Miss Whitney. Lord and Lady Kendal convey their warmest regards. And . . . ah . . . Lord Kendal requests that you return to Candale. We have come to escort you."

She went cold with dread. "Has there been trouble regarding my uncle?"

"Not that I am aware, ma'am. But several of the guests have gone into Scotland—for the fishing, I believe—and the house is no longer filled to the rafters. Lord Kendal suggests that you will be more comfortable at Candale than here."

"I see." She could not restrain a small sigh. "Then I suppose I have no choice."

"As to that, ma'am, his lordship also said that if you preferred to remain at Lakeview, which was more than likely, I was to stay and be of service to you." He gestured to the maid. "Betsy as well."

"I do indeed prefer to stay here," she said, elated. "And the two of you are most welcome, although I'm not sure where to put you. We'll have to open up two more rooms." And what of the colonel? she wanted desperately to ask. Servants always knew the latest gossip.

Carver drew a small parcel from his coat. "Lady Kendal asked me to give you these letters. And you will wish to know that Lord Kendal's brother, Colonel Valliant, has returned from South America."

"Indeed?" she said too brightly. "He has been gone a very long time, or so I understand. Lord Kendal must be pleased to have him home again. Although now that I think on it, Lakeview belongs to Colonel Valliant, does it not?"

"I cannot say, ma'am. I have not heard that he means to come here, if that is what concerns you. Perhaps Lady Kendal's letter will provide more information."

Butlers were annoyingly discreet, she thought, knowing she'd get no more from Thomas Carver. And ladies, after all, ought not to be interrogating the servants. "Well, we must get you settled in. Go along to the kitchen for a cup of tea while Miss Wigglesworth and I choose the most suitable rooms."

Carver bowed again. "One more thing, Miss Whitney. Lady Kendal thought you might like to have your mare. I've put her in the stable."

"Oh, but that is *wonderful*!" She clapped her hands. "I have so missed riding. I shall take her out this very afternoon."

"As you wish, but Lord Kendal has given me strict instructions in that regard. I am to accompany you whenever you ride, and for that matter, whenever you leave Lakeview for any reason."

"A good thing, too," Miss Wigglesworth put in, slicing her a knowing look. Diana Whitney's reputation was already in shreds, it said plain as day. There would be no haring about the countryside on her own.

She concealed her disappointment with a smile. "In that case, I shall have to postpone my ride. But we shall go exploring tomorrow, Carver. Be ready first thing after breakfast."

It had rained during the night, and Diana feared her ride would have to be delayed yet again. But the sun was breaking through the clouds when she set out, Carver in tow, to see what lay beyond the grounds of Lakeview. Since arriving, she had not left the small estate, not even to walk the two miles into Coniston.

A crisp morning breeze played with the veil on her blue felt bonnet. By now, she supposed, everyone for miles around knew precisely what was to be seen beneath the veil. The Coniston Cats had doubtless spread the word, and she could well imagine how they spoke of her.

Oh, yes, they would say. They had seen it with their own eyes, and a dreadful sight it was. Miss Whitney bore the mark of the devil on her face. Wicked Miss Whitney, who had taken at least one man into her bedchamber. They had seen the man, unshaven and thoroughly disreputable. And rude. He had ordered them from the house. Oh dear, oh dear. What was this world coming to?

She wanted not to care what they thought of her. She had quite made up her mind not to care. And to prove it, she would no longer keep herself prisoner at Lakeview. Today, she was making a start at getting along in the world. She was striking out on her own for the first time since, well . . . for the first time.

What a lowering thought, and so dizzyingly true. Miss Diana Whitney, spoiled child of doting parents, had never taken a decision for herself. No one had expected her to. She willingly obeyed the wishes of her mother and father. At school she obeyed her teachers. She was a good, obedient girl.

And she hadn't minded in the least, because everyone took pains to make life pleasant for her. When she was at home, a maid laid out what she was to wear. Cook prepared her favorite foods. She was given puppies and kittens to cosset and ponies to ride. When she was sent off to Miss Wetherwood's Academy for Young Ladies, she had a room of her own, unlike most of the other girls, and she always got good marks in her classes. She excelled at music and drawing and dancing. She did what she was told. Always she was a good, a *very* good girl.

There was no reason to be otherwise. She knew that she was being prepared to make the one and only important decision of her life. When she was ten-and-seven her parents would take her to London for the Season. She would be presented at court, and go to balls and routs and to Almack's, the Marriage Mart, where she would be an Incomparable. She had been assured that she would be an Incomparable. She never doubted it.

Young men would flock to her. She never doubted that, either. Her father, wiser than she, would turn away the scoundrels and fortune hunters. The others, all of them titled and eligible and rich, would be laid out before her like a banquet. They would be madly in love with her, of course. They would woo her. Send her flowers. Write poems in praise of her beauty. Steal kisses in garden arbors and hold her a trifle too closely when they danced the scandalous waltz.

And finally, feted and courted and made much of, she would choose from among all these men the one who would be her husband. That decision was to be hers alone, her parents had promised. Their greatest wish for her had been that she would marry for love, as they had done. And with their happiness as a model for the life she wanted for herself, she'd been certain that she would make the right choice. After that, of course, she would do her husband's bidding. And live happily ever after.

With a grim laugh, Diana wrenched her thoughts from dreamland. It only pained her to dwell on what she had lost.

For the first hour she kept to the road that ran alongside Coniston Water, following it all the way to where it narrowed into the River Crake. Then she turned off and wound her way back along a narrow track set against the hills, following the route Mr. Beadle had suggested. She'd gone down to meet him just after dawn, when he passed Lakeview as he always did, and asked him to direct her to where the country folk lived.

She was looking for something. That was all she knew. It would help greatly, though, if she had some notion what it was that she sought. Should she chance to stumble upon it, she hoped that it would have the kindness to pop up and identify itself.

Directly ahead, a swift-flowing beck emerged from the fold between two low hills, rattling over worn rocks and pebbles before vanishing into a stand of beeches. She let Sparkles enjoy a drink before guiding the mare carefully over the narrow footbridge, which was no more than a few planks tied together with cord. Just the other side, she saw a lane cutting through the trees and decided to see where it led.

When she came out of the spinney, she was startled to find herself in a forest of fluttering linens. Sheets, towels, duvets, pillow casings, and all manner of clothing were suspended from a dozen lines attached to poles driven into the ground. Sparkles shied, spooked by the flapping linens, and Diana quickly steered her to open ground. There, alongside the beck, she saw an enormous metal vat on props above a fire. Beside it, a tall woman with graying hair was stirring its contents with a wooden paddle. She looked up when Diana appeared from behind the screen of sheets.

"Good morning," Diana said, wondering why the woman was glowering at her. Then she realized the glare was directed to a point behind her, where Carver had got himself tangled in the clotheslines. His face red as holly berries, he extricated himself and mumbled an apology to the laundress.

"Well, that's all right then," she said, letting go her paddle and wiping her hands on her apron. "If you be lookin' for Annie Jellicoe, you found 'er. But I be takin' no more customers, never mind the money would come welcome. Got all I c'n manage now and a bit more."

Diana glanced back at the waving rows of laundry. "I should say that you do! Is there no one to assist you?"

"Assist?" She laughed heartily. "And where would I be findin' such a creature? You don't hail from these parts, I warrant. Be you on a tour of the lakes?"

"Actually, I am in residence within a few miles of here, although it's true that I've only recently arrived." Passing Sparkles's reins to Carver, Diana slid from the saddle and looked about with interest. Firewood was stacked against a small tin-roofed shed that was used, she guessed, to store supplies. There was a rough-hewn table covered with oilcloth, and beside it, a number of large willow baskets. Some were piled with folded laundry.

"Ah, then you be the lady what is stayin' at the big gray house. The lady what the old Alcorn goat keeps yammerin' about."

"Diana Whitney," she said with a sinking heart. "Mrs. Alcorn does not approve of me, I'm afraid."

"That be a feather in your cap, to my way o' thinkin'. 'Tis a pleasure to meet you, Miss Whitney. Call me Annie if you like, or Mrs. Jellicoe if that suits you better." She took up her paddle and went back to stirring the soapy contents of the vat. "Be there somethin' I c'n do fer you, so long as it's nowt to do with laundry?"

"In fact, Mrs. Jellicoe, I was trying to learn something about this area. I am given to understand by a gentleman of my acquaintance, Mr. Beadle, that many of the residents are unable to find work."

"Oh, aye. We all know Mr. Beadle. He built that shed and planted the poles for my lines, so I do 'is washin' for free. Not that there's very much of it. He's right about the jobs. None to be found. I be Yorkshire born, but I married a Lancashire man and we come to live here so as he could work in the copper mine. But it closed, and he couldn't get no other work, so he went inter the army and got 'imself killed." She wiped her forehead with her sleeve. "It were much the same for 'alf the women in these hills. You ride around and 'ave a look, Miss Whitney. You won't be seein' many men."

"They were lost in the war?"

"A good number of them. Others be gone south to work in the factories. Some be rascals and just took off, leavin' their families high 'n dry. That be what 'appened to Meggie Doyle, who lives just yonder. You c'n see the smoke from 'er chimney.

In the cottage past that is Dora Fellson, what be a widow. Same for Jane Renfrew, down the way a bit."

"But however do they survive?"

"On the parish," Mrs. Jellicoe said grimly. "They scrape by what ways they can. Dora has three milk cows, and Jane keeps chickens. Meggie's scrap of land is good for plantin', not like most around here, but she's got nobody to work it. 'Tis all she can do to keep after her youngsters."

"Do you think they'd mind if I called on them?" Diana asked hesitantly.

"They would if you came offerin' charity. It's shame enough bein' on the parish dole. And bein' poor don't mean they ain't proud."

"Thank you for telling me. I should not wish to offend them. Perhaps I will ride in that direction, though, and make their acquaintance. And may I visit you again, Mrs. Jellicoe?"

"When the sun be shining, I be here. If there's rain, come on down to the cottage and I'll make a pot of tea." She smiled, revealing surprisingly white teeth. "Should you be goin' by Meggie's place, mebbe your man there could take up a basket and give it to her. She'll be needin' the nappies, I warrant."

"It will be our pleasure." Diana beckoned to Carver, who helped her onto the saddle. "I shall come again very soon, Mrs. Jellicoe."

When Carver was mounted, the laundress passed him a round willow basket. "If the others don't be welcomin'," she called as they rode away, "take no mind of it. They don't be used to minglin' with the gentry."

That became painfully clear as Diana went from one cottage to the next. The women, two of them with children clutching at their skirts, mumbled a greeting when she introduced herself and then stared fixedly at the ground. Realizing that her presence made them uncomfortable, Diana promptly bid them farewell and rode on.

Only Mrs. Doyle spoke audibly. After passing the infant in her arms to a little girl, no more than five or six, she took the basket from Carver's hands and turned to Diana. "Thank you, m'lady," she said in a shy voice. Then she fled into the cottage, followed by all but one of the children.

A too thin freckled boy stayed behind, gaping up at Diana. "Why you got that thing in front o' yer face?" he piped.

She was fumbling for a response when Mrs. Doyle stuck her head out the door. "Come in here this instant, Willie!"

"B-but she looks funny, Mama."

"Now!"

He scampered into the cottage and the door closed firmly behind him.

Diana saw his face at the window as she rode past. Not sure if she ought, she raised a hand and waved at him. To her delight, he grinned and waved back.

All the way home she thought about what she had seen and heard. And by the time she arrived at Lakeview, the glimmer of an idea had begun to take form. She rushed past a surprised Miss Wigglesworth, who had come down to greet her, and closed herself in her room.

Miss Wigglesworth was not to be denied, though. She knocked just as Diana was pulling off her riding habit and entered before she could be told not to. "Has something happened, my dear?" he asked, her face creased with worry.

"Oh, I have had *such* a day!" Diana smiled. "It has given me so much to think about. Please excuse me for being rude, but I wish to be alone for a while. Perhaps the rest of the day, and probably the evening as well. May I have supper on a tray, Miss Wigglesworth? And a pot of tea now, with some biscuits and a slice of Mrs. Cleese's apple cake, if there's any left."

"I'll see to it. But you *will* tell me if I can be of assistance?"

"Yes indeed." Diana sat on the bed to remove her half boots. "It's far too soon to say at the moment, but I rather expect you will find yourself being a great deal of help. More than you can imagine."

"My, my. Well, be mysterious if you must, so long as that lovely light remains in your eyes."

When Miss Wigglesworth was gone, Diana put a hand over her scar and went to the mirror. There *was* a glow in her eyes, she thought before turning quickly away. Fancy that! And she felt exhilarated, the way she used to when she had something good to look forward to.

Now if only she could pull together the tumble of ideas in her head and make some sense of them!

When she was comfortable in her eiderdown dressing gown and slippers, she went to the writing table where she had begun the day. Gracious, it seemed ages ago that she inscribed her paltry list of talents and skills. Once again she stacked clean sheets of paper atop the desk, removed the stopper from the inkwell, and sharpened her pen.

Then she paused, bowing her head. "Please, dear Lord, help me find what I am seeking," she begged. "Show me how to do what needs to be done. And if You don't mind, could You tell me precisely what that is?"

Chapter 5

Alex was pleased to see his brother after so long a time and to meet the new Lady Kendal, who was in every way an improvement over the previous countess. He'd a new nephew as well, and the heir, now a robust ten-year-old, was brought up from Harrow to renew acquaintance with his uncle.

For the first few days, family and Kendal's houseguests provided distraction from his dour thoughts. But when the guests departed and Charley had returned to school, the house seemed to close in around him. All that domestic bliss began to cloy, and feeling an outsider in the only home he had ever known, he took to spending his days walking the fells. Sometimes, if the night was clear, he would remain in the high country and sleep under the stars.

He knew that at some point he must separate himself from the army, and resigning ought to be a simple enough matter. He still had the letter excusing him from duty on his own recognizance, although Ross could hardly have expected him to vanish for two years. But the general had been killed shortly after penning the orders, and following Bonaparte's escape from Elba, no one had cared what was transpiring in the American War.

Alex Valliant was a paper soldier now, an unpleasant reminder of a conflict everyone would prefer to forget—no one more than he. But somewhere in an office at Horse Guards he still held his commission, and the habit of military discipline would not permit him to leave loose ends to dangle, however painful the tying off of them.

There was no reason to keep putting it aside, he supposed. In the month he'd been at Candale, he had succeeded only in reac-quainting himself with the lakelands and disrupting his family. Celia had done her best to make him welcome, to be sure, and gone so far as to take him under her wing. She deliberately sought his company in the evenings and chattered away, fully at ease, while he struggled to think of something to say. Fortunately, she never seemed to mind his abrupt, chilling responses.

"You are the quiet one," she informed him, as if he didn't know that already. "James and Kit probably never let you get a word in when you were growing up together."

That wasn't the case, although he allowed her to go on thinking so. Unlike his brothers, both of them articulate and witty, he had always been solitary by nature. A throwback to some stolid, unimaginative distant ancestor, he expected, since his parents were reputed to have been as charming as his brothers.

As befitted the second son of an earl, he had dutifully taken up a career in the military and found himself surprisingly suited for it. In retrospect, he supposed it lucky for him that he'd been driven into the army before finishing his studies at Cambridge. The only commission he could buy on sudden notice was in the 44th Foot, not the glamorous cavalry regiment he had hoped to join, but with less competition from influential fellow officers, promotions came rapidly. He was a major at age twenty-seven and a lieutenant colonel not long after.

He was doing it again, he thought as the Candale gatehouse came into view. Dwelling on the past. And in light of its inglo-rious end, his military career was the last thing he ought to be calling to mind.

Better to concentrate on his new horse, a large, tempera-mental bay that suited him exactly. The search had taken him all the way to Doncaster, and with an excess of time on his hands, he had remained at the breeding farm for several days, putting the steed through his paces and enjoying long rides on the open moorlands.

At least he was returning to Candale in a better mood than when he departed, which Kendal and Celia would doubtless ap-preciate. Having a brooding, bad-tempered relation hanging about, even one who spent little time at the house, could not have been a great pleasure for them.

Timmy darted from the stable as Alex reined in and dismounted. "Ooo, he's a good 'un, sir. Best I seen since I been workin' here."

"I'm glad you approve," Alex said dryly, handing over the reins. "Give him a rubdown, will you?"

"Yes, sir. I'll be takin' good care of this 'un. What's 'is name?"

Alex tossed a coin to the impertinent stableboy, who flashed him a grin of thanks. "The breeding farm listed him as Number Seven out of Courageous and Miss Buttercup. Any ideas what I should call him?"

"I never got to name a horse before." The narrow face wrinkled in thought. " 'Ows about Thunder?"

Alex removed the saddle pack and slung it over his shoulder. "Thunder it is."

He had grown fond of the boy, Alex was thinking as he walked up the path from the stable to the front door of the house. Timmy had aspirations to be a jockey if he continued small, or a trainer if he grew as his five brothers had done.

A flashing thought—Alex Valliant as the owner of a horse-breeding farm—stopped him in his tracks. Yes. Possibly. He'd no money to finance such an enterprise, of course, but if he sold the house at Coniston Water, he could make a small beginning. And his commission might be worth something, although he expected that adjustments had been made to the system after the war. What with scores of officers wanting to sell out, colors must be going a-begging.

Well, it was worth considering, the horse farm. Nothing else had the slightest appeal to him, and he felt an unaccustomed spark of enthusiasm at the prospect. If it was not soon extinguished, perhaps he'd swallow his pride and ask Kendal for a loan.

Alex let himself into the house, surprised to see two men waiting in the entrance hall. One, a portly fellow with a red face and a receding hairline, was slumped on a bench with his arms dangling between splayed knees.

The other was pacing the black-and-white-tiled hall, hands clasped behind his back. Tall, lean, and hawk-faced, he spun around as Alex closed the door and fixed him with a belligerent glare.

"Are you a servant in this household?" he inquired sharply.

Clothed as he was, with a saddle pack thrown over his shoulder, Alex supposed he could be mistaken for one. Then again, a servant would hardly be using the front entrance. "No," he said coolly. "Do you require one?"

"I most certainly do. The butler left us here like common tradesmen nearly an hour ago, and I have pulled the bell rope a dozen times thereafter. Why has he failed to respond?"

"I have no idea. Why are you here?"

The man's slate-gray eyes narrowed unpleasantly. "We have come to speak with Lord Kendal on a matter of importance."

"Indeed. Well, I've no doubt that Geeson has informed him of your presence." Alex felt the man's glare prong him in the back as he mounted the stairs. At the top he turned in the direction of the study, where Kendal was generally to be found at this time of day.

The earl was seated at his desk with a number of documents spread out across the blotter in front of him. "Ah, good," he said when Alex came into the room. "I'd hoped you would be here in time for the fireworks display."

Alex dropped his saddle pack on the floor. "You refer to the pair of idiots bivouacked in the entrance hall?"

"I'm afraid so. The tall one, Sir Basil Crawley, is a particularly repellent mushroom. The other is Lord Whitney, uncle to the young lady now in residence at Lakeview. You may recall that I mentioned her to you some weeks ago?"

"Vaguely. She is your ward, I believe."

"That is, in fact, open to some question. My arrangement with Lord Whitney was more in the nature of a gentleman's agreement than a strictly legal transfer of guardianship. There was always the chance he'd take up the matter with Chancery Court, and it appears that he has done so." Kendal thumbed through the sheaf of documents. "Amid all this lawyerly blather, two things are abundantly clear. The court, which

47

means to take up the case, has ordered the concerned parties to make themselves available in London. Moreover, until a judgment is rendered and in accordance with the terms of her father's will, Miss Whitney is to be returned to Lord Whitney's custody. The gentlemen waiting downstairs have come, I would imagine, to collect her."

"You don't mean to hand her over to them?"

"Well, she's not here, is she? But the authorities will have every right to seek her out and seize her, should Whitney demand that the magistrate enforce the pronouncement of the court. I expect that he will."

Alex went to the sideboard. "And what has Crawley to do with all this?"

"I'll have a brandy, so long as you are pouring." Kendal leaned back in his chair. "Left to his own devices, Whitney is a drunken, witless boor with debts up to his eyebrows. Not coincidentally, most are owed to Sir Basil, who made a point of buying up his gaming vouchers." He accepted the glass Alex handed him and took a drink. "Since I mean to keep them waiting as long as possible, would you care to hear about the events leading up to this confrontation?"

Damn right he would. He had developed a proprietary interest in Miss Whitney's affairs, if only because she was the only female he had ever proposed to. She was certainly the only female who'd ever whacked him with a skillet. "If you wish to tell me," he said with studied indifference.

Kendal glanced over at the clock on the mantelpiece. "A summary, then. Only Kit knows the whole of it, since I did not become involved until near the end. And for some reason, no one is willing to give me the details of her rescue."

"If Kit was involved, I can well imagine why."

"Where our little brother is concerned," Kendal said with a smile, "there are a great many things I'd rather not know. But to the subject at hand. When Miss Whitney's parents died of typhus a bit more than a year ago, the title passed to Lord Whitney's brother. The new baron was living in London at the time, trading on his expectations and apparently unaware that he was to receive none of the family's considerable fortune. Only the land and the house are his, and being entailed, he can neither sell nor mortgage them."

Alex paced the room. "I take it that Crawley means to wed the heiress?"

"He has offered for her, but not, as you might expect, to get his hands on her money. It is her birth and breeding that prompt him, for she is descended from a line dating back to the Conquest. Moreover, her family has always lived in Lancashire, where most of Crawley's business interests are centered."

"But if she refused him, which I assume she did, is not that an end to it? Whitney cannot force her to marry against her will."

"No. But he can make her life devilish miserable, which he has already done." Kendal steepled his hands beneath his chin. "Crawley offered to forgive his debts and provide a hefty marriage settlement, but if Whitney failed to produce her, he would be ruined. One evening, blind drunk, he roared into her bedchamber and demanded that she accept Crawley's proposal. When she continued to defy him, he struck her. It was the first and only time, she has always insisted, but the consequences were . . . appalling. By ill luck, she fell against a fragile glass dish that shattered against her face and left a prominent scar."

Alex took a long drink of brandy, remembering the spider-web of scars on her cheek. After the first look, he had paid them little mind. A soldier soon grew accustomed to scars, his own and those of his fellows, and held them to be badges of honor.

His vision clouded. He thought of the brutal uncle slumped on a bench downstairs, only a short distance from the reach of his fists. He thought of pounding those fists into that pudgy red face until it burst like a melon.

Kendal's voice reached him when he had one hand on the door latch. "Don't, Alex."

"Why the devil not? He deserves no less."

"Unquestionably. But punishing him will not help the young lady, whose welfare is our primary concern. If we behave as brutally as we claim Lord Whitney to have done, it will only give him more credence with the courts. Besides, Crawley is our real problem."

"Then I'll put him out of commission, too." But Alex knew

better than to rush into action while fury was driving him. With a muttered oath, he let go the latch and turned, propping his shoulders against the oak door. "I cannot credit that a cit and a drunkard baron have got the better of you, James. Tell me that you have a plan to scotch them."

"Would that I did. But I confess to underestimating Crawley. Once Whitney had signed his niece into my custody, I frankly assumed the business to be settled."

"Then why isn't it? If Crawley requires a wife with aristocratic connections, there must be scores of them to choose from. Why must he have this one in particular?"

"Because she was denied to him, I suppose. He is not a man to accept defeat, most especially at the hands of a family like ours. We have, by simple right of birth, what he most covets. And I have sharpened his resentment, I'm afraid, by conducting an investigation into his business practices. I'd not have meddled further with him, you understand, had he not purchased an estate nearby and set about taking control of several canals and turnpike roads. I've a responsibility to the citizens of this county, and have already thrown a spanner into more than one of his pet projects. Indeed, I am resolved to drive him from Westmoreland if I possibly can. Or that was my intention, until he presented me with these documents."

Kendal looked grim. "Plainly I should have waited until Miss Whitney came of age, but I failed to anticipate the level to which he would sink. Kit might have expected it, being better acquainted with the fellow. But off he went on his wedding trip, I falsely assumed Miss Whitney safe in my custody, and now— as Celia would say—we are in the soup. I can tell you that I do not look forward to giving her the news. She will have my head on a platter."

"Much as I'd like to see that," Alex said, "we'll do better to extricate ourselves from the soup pot. Let's hear from the enemy, shall we?"

"You're nearest the bell rope."

Alex rang for the butler, who must have been anticipating the summons. Despite his arthritic knees, Geeson arrived quickly to get his orders and soon returned with Lord Whitney and Sir Basil Crawley in tow. Alex had barely refilled his brandy glass and settled on a wingback chair when they were announced.

Crawley immediately launched the attack. "You kept us waiting overlong, Lord Kendal. I would have expected more courtesy."

"Indeed?" Kendal raised a brow. "I cannot think why, since you appeared on my doorstep without notice. And naturally I required time to read through the considerable mass of documents you have delivered to me."

Lord Whitney backed himself into a shadowed corner. This is all Crawley's doing, his expression said apprehensively.

Kendal was more than a match for Sir Basil, of course. While they exchanged veiled insults, Alex sat back and quietly took Crawley's measure.

He had seen his sort before—clever, ruthless, and occasionally petty. Much like the French-loyalist mayor of a Spanish town Alex's regiment had once occupied, who gave orders that every sheep, goat, pig, and chicken be incinerated to prevent the British invaders from making a supper of them. Never mind that, unlike the French, Wellington's troops did not live off the land, or that the town's citizens would starve when the soldiers had moved on to their next objective. For vanity's sake alone, Señor Viscaya asserted his power, and others suffered because of it.

"Miss Whitney will return with us to her home," Crawley was saying.

"Not today," Kendal said mildly. "You will pardon my lamentable unfamiliarity with Chancery statutes and edicts. Naturally my solicitors must examine the documents and advise me what steps are to be taken."

"The court's directions are perfectly clear," Crawley said. "Lord Whitney intends to see them enforced by whatever means you compel him to use. But we are civilized men, sir. This matter should be resolved in a civilized manner. Or do you prefer that the young lady be hauled away by officers of the law? I assure you that if you refuse to turn Miss Whitney over to her rightful guardian immediately, you may expect constables and Bow Street Runners on your doorstep before tomorrow noon."

"I see. Well, you have made yourself clear, Sir Basil. Now take yourself off my estate before I summon a few exceptionally large footmen to throw you off."

With a discernible moan, Whitney shuffled to the door and let himself out.

Crawley watched him go, a look of disgust on his face, before turning back to Kendal. "You have interfered in matters that do not concern you, my lord. Perhaps you imagine that your rank puts you above the law. But even those not born into a privileged class have the right to conduct business without being trampled on by arrogant aristocrats. One day, someone with the determination and the means will contrive to bring you down."

"How very melodramatic. Should your other enterprises fail, Sir Basil, which I expect they will, might I suggest you consider a career on the stage?"

Alex saw the color leach from Crawley's face, but there was no mistaking the fury in his eyes. With a curt bow, he turned on his heel and strode decisively from the room.

"Well," Kendal said when he was gone, "what do you think?"

"Were he a gentleman, I'd call him out."

"Not very helpful, Alex. Do concentrate. You may be sure that in the long term, I have the means to render Crawley harmless. But where Miss Whitney's immediate fate is concerned, he holds the trump cards. We can expect a search of the estate tomorrow, and when she is not discovered, he will cast his net over all the properties belonging to the family."

"In his place," Alex said thoughtfully, "I wouldn't limit tomorrow's search to Candale. I'd have a constable at Lakeview first thing in the morning, and another at Kit's cottage in Hawkhurst. I'd also set guards on the road just beyond the gatehouse, in case we tried to make a run for it tonight." Alex rubbed the back of his neck. "If he is so clever, why doesn't he know that Miss Whitney is not in residence here?"

"Because he has only just returned from London with this damnable court order, I presume. In any case, if an enemy never made a mistake, he would be invincible. Let's agree that we've a few hours of grace to devise a plan. Should we spirit her away to Scotland?"

Alex's blood ran cold. The family owned an estate in the Highlands, but none of the Valliant brothers had ever set foot there. On one of their annual visits, his parents were caught in a snowstorm on Rannock Moor and perished, along with the servants and the horses. He was nine years old then, and remembered when the news was brought to Candale. James, only twelve, was suddenly Earl of Kendal. Kit had been too young to understand what had transpired.

Caretakers managed the Highland estate now, and he supposed Miss Whitney might be concealed there for a time. But an enterprising Bow Street Runner would eventually track her down, and Crawley was perfectly capable of going there himself and dragging her back across the border.

"That won't do," Alex said finally. "We can't hide her. Crawley will harry her until she is run to ground. She has to be put beyond the control of her guardian, and of the courts as well."

"A lovely idea, to be sure. But how are we to accomplish such a feat?"

Alex took a deep breath. "I shall marry her."

For the first time in his life, he saw his elegant, invariably composed brother gape with openmouthed astonishment.

Kendal picked up his glass and swallowed the last of his brandy in a single gulp. "N-no," he managed to say on a cough. "Impossible."

"How so?" Alex warmed to the idea with startling speed. "Your mention of Scotland gave me the idea. A speedy wedding at Gretna Green will turn the trick, so long as we can get her across the border before Crawley puts his hands on her. It's the obvious solution, James. The *only* solution."

His composure recovered, Kendal propped his chin atop steepled fingers and regarded his brother with cool blue eyes. "It's madness. She will never agree to it. And what in blazes has put such a notion into your head? I've no doubt you are a gallant fellow, but you needn't throw yourself on your sword to save a young woman you have never even clapped eyes on."

Alex leaned back against the chair, making a few swift

calculations. He had made promises to Miss Whitney, but under the circumstances, they would have to be broken. James had to hear the truth or he'd not agree to cooperate with a plan that was suddenly—inexplicably—a plan that Alex had taken to heart. He didn't want to explore the reasons. He had no good reasons. He wanted only to do the thing and deal with the consequences later.

"As a matter of fact," he said, not meeting his brother's intent gaze, "Miss Whitney and I are acquainted. What's more, I have already made her an offer of marriage. She refused me, understandably, but perhaps I'll have better luck on my second attempt."

"I think you had better explain, Alex."

"Very well, although I'd prefer to get on with the business at hand. While I was in Liverpool arranging for my luggage to be sent north, a clerk mentioned that he had made similar provisions in the weeks just past. Lord Kendal was hosting a house party, he said. So far he knew of a duke, two earls, and several lesser members of the Quality gone to Candale, not to mention their families and servants. Naturally I chose not to descend on you while you were preoccupied with your guests."

"Damn the lot of them. If I'd any notion you were on the way home—"

"It doesn't matter, James. Truth be told, I was somewhat unsettled about seeing you again after so many years, and Coniston seemed a good place to wait until the coast was clear. I expected the house to be empty, of course. But I'd no sooner arrived than I fell ill—nothing of consequence—and an apothecary was summoned. One way or another, the news spread through the neighborhood and a few of the local gossips transformed an insignificant incident into a scandal."

"I see. Was not Miss Wigglesworth in residence at the time?"

"Certainly. As I said, the uproar was out of all proportion to the circumstances. Nevertheless, I considered myself bound in honor to make a proposal, which was summarily declined."

"And there was some reason you chose not to mention this before now?"

"Bloody hell, James, what was the point?"

"Until the court snatches her away, I am charged with Diana's welfare."

"And a damnable job you've made of it, permitting her to reside in a decrepit country house with an old woman her sole protection. Miss Whitney has no more worldly sense than a kitten. Make that a mouse. She trembles at a puff of wind."

Kendal fixed his cool, blue-eyed gaze on Alex's face. "Were that the case, you would be crying the banns even now. She had the strength of will to refuse your proposal, just as she refused Sir Basil's—"

"The two offers of marriage are hardly to be compared!"

"I know she looks as if she'd melt under a harsh word," Kendal continued more gently. "She often behaves like a frightened rabbit. Kitten. Mouse. Whatever small creature comes to your mind. But I assure you that Miss Whitney has a will of iron. I also suspect she is unaware of it, even when she quietly defies my wishes and most charmingly goes about having her own way."

"She cannot have it when she is wrong. Would you permit her to jump off a cliff if she insisted on doing so?"

"I might have held her here at Candale, under duress," Kendal said in a level voice. "But she has suffered much at the hands of less benevolent men who were charged with her care. At the time, I was persuaded that she would do better to try her wings in what I considered to be a safe environment. And unless I am much mistaken, Alex, she was doing well enough until you paid an unannounced call."

He should have known better than to debate his diplomat brother on points of logic. Not that logic had much to do with any of this. He had resolved, for reasons that did not bear close scrutiny, to marry her. And so far as he was concerned, that was that. "We are wasting valuable time, my lord earl. Do you mean to help me or not?"

Kendal regarded him in silence for what seemed a very long time. Then he released a sigh. "No good can come of us working at cross-purposes, that is certain. But before you go haring off to Lakeview, let us contrive a plan. Do you really believe that you can persuade Miss Whitney to marry you?"

"Yes!" Alex said immediately. And untruthfully, he was

55

forced to acknowledge, although not aloud. "At the least, I can bring her into Scotland. We shall assume the best and prepare for what is to happen when we get there."

Chapter 6

Alex arrived at Lakeview in the early afternoon, surprised to find two pony carts, a gig, and a battered carriage drawn up in the stable yard. A grizzled postilion, snoozing under a tree, opened one eye and closed it again.

Bloody damn. Whoever they were, the people belonging to those vehicles, he had to get rid of them without alarming Miss Whitney.

Carver directed him to the kitchen, which struck him as a devilish odd place to be entertaining guests. He heard her voice as he came to the end of the passageway, stopping just short of the open door where he could look inside without being observed.

Wearing a stained apron over a brown dress, Miss Whitney was standing at a butcher's block with bowls, cutlery, and small jars spread out in front of her. Tendrils of hair, come loose from the knot atop her head, dangled at her nape and over her ears. She was addressing an audience of eight females seated around the trestle table directly across from her.

"I wish to thank Miss Gladys Yoodle for donating the perfume," she said, "and Mrs. Pottle for allowing us to borrow her earthenware pipkin. Our first batch of Paste of Palermo appears to be successful, but in the next week you must all test its effectiveness. Be sure to take a jar with you, and apply the concoction each day without fail."

"I'll be takin' a double helping," said a worn-looking female, holding out her hands and wriggling her fingers.

The others laughed.

"An excellent suggestion, Mrs. Jellicoe. There can be no better trial than the hands of a laundress. Now, as all of you know, we shall meet again Thursday next, and for our project I have selected Eau de Veau. If you are able to provide one of the ingredients, please raise your hand." She picked up a piece of paper and read from it. "Two calves' feet."

Calves' feet? Alex wondered if he'd stumbled into a coven of witches.

"No? Well, I'll procure those, along with the rice. A loaf of white bread? Thank you, Mrs. Jellicoe. A gallon of milk? Mrs. Fellson. Ten fresh eggs? Mrs. Renfrew. Two pounds of fresh butter? Mrs. Fellson again. Thank heavens for your cows, ma'am. Mr. Beadle will procure camphor and alum from the apothecary, and then we shall be ready to proceed."

"Be we testin' the odevo?" The Jellicoe woman frowned. "It don't sound so nice as the paste with the perfume in it."

"No, it certainly does not," Miss Whitney agreed. "But according to the receipt, Eau de Veau serves much the same purpose as Paste of Palermo, which is rather expensive to make because of the perfume. If it works as well as the paste, we'll simply give it a fancy new name."

"Better not tell folks what be in it," Mrs. Jellicoe advised laconically.

"Dear me no. How we do what we do will be entirely our secret. Now, are there any questions or suggestions before we close the lesson? No? Very well, then. I shall inform Carver that you are ready to depart. Mrs. Renfrew, don't forget to take an extra jar for Mrs. Phelps, and tell her we hope she will soon be feeling more the thing."

Alex quickly made his way to the entrance hall. "I've only just arrived," he told the startled butler. "Please inform Miss Whitney that I am waiting in the parlor."

She appeared at the door not long after, a worried look in her eyes. "Colonel Valliant?"

He bowed. "Pardon me for intruding while you have guests, Miss Whitney, but I must speak with you on a matter of some urgency."

"Of course." She closed the door. "What is it, sir?"

She was putting a brave front on it, but her face was ashen and her hands gripped at her skirts. Suddenly the well-ordered speech he'd planned to deliver went completely from his mind. "Perhaps you would like to be seated," he said after a moment.

That frightened her all the more, he could tell, but she shook her head. "Pray go on, Colonel. I shan't swoon, I promise you. Has this to do with my uncle?"

"I'm afraid so. He has made application to Chancery Court, which has agreed to consider the matter. You are summoned to London, along with the other parties concerned, and pending a ruling, his rights as legal guardian have been reaffirmed. Kendal is ordered to return you to his custody."

"I see." Her hands dropped to her sides. "Then I must go to him at once. Will tomorrow morning be acceptable, do you suppose? I should like to pack a few things. But I can be ready to depart within the hour, if you have come to escort me back."

"It's not so simple as that."

She cast him a reproachful look. "Believe me, sir, I find the prospect of returning to my home—my uncle's home—anything but *simple*."

"No. Of course it is not." Alex fumbled for words, but they slithered away. "I meant . . . something else."

"What, then? I am perfectly resigned to the circumstances, however much I regret them. 'Tis only for eleven months, and Lord Whitney would not dare to do me harm while he is under the scrutiny of the court."

"On his own account, no. But if ever he had a will of his own, it has long since been drowned in hock. Whitney is Sir Basil's creature now, and I suspect he will do as he is told."

"Perhaps he will try. But since he cannot compel me to marry Sir Basil, which is the only thing either of them wants of me, there is no reason for concern."

"I fear this has gone far beyond Crawley's intention to have you to wife, madam. Kendal's interference has set him on something of a vendetta against the family, and we believe that Crawley means to use you as the instrument of his revenge."

"Dear heavens." She leaned her back against the door for support. "After all that Lord Kendal has done for me, to have it come to this. I am so dreadfully sorry. What can I do to spare him further difficulties on my behalf? Will Sir Basil call it off if I wed him, do you think?"

She would give herself to that blackguard in hopes of protecting Kendal? Alex had seen men sacrifice themselves on the battlefield to save their fellows, but never expected to find that sort of courage in a young girl. "There can be no question of you marrying Crawley," he said gruffly. "Before permitting such an abomination, I would dispose of him."

She blanched. "You would do me no kindness, sir, to put a man's death on my conscience."

"I expect it won't come to that. But you are to forget any notion of returning to your uncle's custody. Kendal is resolved that you shall not, as am I, and you cannot stand against us both."

"But if Lord Kendal has been instructed by the court to hand me over, what will happen if he fails to obey?"

"He'll not be chained up in the Tower of London, if that is what you are imagining. I assure you that Kendal is well able to deal with the consequences, whatever they may be, of defying the Lord Chancellor's order. You are not to concern yourself with him. Understood?"

She wanted to object, that was evident. But she lowered her head, her gaze fixed on the threadbare carpet. "Am I to go into hiding, then? If Lord Kendal will advance me the funds, I could travel south and hire a cottage in some out-of-the-way village. Perhaps in Devon or Cornwall—"

"That can be arranged, of course. But it's not a good idea. Crawley has employed Bow Street Runners to hunt you down."

She gave a small shrug. "He did so before, you know. And the Runner found where Kit had concealed me. But in the end, nothing came of it."

"Indeed? Well, I know little of your prior experiences, but the next time you may not be so fortunate."

"Perhaps." She raised her head, a smile wavering on her lips. "You won't allow me to marry Sir Basil, nor may I return to my uncle. What other choice have I, then, but to hide from them?"

And now, finally, they were come to the point. Cold perspiration formed at his neck and trickled into his collar. How to say it? He was astounded to realize how important it was for her to agree. How very much he wanted her to agree, although he could not have said why.

She was regarding him quizzically, still with that gallant little smile on her lips. Were he in possession of a heart, he thought, it would have cracked in the presence of that smile. As it was, his chest felt wrapped about with knotted ropes. Bracing himself, he snatched a shallow breath of air and said softly, "You could marry *me*."

Her eyes went wide. Plainly that was the last thing on earth she had expected to hear. Shock and bewilderment and something he could not put a name to—fear, most like—washed over her face.

"I—no. You *mustn't*. Why would you even suggest it? Well, you did so once before, to be sure. But there is no more reason now than then. You keep trying to save me by marrying me, sir, but what would become of you if you did? It is most kind to make such an offer, of course. Thank you. Terribly kind. No."

Is the thought so repellent to you? he wanted to ask, as if she hadn't just said so as politely as she could. I am not kind, he wanted to say, but she already knew that.

All the way to Lakeview he had tried to convince himself that she had no choice but to accept his offer. The poor child was backed into a corner. As he had told his brother, what else could she do but marry him?

Now he'd found out. She could say no.

He pulled together what remained of his pride. "I cannot blame you for refusing, Miss Whitney. You do not know me. And if you did, you would be all the more unwilling to endure my company. But the fact remains that you have been dealt poor cards, and now you must play them as best you can. With our help, to be sure. Content yourself to be in our hands, madam, at least until we have got you away from Lakeview. There will be time later for a discussion of what we are to do next."

She stood away from the door. "May I ask where you mean to take me?"

"North, into Scotland. We'll go on horseback as far as you are able and hire a post chaise from there. Kendal and Celia are already on their way. We'll join up with them just across the border at Gretna Green."

The significance of their destination wasn't lost on her. "If they are expecting to witness our marriage, sir, they will be disappointed."

"So it seems." But not nearly so disappointed as the rejected groom, he thought, even as he wondered why he thought it. Wedding Diana Whitney would be, after all, something on the order of adopting a stray kitten. And he rather suspected that this particular kitten, if roused, could unsheathe a formidable set of claws. A smart man would stay clear of them.

He was well free of her. Of course he was. But though he meant to tell her to change into warm clothing and prepare herself for a long ride, he heard himself saying something quite different. "I'll not exhort you to accept my offer, madam. I suspect that it would distress you if I spoke of it again. But it remains open nonetheless, and as we ride to Gretna, I would ask you to give it further consideration."

Her gaze slid away. "What is to be done with me, sir, if there is no marriage?"

"I don't know," he said frankly. "Perhaps Kendal will have devised a plan. My task is to get you there, and we must depart at once. Make yourself ready now and dress warmly, for we'll be traveling well into the night. Meantime I shall explain the circumstances to Miss Wigglesworth and see your horse saddled."

"Yes, sir." She curtsied and turned to the door, pausing with her hand on the latch. Her head was inclined, and he wondered for a moment if she was weeping. But she soon straightened, and let herself into the passageway without a backward look.

Chapter 7

"Welcome to Gretna Hall, sir. Madam." The slender gentleman bowed with grave courtesy and ushered them inside. "How may I be of service?"

"Colonel Alexander Valliant," came the curt reply.

"Ah, yes. You are expected. Follow me, please."

Diana gazed around her as he led them across the reception hall and through an arched doorway, surprised to find herself in such a large, impressive establishment. She had expected something quite different, although she could not have said what. A blacksmith's shop, perhaps. Were not Gretna marriages said to be conducted over an anvil?

"Lord and Lady Kendal await you in the Green Parlor," the gentleman said, pausing before a carved oak door. After knocking lightly, he opened it and stepped aside to let them enter.

Kendal had been embracing his wife, Diana saw at once. Although he rose from the sofa with his usual dignity and bowed to her, color was high on his cheeks. Behind him, Lady Kendal combed her fingers through disarrayed blond curls.

Kendal crossed to shake his brother's hand. "You made excellent time, I must say. We didn't expect you until well after midnight."

"Miss Whitney is a superb rider," the colonel said with one of his almost-smiles. "I was hard put to keep up with her."

"Since we'd no idea when you would arrive, it was naturally impossible to make arrangements for the ceremony. But Mr. Lang has promised to come whenever we send for him, no matter the hour." Kendal gave the colonel a steady look. "It would do well, I believe, to proceed immediately."

Ghosting behind the words, Diana sensed, was a private communication between them. But . . . *immediately*?

She felt light-headed. Nothing must happen immediately! She plucked at Colonel Valliant's sleeve.

He sliced a brief glance at her. "Not right away, James. After the long journey, Miss Whitney will require time to catch her breath. I certainly do."

Looking mildly displeased, Kendal nodded. "In that case, perhaps the ladies should withdraw upstairs."

No! She desperately summoned the will to protest, but it declined to respond.

Lady Kendal appeared at her side. "Come, my dear. I expect these gentlemen mean to apply themselves to a bottle of brandy, and you must be longing for a cup of tea. Please have a tray sent to us, James."

All in a fog, Diana was swept from the parlor, up the stairs, and into a large bedchamber. Every ounce of the energy that had carried her this far suddenly flooded out of her. She stood, limp as rags, while the countess removed her cloak and bonnet and gloves. When told to be seated, she went on legs of jelly to a chair by the fireplace and sank down with a sigh.

Dear heavens, what was she to *do*? Evidently Lord and Lady Kendal assumed she had come here to marry Colonel Valliant, and for some unspoken reason, the earl was in a great hurry to get on with it.

This is what it must be like, she thought, to be caught up in a whirlwind. One word from her—a firm *no*—would put a stop to this. But she couldn't bring herself to say it, any more than she could produce the *yes* that sometimes trembled, unwelcome, on her lips.

For hours and hours, for all the miles up the steep winding road over Kirkstone Pass and down again, along narrow tracks and across fields as they proceeded to Scotland without ever venturing onto the Great North Road, she had prayed for an answer to be given her. The smallest sign would do. If she saw a falling star before she counted to a hundred, she would wed the colonel.

She counted and watched the sky, but no stars fell. So she made another deal, offering Heaven a bit more latitude this time. If a rabbit ran across the road *or* a star fell, she would say yes. And this time she'd count to a thousand.

Next it was two thousand, and she threw in catching sight of a cow or a deer. By the time she increased the count to five thousand, she was willing to settle for a sheep. Surely she would see one miserable sheep!

When that failed, she tried turning her bargain the other way around. She would count again to five thousand, and promised at first sight of rabbit, falling star, cow, deer, or sheep to irrevocably decline the colonel's offer.

But there were no signs from Heaven, no miracles to be had. No answers. Nothing but the man riding beside her, more silent and remote than the stars.

Lady Kendal tugged a leather ottoman across the carpet and sat beside Diana's knee. "This must be a great trial for you," she said. "I am so very sorry for it. We had thought you to be safe, but I fear that is no longer the case. Kendal will not tell you this, because men have the addled notion that women wish to be spared hard truths, but our carriage was twice stopped and searched on the way here. I think the constable suspected we were hiding you under the floorboards, or perhaps in one of the portmanteaus, for he was quite thorough."

"But *why*, Lady Kendal?" Those were the first words Diana had spoken for several hours, and they came out in a froggy croak. "My uncle can do no more harm to me than he's already done. I'm sure he would never dare to beat me, and even if he did, I would refuse to marry Sir Basil until my dying breath."

"Well, it won't come to that, I assure you. And I quite enjoyed our little adventure on the journey to Gretna. A Bow Street Runner followed us across the border, you know. Not Mr. Pugg, unfortunately. Sir Basil has employed a less kindly man this time. Kendal reasoned he would track us until convinced we truly meant to visit the Highland estate, so we kept on going right past Gretna and all the way to Moffet before he finally gave up. When we were sure he had turned back, we waited a few hours at an inn before retracing our way to Gretna Hall."

"Where is he now, do you suppose?"

"Possibly he has gone back to look for you at Candale, or

Lakeview, or any other place you might be found. But Kendal is fairly certain he is still lurking about Gretna. Sir Basil and his Runner must realize that we are plotting your escape, for it cannot be a coincidence that we set out for Scotland so soon after learning of the court's ruling. When they failed to find you in our company, they surely mounted guards near the border. Indeed, I thought the Runner would plant himself directly center of the bridge to waylay you. But you crossed without difficulty, so it seems we have thrown him off the scent."

"Colonel Valliant thought it too dangerous to use the bridge," Diana said. "We followed the river until we found a place shallow enough to ford."

"Oh, well done! Naturally Alex would anticipate a trap. But the Runner may think to check here again, and should he find you before you are securely wed, he has the authority to snatch you away. I expect you noticed that Kendal is in something of a hurry to proceed with the ceremony."

"Yes." If there was to be a wedding at all. Why were they not considering other possibilities, such as taking her deeper into Scotland or dispatching her to Cornwall? Or even casting her off to fend for herself? Colonel Valliant had said they would discuss it further, the question of their marriage, when they reached Gretna. But nobody was discussing anything. Not with her, at any rate. Everybody was assuming she'd go to the altar or the anvil or wherever she was led and do what she was told to do.

And most likely she would.

Why could she not turn him away? In all good conscience, that was the reasonable—the *decent*—choice. It was her moral obligation, was it not, to save the colonel from this act of folly? But while a servant bustled into the room with a tray and laid out cups and saucers and the teapot and the rest, she gazed up at the plaster ceiling and hoped for a shooting star.

Lady Kendal pressed a warm cup into her hands. "Drink this, my dear. And then we must get you dressed. I knew you would be traveling without luggage, so I packed several of the gowns you had left at Candale and brought them along. Three have been pressed, and of course, you must choose whichever you prefer. But I quite favor the pale moss green. It looks so well with your hair."

She remembered the gown, one of a large number already made up for her London Season before her parents died. All were two years out of fashion, of course, and far better suited for a carefree young girl eagerly looking forward to her come-out. The girl she had been.

She felt a great deal older tonight. Aeons older. But very little wiser, alas. While they lived, her parents had made every significant decision for her. Now strangers ordered her life while she sipped tea and dithered.

Lady Kendal placed a reassuring hand on her knee. "All will work out for the best, you know."

Diana set down her cup, sloshing tea into the saucer. "You mean well," she said in a raw voice. "All of you mean well, and I'm ever so grateful. But I cannot marry Colonel Valliant."

"Ah." The countess tapped a manicured nail against her chin. "You dislike him, then?"

"By no means. Not . . . precisely. I confess that I find him more than a little . . . well, formidable. But the fault is all mine. He has always been exceedingly kind."

"In an abrupt, military sort of way." Lady Kendal smiled. "Alex is another of those obstinate I-know-what's-best-so-do-as-I-tell-you men who will run roughshod over you should you permit him to. Kendal is much the same. I vow that sometimes he makes my teeth ache! And Kit is no better. It must be a family trait, this penchant for issuing orders and expecting them to be obeyed without question. But one soon learns how to deal with excessively strong-minded husbands. It's rather amusing to let them imagine they are having their own way while all along, you are having yours."

"But it's not the same with me, Lady Kendal. You and Lucy had far more experience of life when you were wed. You are possessed of stronger characters than I shall ever have. And you married for love, while Colonel Valliant is—oh, I don't know *what* he is doing! Sacrificing himself at the altar, I suppose, for the sake of his brother's not-quite-legal ward. And if I permit him to do so, he'll be stuck with me *forever*! He is certain to regret it. We don't know the least little thing about each other. I have met him only twice, under difficult circumstances, and—"

"And both times he proposed marriage." Lady Kendal stirred honey into her tea. "Is that not extraordinary, Diana? Bringing a man to scratch once is strenuous enough. Twice is a marvel. It's perfectly obvious that Alex wishes to be *stuck* with you."

"I believe, Lady Kendal, that you are mistaken. He is impelled by a misguided sense of honor, or duty, or whatever causes gentlemen to behave in so irrational a manner. I haven't the slightest notion what he is thinking. Not ever. All the way here he said practically nothing to me. Whenever we stopped to rest the horses, he wandered off by himself." Her voice faltered. "As if he could not bear my company."

"Oh, I assure you that is not the case. He behaved in very much the same way at Candale. We rarely saw him, and he seldom spoke unless asked a direct question. It was my feeling—only guesswork, you understand—that something deeply troubles him. Perhaps you will be able to discover what it is, if indeed it be anything at all. Kendal says that Alex has always been reserved, so you must not imagine that he suddenly fell silent on your account."

Diana mustered a faint smile. "We would have a quiet household, then. Colonel Valliant has no inclination to engage in conversation, and I dare not say a word to him. Perhaps that is why he is willing to enter into a marriage of convenience. He has found himself a wife who will leave him in peace."

"Give me leave to doubt that," Lady Kendal said, laughing as she rose from the ottoman. "And so, my dear, will it be the green dress?"

Much to Diana's embarrassment, Lady Kendal cheerfully played lady's maid, helping her pull on silk stockings and the veriest wisp of a chemise. She had been concerned about the green muslin dress, a summer frock with embroidered cap sleeves and a band of dark green ribbon tied under her breasts, but it still fit her even without the corset Lady Kendal had forgot to pack. She'd forgot to bring the long kidskin gloves as well, the ones dyed to match the ribbon, so Diana's arms and hands would have to go bare. At least she was relatively clean, after sponging herself from scalp to toe with lukewarm water from a basin, and she'd washed her hair that very morning.

While Lady Kendal was arranging her tangled locks, she slumped dejectedly on the chair in front of the dressing table, making sure never to glance up at the mirror. "Why are we taking such trouble to rig me out for a slapdash Gretna wedding?" she asked. "Especially with Lord Kendal in so great a hurry to get on with it?"

"Ah, my dear, this is perhaps the most significant event of your life. Don't you think it merits a bit of trouble? And Kendal has always been rather formal when it comes to—well, to just about anything. Certainly a wedding in the family requires a proper ceremony, as best we can manage under the circumstances. He brought along something for Alex to wear, I believe, so you needn't fear that your bridegroom will be standing there in all his dirt."

When Lady Kendal finished pinning up Diana's hair in what she described as a style of "relaxed elegance," she handed her a small bouquet of tulips. "I picked these in the garden this afternoon," she said, brushing a kiss against her cold cheek. "Are you ready to go downstairs?"

No. No. No.

"Yes," she replied, her heart plunging to somewhere in the vicinity of her ankles. "But how can it be that I seem to have come to a decision without ever making up my mind?"

"Put it down to instinct," Lady Kendal advised. "I knew that I wanted Kendal the very first moment I saw him, which happened to be on the day of his wedding to another woman. I was ten-and-seven and married to another man. Nine years passed before I saw him again, at which time I made his acquaintance in the most humiliating way, and from there the tale becomes even more unconventional."

"Is this meant to reassure me?" Diana murmured into her bouquet.

"Well, it might if we'd time for you to hear the entire story. The point is, you have seen us as we are now, despite the unpromising beginning we made. It may well be the same for you. Wilberta Wigglesworth once told me something that I knew by experience but had failed to comprehend. One can fall in love in the space between heartbeats."

"But I'm not the least bit in love with Colonel Valliant!"

"She didn't specify *which* heartbeats, my dear." Lady Kendal took her arm and led her from the room. "Have you read *Hamlet*?"

Startled, Diana could only nod.

"Then remember, 'If it is not now, yet it will come. The readiness is all.' "

Her bad luck then, for she was not at all ready. Indeed, she'd not have objected overmuch if Sir Basil's Bow Street Runner put a stop to the wedding and swept her off to some less terrifying fate. But only a footman appeared, to escort them to the reception hall. And when she stepped inside, her heart bounded to her throat.

Colonel Valliant was standing directly across the room, a tall impressive figure in scarlet coat, white breeches, and high black boots. One white-gloved hand rested on the hilt of his sword, and his other arm was folded behind his back.

In his regimentals, the colonel was positively dazzling. Light from the chandelier directly overhead gleamed off silver epaulets, silver buttons, the silver braid across the front of his coat, and the yellow and silver braided sash at his waist. Most striking of all, it shone on the bright silver sword at his left hip. He stood as rigidly as the high stand-up collar he wore, his face without expression, his eyes watchful.

Suddenly aware that she had been gawping at him like a schoolgirl, Diana wrenched her gaze to Lord Kendal. Beside him stood a gray-haired man dressed in a black frock coat and loosely knotted cravat.

Kendal smiled. "You look lovely, my dear. May I present Mr. David Lang, the . . . er—"

"Priest," Lang supplied. "I'm no cleric, but 'priests' is what we be called."

"I am pleased to make your acquaintance," Diana murmured, wondering how she was supposed to conduct herself in these excessively odd circumstances.

Lang pulled a thin, tattered book from an inside pocket. "Are you here of your own consent, miss?"

Surprised by the abrupt question, she managed to nod.

"Be there impediments to this marriage?"

Not sure what those might consist of, she said, "None that I know of, sir."

"Shall we proceed, then?" He flipped open the small book and waited expectantly.

Colonel Valliant moved to stand beside her, his gazed focused directly forward. The top of her head was no more than an inch higher than his shoulder, and this close to him, she was more conscious than ever that he was, by nature and experience, a warrior.

Mr. Lang had begun to speak, but his voice seemed to be coming from a vast distance. The colonel spoke as well, in a soft baritone, and as he did, something brushed lightly against her. She slid a glance to where his sleeve touched her arm from elbow to wrist, scarlet wool against pale, goose-pimply skin. It was warm, the sleeve, and slightly scratchy. It entranced her. Not a speck of lint on it, she thought in wonder. When it pressed more firmly against her arm, she liked the feel of it and of the muscles swelling inside it as his hand drew into a fist.

Her gaze dropped to the white knit glove stretched tautly over his knuckles.

"Well?" Mr. Lang said, his voice sharp. "Will you or won't you?"

She looked up at him blankly. Was he speaking to her? Then she saw Lady Kendal, who was standing a little way behind him, nodding vigorously.

"Yes," the countess mouthed silently.

"Y-yes," Diana said.

"Very well, then," said Mr. Lang. "Have you a ring, sir?"

Turning slightly, Colonel Valliant raised her left hand and slid a gold band onto her finger, repeating very softly the words Mr. Lang gave him to say.

When he was done, he turned again to face the priest. But he kept hold of her hand, which felt impossibly small encased in his.

"You being sworn to each other," Mr. Lang intoned, "I declare you rightly married by the form of the Kirk of Scotland and agreeable to the Church of England." He snapped his book closed and returned it to his pocket. "Now if ye'll sign the register and the papers, I can go back to me bed."

Colonel Valliant led her to a small table strewn with documents and let go her hand to take the pen offered him by the innkeeper.

Had he been here all this time? Diana accepted his good wishes with a distracted smile, watching her husband—her *husband*!—inscribe his name in bold letters. Alexander Rutherford Valliant. He wrote it thrice more before giving her the pen and stepping aside.

"Directly under his," the innkeeper said when she hesitated, wanting to read what was written on the papers she was signing. But everyone was looking at her, waiting for her, so she hastily scrawled her name where she'd been told.

Mr. Lang added his signature, a rough scribble, and the innkeeper applied a wax seal at the bottom of each page.

"All right and tight," he said with satisfaction, handing the documents to Lord Kendal. "Now if you'll pardon me, I shall see to the other arrangements." With a bow he left the room, followed by Mr. Lang.

What other arrangements? Diana thought, feeling more like a footstool than a bride as everyone carried on as if she weren't there. Kendal drew the colonel aside, where they spoke in voices too low for her to make out what they were saying. She saw Kendal give over one of the papers and slip the others inside his coat.

"For a moment," Lady Kendal said, coming to stand beside her, "I thought you meant to bring a halt to the wedding."

"My mind wandered, is all." She sighed. "It happened so quickly. I was scarcely aware we had begun, and then in a flash it was finished." Lifting her hand, she gazed bemusedly at her wedding ring. It was of chased gold set with a teardrop-shaped emerald. "I *am* married now, I suppose."

"Oh, yes. The ring belonged to Alex's grandmother. It's lovely, don't you think?"

"Indeed." She shivered. The room had gone frightfully cold. "But what is to happen now, Lady Kendal?" She gestured to the men, whose backs were now turned to her as they conversed.

"Whatever can they be talking about that I am not permitted to hear?"

"Of course you are permitted, and I assure you there is nothing confidential about what they are saying. But when gentlemen are discussing business, they've a lamentable tendency to forget that we exist. Shall we go over there and remind them?"

Gazing at Colonel Valliant's wide shoulders, the dark hair brushing against his stiff collar, the long legs planted slightly apart, she felt safer keeping her distance. "No, Lady Kendal. I shouldn't care to interrupt them."

"As you wish. They are merely deciding the most expedient way to notify your trustees, your uncle, the magistrate, Chancery Court, and anyone else who ought to learn of the marriage. For that very purpose, Kendal had the proprietor supply several copies of the marriage lines. And I expect they have a few loose ends to tie as well, for Kendal and I shall be departing within a few minutes. Our luggage is being put onto the carriage even now."

"But why?" Diana's voice was shrill with panic. "Surely you cannot mean to travel at night? And how can we go with you? Our horses won't bear another long journey so soon."

"Kendal thinks it best we return immediately with proof of the marriage, lest the constables descend on Candale with a warrant to search the house. I shouldn't like to imagine them barging about, especially in the nursery, before we can arrive to stop them. You will remain here with Alex, of course. A light supper is being laid out in your room, and the things I packed for you have already been taken there."

The whirlwind caught her up again. She hadn't thought what would happen after the wedding. Heavens, she still had not decided to marry him—never mind that she'd already done so.

The innkeeper swept through the door, all smiles and courtly grace as he bowed to the earl.

"He has been well paid for his services," Lady Kendal whispered, drawing Diana across the room to join the men. "Ask of him anything you require while you remain at Gretna Hall."

Lord Kendal turned to greet them. "The carriage is ready to depart, Celia, and a servant is waiting in the foyer with your cloak and bonnet. I shall join you in a moment."

73

The countess pulled Diana into a warm embrace. "Now we are sisters, you know, and I am so very glad of it. Perhaps at long last you will consent to address me as Celia!"

Heart sinking, Diana watched her sole ally disappear through the door. *Please* take me with you, she begged silently. Don't leave me here alone with *him*.

Lord Kendal took hold of her limp hand and held it between his. "I hope you will be very happy, my dear. And it is my conviction that Alex could not have chosen better if he'd searched a thousand years. Military men, it seems, have a talent for recognizing a desirable objective."

"They sometimes make mistakes, my lord."

"Even the best of them," Kendal agreed mildly. "We are pleased to welcome you into the family, Diana Valliant, but we shall save the speeches and toasts until you arrive at Candale." With a bow, he took his leave.

"I'll walk out with you," Alex said, passing directly by Diana as if she were a doorstop.

She must have been glaring at him, because her expression appeared to startle the maid who entered the room a moment later.

The girl dipped a curtsy, color blazing on her cheeks. "I come to take you upstairs, ma'am. To the Bridal Chamber."

Chapter 8

Diana had seen larger beds, she supposed, but none that dominated a room in such a way as the one in the Bridal Chamber. She kept her distance, hovering against the opposite wall and deliberately not looking at it.

Instead, she inventoried the rest of the furnishings. In two vases atop the mantelpiece, spring flowers were somewhat wilted from the fire blazing just beneath them. A lacquered screen in the Chinese style was folded in one corner. Candles flickered from a pair of wall sconces and a silver brace on the marble-topped dressing table. The maid had opened the armoire to show her that her dresses were there, and her stockings, underthings, and a night rail were folded in a stand of drawers.

Had she been left here alone to change into that decidedly flimsy night rail? Like the dresses, it was part of her London wardrobe and had never been worn. Nor did she wish to wear it tonight, not unless all the lights had been extinguished.

The supper Lady Kendal had spoken of was laid out on a small round table near the center of the room. Beside it were two graceful wooden chairs and a tripod that held a silver pail filled with ice chips and a bottle of champagne. As she gazed at the basket of pastries, the lobster patties and sliced meats, the open syllabub tart and wedges of cheese, her stomach roiled.

There was a sharp rap at the door. Without waiting for a response, Colonel Valliant strode in, closed the door behind him, and gave her a perfunctory bow. "Is everything to your satisfaction, madam?"

"Y-yes indeed. The chamber is most elegant, don't you think?"

He glanced around indifferently. "It's well enough, I suppose."

Having exhausted her meager supply of polite bedroom conversation, she watched with growing apprehension as he unbuckled his sword belt. He held it in one hand for a moment, as if deciding what to do with it, and finally tossed it onto the bed.

Her gaze fixed on the sword. Silver and leather against maroon and gold brocade.

"If you are considering making a run for it," he said, a trace of amusement in his voice, "there is no need. I have secured a second bedchamber for myself."

Chagrined, she drew herself away from the wall and squared her shoulders. "I had no thought of fleeing, sir."

"Did you not?" A faint smile lifted the corners of his mouth. "You put me forcibly in mind of a raw recruit about to panic at first sight of the enemy."

Enemy? "You are quite mistaken, Colonel Valliant. I stand firmly prepared to do my duty as your wife."

The smile broadened. "I'm afraid that if you stand firmly, my dear, we shall have no little difficulty carrying through."

"You know very well what I meant, sir!" Heat flooded her cheeks. "And this is hardly the time for word games. I was never any good at them, and they accomplish nothing."

"To the contrary." He stripped off his gloves. "Until I made you angry, you were undeniably afraid."

"Well, now I am angry *and* afraid."

"So I see. One of your hands is clutching at your skirts, and the other is knotted into a fist."

She glanced down in surprise. Good heavens! Hastily, she clasped her hands behind her back.

"Better if you had made two fists," he advised her, the smile gone. "Be angry when you will, madam. But if you fear me, we shall have very rough going."

"I don't fear you!" she said immediately. "Well, not terribly much," she added in strictest honesty. "The thing is, I don't *know* you. And now, willy-nilly, I am *married* to you. I do find that fearsome, sir."

"Quite." He folded his gloves over his sash. "As a matter of fact, I had become convinced you didn't mean to go through with it. You had made it clear you'd no intention of doing so, and while I had some hope you would change your mind, I cannot say that I expected that you would." His eyes narrowed. "You were closeted with Lady Kendal for rather a long time— one hour and eighteen minutes, to be precise—before sending word that Mr. Lang was to be called. Tell me the truth, please. Did she talk you into this?"

"Not exactly." Diana tried to recall their conversation. "Did you *wish* me to refuse?"

He crossed to the ice bucket and pulled out the bottle of champagne. In silence, his expression unreadable, he removed the cork.

"You have not answered my question, sir."

"I beg your pardon. To my mind the answer was perfectly clear. I said that I *expected* you to decline my offer, not that I wished it. Were I reluctant to marry you, you may be sure the offer would never have been made."

"I don't understand. How could you possibly have wanted to marry me? You know me no better than I know you."

He filled two flutes with champagne. "We have chosen an odd time for this conversation, don't you think? Why is it, do you suppose, that we married first and only began to debate the wisdom of our decision over our wedding supper?"

"I wish I knew," she said on a long sigh. "But here we are. And neither of us seems to know why."

He looked up at her, holding her gaze. "We can come to no conclusions tonight, Diana. You are exhausted and confused. I am . . . well, very much the same. But I believe that neither of us will sleep until we have made a beginning of some sort. At the very least, shall we drink a toast to our marriage?"

When he stayed in place and held out a glass of champagne, she understood that he meant for her to come to him. The distance between them was no more than a few steps, but he seemed to her very far away and impossible to reach. Then, without knowing quite how she got there, she was standing directly in front of him and he was pressing the glass into her hand. When she looked straight ahead, she saw the silver braid on his crimson collar and the black stock at his throat.

Slowly she lifted her gaze to his chin, and to his lips, and finally to his eyes.

He touched his glass to hers. "To my reluctant bride," he said with another of his faint, enigmatic smiles. "And to her remarkable courage."

She swallowed the lump in her throat. "To my equally reluctant groom," she replied softly. "And to his noble sacrifice."

Stepping back, he frowned at her. "I'll not drink to that, madam. You are very much mistaken to think me remotely chivalrous, and I am disinclined to martyrdom. Let us not pluck that crow again." After setting his glass on the table, he pulled out a chair and gestured for her to be seated.

"I meant no insult," she murmured, sinking down under his stern glare and watching him take the chair across from her. "And it is no more than the truth."

"Have we not agreed that neither of us knows the truth?" he countered in a level voice.

"But certain things are implied, are they not? Had my uncle left me in peace, you would never have considered marrying me."

"No? I distinctly recall making you an offer before I knew of his existence. I could as easily accuse you of accepting my proposal solely to escape him. Is that the case?"

She put down her glass. "I would hate to think I had done such a cowardly thing, but it may well be that I did. How can I explain myself to you when I've no idea what sort of creature I am? You have made a bad bargain, sir. You have wed a *nothing*."

"I promise that you have drawn the shorter straw," he said with a harsh laugh. "Unlike you, I do know what I am. And while you can yet become anything you choose to be, I have already cast my lot with the devil."

"Rubbish. You *could* not!"

"Don't be so sure of that." He raised a mocking eyebrow. "It's not too late, you know. The papers are easily torn up. Mr. Lang, if I read him aright, can be bribed to forget the marriage ever took place."

"But it *is* too late. Lord Kendal is already on his way south to spread the news." She took a deep breath. "Besides, I don't wish to tear up the papers and forget what we did tonight. I simply want to know what to do next."

It might have been her imagination, but he appeared to relax. Infinitesimally, to be sure, but she supposed that soldiers never relaxed to any great extent.

"We have got off to a rocky start," he said, propping his elbows on the table and resting his chin on his folded hands. "I meant for us to find common ground tonight, but we appear to have dug ourselves into separate trenches. And as you plainly see, I have no talent for conversation, particularly with a young woman who is trying very hard not to regret becoming my wife."

"I am fairly sure I've no regrets, sir. What concerns me are *your* regrets."

"Ah. Will it help if I promise to tell you the moment I have any?"

"Dear me, no." She shuddered. "Each time you spoke to me, I'd be expecting the ax to drop. But you must always correct me when I displease you, and instruct me how to mend my character. I shan't mind that in the least."

His eyes shadowed. "I'll not be reading you any lectures, madam, save this one. Fear invariably displeases me, unless I see it on the face of an enemy. Even then I have a disgust of it, although I have been afraid more times than I can count. For that very reason I will never sit judgment over you, and if you perceive me doing so, put it down to my bad temper and pay me no mind. Is that understood?"

She made a vague gesture, still trying to imagine Colonel Valliant in fear of *anything*. It was beyond her power. She did understand, painfully, that he despised cowards, and now he had married one. Whatever was to become of them?

"Drink your champagne," he said, not unkindly. "It will help you to sleep tonight."

She obeyed, wondering if he could hear her teeth chattering against the rim of the glass. Then the bubbles went up her nose and she sneezed. Mortified, she took the handkerchief he offered her and buried her face in it. "I shall be stronger tomorrow," she mumbled. "I promise you that I will."

"And what do you wish to do tomorrow? Kendal assumes

that we will proceed directly to Candale, but when he said so, you appeared to dislike the plan."

She was astonished that he had noticed. "Would you mind very much if we returned to Lakeview instead?" she asked, peering at him over the top of the handkerchief.

"Not at all." He gave her a wry smile. "You see how easy it is? What else do you want to ask of me?"

His mood had softened, she realized, and there might never be a better time to approach the second most important thing on her mind. "Well, there is one matter I had hoped to mention, sir. I should very much like your permission to continue working on several projects that Miss Wigglesworth and I have undertaken. Oh!" She clapped one hand over her mouth. Until this moment, she had not considered that he might object to Miss Wigglesworth living with them.

"You will need to define *oh!* for me," he said when she failed to continue.

"M-may she remain at Lakeview?"

"Why not? I like her. She speaks her mind."

Taking heart to find him so unexpectedly agreeable, she plunged ahead. "And may we proceed with our venture? Of now it is little more than a seed, but I've no end of schemes to make it grow."

"Then do so." He refilled her glass. "What else, madam?"

"Nothing more, sir. Thank you. Except . . ."

She could not ask him. She wasn't even sure what it was she had to know. How were they to live together? What did he expect of her?

"Blurt it out, Diana." He looked mildly amused. "Before it chokes you."

It all but paralyzed her. "Is this to be a r-real marriage, Colonel Valliant?"

"If you mean will I bed you, the answer is yes."

"No." She waved a hand. "I mean, that is not what I meant. I always assumed that you would."

"Then what are you asking? I have every intention of keeping to the vows I made you, in case you were imagining otherwise. There is no love between us, of course, but we, too, have planted a seed. Perhaps it will grow and flourish. I must warn you, however, that it would be unwise to expect a great deal of me. I shall be faithful, yes, and protect you and honor you. More than that, I cannot promise."

It was what she had needed to know, she supposed. He was an honorable man, and she could safely depend on him to keep to every letter of the wedding vows. Well, save for the one than mentioned love. She presumed that love had been mentioned, although she had no recollection of it.

She had never considered the possibility he'd fallen in love with her, nor dared she to dream that he might come to love her sometime in the future. Really, she ought not to care that he had put into words what she already knew. But she did care.

Forlorn Hope.

He touched her hand. "I believe we will make no more progress this night, madam. Shall we start afresh tomorrow? Sleep as late as you like, and we'll head out for Coniston whenever you are ready."

"I'm an early riser, sir."

"Excellent. More common ground." He went to the bed and retrieved his sword. "It won't be so bad as you are thinking, you know. Remember, you have only to tell me what you want. Don't make me guess. I have lived in the company of men all my life, and what I know of females wouldn't fill a canteen."

"Then you are far advanced of me, sir." Standing, she brushed at her skirts with quaking hands. "What I know of men wouldn't fill a thimble."

To her astonishment, he came directly up to her and brushed the lightest of kisses on her forehead. "Then we must stumble along in harness, madam wife, and make the best we can of this marriage. For now, I hope you will sleep well."

The words bubbled to her throat of their own accord. Heaven knew she hadn't formed them in her mind, but out they came. "Stay. If you wish. If you want to . . . to . . ."

She couldn't finish. But he knew what she meant. She saw the light flash in his eyes. And then it was gone.

His smile was singularly sweet, though. She had not seen such a smile on his face before.

"I always want to, " he said. "I am a man, and men are fairly predictable in that way. But I'm not a beast, Diana, and you are not ready."

Yes I am!

But she couldn't say such a thing, and it probably wasn't true. What she wanted, emphatically, was to get it *over* with. She would not feel married until they did what married people did together, which she knew about in theory but had trouble imagining in actual practice.

It seemed so very . . . intimate. Invasive. He would put himself into her body! Perhaps he was right. When she considered what was to happen, she wasn't the slightest bit ready for it.

"Very well, sir." She forced herself to smile. "I bid you good night."

Chapter 9

Diana was on her way downstairs when her husband stalked into the house, his jaw set and a leather portfolio clutched under his arm. Pausing with one hand on the newel post, she watched him toss his hat and gloves to Carver.

He barely glanced at her. "I wish to speak with you, madam. Carver, see to it there is a decanter of brandy in the study and inform Miss Wigglesworth that we are not to be disturbed."

Crimson-faced, the butler hurried down the passageway.

Diana, greatly wishing that she could go with him, studied the wintry look on Colonel Valliant's face. He was in a black mood, that was perfectly evident, although she could not begin to think why. This day had been exactly like all the others since their marriage. He'd left the house after a breakfast taken in solitude and returned not much later than he usually did.

She never asked where he was going, or how long he'd be gone, or what he did with his time. If he wanted her to know, no doubt he would tell her. And because he expressed no interest in her affairs, she dared not meddle with his.

Clinging to the newel post for support, she waited, as he waited, for Carver to bring a decanter to the library and ignite the lamps. The colonel stood in rigid silence, his gaze fixed on the floor. At length he turned and strode with military assertiveness down the passageway, plainly expecting her to follow.

She would, yes she would, just as soon as her legs steadied under her.

There were scores of reasons, she supposed, for him to be displeased with her. He had married her on a gallant impulse, and what had he gained but a wife he didn't want and a ramshackle household overrun with the sort of people not generally admitted to aristocratic drawing rooms.

All in all, she readily admitted, he had been remarkably patient with her these last few weeks. He never interfered with her activities. He asked nothing of her, not even his rights as a husband. But she ought to have prepared herself for when his patience ran out, because it was inevitable that sooner or later he'd take control of the house. And her.

She had been careful not to think of it. She could not bear to. He engulfed her. Overwhelmed her. He filled every room when he wasn't even there. And when he was, the effect on her was cataclysmic. He was too powerful. Too intimidating. Too *male*.

Diligently she hid from him. Her days were spent among the women, who provided an effective shield, and in the evenings she closeted herself with Miss Wigglesworth. But she couldn't always escape, not altogether. Occasionally he joined them in the drawing room after dinner, settling in a chair by the fireplace to read his book.

She often glanced over to see his gaze fixed on her. She could *feel* him looking at her. Not merely sense it, but actually feel it, like a touch.

And now he was angry. Dear heavens. She would sooner face a rampaging boar than Colonel Valliant in a temper. But no rampaging boars came to her rescue, so she was forced to make the long walk down the passageway and into his study.

He was standing beside his desk, looking excessively severe. "I have been to Lancaster," he said. "Your trustees wished to consult with me regarding the disposition of your inheritance. They have provided me a detailed accounting of their stewardship and a list of your assets."

"Oh?" she said warily. The trustees had been selected by her father, and she'd always assumed them to be reliable. "Has there been some difficulty?"

"Not that I am aware. For the time being they will continue to manage your inheritance. I was prepared to make disposition of the funds then and there, but was persuaded to speak with you beforehand."

That explained why he was so out of temper, she thought, sitting when he pointed to a chair. Colonel Valliant would not appreciate lessons in conduct from his wife's solicitors. "I know nothing whatever about matters of finance," she said. "You must do as you like."

He opened the folio, withdrew a sheaf of papers, and spread them over the desk. "You are an heiress," he informed her brusquely, as if she were unaware of the fact.

"That has never been a secret, sir. Surely you were told the conditions of my father's will."

"The terms were perfectly clear. But no one saw fit to mention the *amount* in question. I certainly never expected a rural Lancashire baron with an insignificant estate to have amassed a substantial fortune."

"Well, the family has been about it for several hundred years, you know. And the estate itself was of considerable size until my great-grandfather sold the unentailed land. He preferred collecting art to farming, so now the Whitneys have very little land and a great many paintings. Excluding the contents of the house, which have not recently been appraised, I believe the total is fifty-eight thousand pounds."

"More than sixty now," he said from the oak sideboard where he was filling his brandy glass. "The funds are currently invested on the Exchange."

"You are displeased with that arrangement, sir?"

"How could I be, knowing virtually nothing about managing large sums of money? Kendal will make an evaluation when he has examined the records."

"He has already done so. But I meant displeased about the amount. One could imagine that you wished the fortune to be significantly . . . smaller."

"Of that, you may be sure." His eyes narrowed. "Had I known the truth, there would have been no question of entering into this marriage."

"Good heavens." Had he taken leave of his senses? "You are affronted because your wife turned out to be *wealthy*? But that is nonsensical. I should think you would be delighted."

"To be thought a fortune hunter? You greatly mistake my character, madam."

"Probably so," she agreed with a sigh. "I know very little about you. But why should anyone believe that you married me for my fortune? I never had such a notion, and at the time we were wed, I assumed you knew all about it."

"It never crossed your mind that I might be looking to line my pockets?" He gave her a look of patent disbelief. "Most men would wed a barn owl if it flew in with a dowry of sixty thousand pounds. Why should I prove an exception? And why the devil are you smiling? This is not in the least amusing."

"I'm sorry, but what you said put me in mind of Fidgets, who was at one time vastly in love with Kit. But Fidgets turned out to be a male, as if being a barn owl were not obstacle enough, and—"

"What in blazes are you talking about?" The colonel mauled his hair. "No. I'm quite sure I don't want to know. Let us return to the subject, if you please."

Diana shrank back on the chair. "I beg your pardon, sir."

"And *stop* that! No apologies, not even if they are due. Understood?"

"When you are looming over me, Colonel Valliant, and shouting at me, I have difficulty understanding much of anything."

"Fair enough." He dropped onto a chair behind the desk. "I'll not loom and shout. But you must confess that I warned you, Diana. I said you would have by far the worst of our bargain, and now you are learning what I meant."

That, she reflected with sudden insight, was the sort of thing *she* might have said. But she would not debate which of them was the least worthy, for the answer was perfectly clear. How achingly discouraging it was to learn that the one thing of worth she had brought to the marriage—her fortune—only displeased him. Gazing at the white-knuckled hand gripping his glass, she wondered how to deal with this stranger who was her husband.

There was one other bond they shared, she thought, astonished when the notion popped into her head. They were both angry. But he was free to show it, while she must guard her tongue. Ladies were not supposed to *have* tempers. Ladies, she had been taught, were invariably polite. If they had strong feelings or controversial opinions, no one—most particularly no gentleman—wanted to hear about them.

Even so, she had observed that Lady Kendal freely spoke her mind, and Lucy could strip paint from a wall with her tongue. Why did the rules of deportment not apply to them? Both had husbands who adored them, which must prove something. It was significant that two of the Valliant brothers had chosen to marry females who had no fear of asserting themselves.

But then, unlike his brothers, Colonel Valliant had not married for love.

"Here." He pushed the glass of brandy across the desk. "Drink the rest of this. You've gone white as chalk."

She obediently took a swallow, disliking the taste immediately, but it was deliciously warm as it slid down her throat and settled inside her. Dangerous stuff, brandy. She set the glass on the floor. "The fortune will not go away simply because you wish it did not exist, Colonel. And it wasn't as if I had a choice in the matter. The money passed from my father to my trustees, and from there to you. I have never touched a shilling of it. Nor can I put a hand on one now, unless you give it me."

"The lot is yours to dispose of as you will." He lifted his gaze, meeting hers. "With one key restriction. For so long as you elect to live with me, I shall provide for you from my own pocket. Which is all but empty, you should be aware, and like to stay that way for a considerable time. What funds I can muster will be directed primarily to the development of the land. Eventually the house will be repaired, although we'll see to the most urgent problems immediately. There will be nothing to spare. No luxuries. Neither of us will have access to the fortune, which will be held in trust for our children. Assuming you ever mean to get about producing any, of course. Am I making myself clear?"

"Oh, perfectly. We are to live in poverty. You imagine that I have embraced chastity. It is certain I have taken a vow to obey you. Lakeview appears to have become something of a monastery, sir." She put aside the remark about children, which hurt far more than she could bear. "Am I permitted to express an objection to your terms?"

He looked startled. "Yes indeed. Say whatever you like. But for practical purposes, the subject is closed."

"And why is that, sir? Because you are too proud to spend my money, even if I wish you to? Am I to do without an abigail? Pin money? Will the chimneys be permitted to smoke and the masonry to crash about our ears for the sake of your *pride*?"

Color stained his high cheekbones. "Naturally I shall make every effort to provide clear chimneys, an abigail, and a reasonable level of comfort. That is my duty, madam wife."

A neat evasion, she acknowledged, of the question relating to his pride. A question he'd no intention of answering. Which meant the answer was *yes*, of course, and that he knew it was *yes* and that he could not in honor deny the truth of what she'd said.

It was enough for now. To push her small advantage would be to lose it, she understood, observing his taut lips and the lines between his drawn-together brows. But if she proceeded cautiously and chose her goals carefully, perhaps he would someday agree to a more flexible arrangement regarding her inheritance.

"I expect you'll want an allowance," he said, propping his elbow on the desk and cupping his chin in his hand. "I am prepared to be reasonable. So long as you do not touch the principle, you may draw a reasonable sum every quarter from the interest. Not a penny, mind you, is to be used for household expenses. Buy fripperies, or spend the money on those women you have apparently adopted. I've no doubt that you will. They have already laid claim to virtually all of your time."

Gracious. Unless she was much mistaken, his tone had been decidedly petulant. Her uncle had sounded very much the same when bemoaning his ill luck at the gaming tables.

Was Colonel Valliant *jealous* of the hours she devoted to her ladies and their welfare? Surely not. The idea was so improbable that she nearly dismissed it out of hand.

But he raised the subject again. "I can't walk five steps

without tripping over one female or another. They cringe into corners when I pass and curl into knots if I chance to enter a room where they have gathered. What the devil are you *doing* with them, Diana? More to the point, why are they always *here*?"

"You gave me permission to invite them," she reminded him nervously. "We discussed this on our w-wedding night."

"Probably. But since my thoughts were decidedly elsewhere at the time, I cannot recall what you said. Did you tell me *why* they would be trooping in and out every damn morning, or why you ride off every afternoon and stay gone the rest of the day?"

How could he know that? *He* was the one who stayed gone the entire day, and she could not imagine him quizzing the servants. "You didn't seem interested, sir. You said I could do as I wished. Have you changed your mind?"

He shrugged. "Even if I had, I'd not dishonor my word. You may go on as you have done, certainly. But if you've no objection, I would very much like to know what it is you are about."

"Gladly." She folded her hands in her lap, searching for the best way to explain. A military man was bound to find her vague, disorganized schemes entirely unacceptable. She knew very well that she was always guessing what she ought to do, and speeding ahead because if she stopped, everything might collapse around her.

"You needn't frown, Diana," he said, his gaze intense. "Nothing will change unless you wish it. I ask no more than an explanation."

"Very well, sir." Brief and to the point, she told herself, before he loses patience. Seizing a deep breath, she began speaking at a rapid pace, taking care not to look at him.

"When first I rode out to explore the countryside, I could not help but see the difficult circumstances under which so many of the people are forced to live. Primarily the women, most of them widowed by the war or left to care for the children while their husbands are elsewhere looking for work. There is none to be found here, so they go to Manchester or Birmingham. And some appear to forget they have families, for they send no money home."

She warmed to her story, which was at the heart of every-thing she dared to let herself care about. "Each woman you have seen here has a different tale to tell, but the endings are very much the same. They have been abandoned. They are without funds. The parish cannot support them all, and few have anywhere else to go. So you see, I have set about helping them find ways to provide for themselves. Which is really quite absurd, when you think of it. Of the lot of us, I am the least capable."

"I rather doubt that," he observed mildly. "But go on. How do you mean to accomplish these marvels?"

"*They* will do the accomplishing, sir. I am merely the one who brings them together. And since I've little idea what ought to be done from one day to the next, we stagger along as best we can."

"Have you not mapped out a plan? There's no use gathering an army and launching an assault without a clear objective."

"Well, we do have a goal of sorts. We are producing mer-chandise to be sold at the Michaelmas Fair in Kendal. But we got off to a late start, and with only a few months to prepare, we are forced to select our products carefully. So far we are mostly experimenting with items we can manufacture quickly and with minimal expense. There is little seed money for our en-deavors, I'm afraid. And the ladies, many of them, have chil-dren to tend to. They can spare no more than a few hours a week learning to make hand creams and the like."

"Hand creams?"

"Among other things," she said quickly. "I am always look-ing out for ideas that offer more stability and better income than selling goods at a fair. Small enterprises, if you will, that permit the ladies to work independently. The Michaelmas Fair is our most immediate objective, but we have many others."

"And are like to achieve none of them," he observed, "with-out coordination of time, effort, and resources. Am I mistaken to think you currently lack organization, madam?"

"Oh, no. You are quite on the mark. Consider that I am the one leading this endeavor, sir, and I scarcely know my left foot from my right. There is a good chance I'll lead the lot of us over a cliff."

He fell silent for a prodigiously long time, looking past her at the wall.

She could not read his expression. Did he mean to tell her to give it up? She squirmed on the chair, wishing he would say something. *Anything,* just so it put an end to this awful suspense.

Would she fight him if he ordered her to abandon her women? She hoped that she would. But the brief fire of anger that had propelled her when they quarreled about her inheritance had long since burned out. She waited with cold dread for his verdict.

"It happens," he said slowly, "that I have a degree of talent for organization. It runs more to marshaling troops than . . . er, matters relating to hand creams, but it is possible I could be of some assistance. If you have any interest in what advice I might offer you, of course. I don't mean to interfere." His gaze went from the wall to the top of the desk, never meeting hers. "Feel free to tell me to go to the devil."

She could scarcely believe her ears. He hadn't ordered her to put an end to her projects. He had offered to help! What was more amazing, she had the distinct impression that he *wanted* to help.

She regarded him with astonishment. Color tinged his cheekbones and his gaze remained firmly planted on the desk, as if . . . but no. It couldn't be. Not Colonel Valliant.

He could not be *shy.*

Were she looking at anyone else, though, that is exactly what she'd have thought.

"*Would* you advise us, sir?" she asked, still unable to credit that he meant what he'd said. "We would be so very grateful. The ladies pretend that they have faith in me, but I know they wonder if this is all a foolish caprice on my part and a waste of time on theirs. Were you in charge, they would have a great deal more confidence."

"*They* mean nothing to me." He still refused to look at her. "How do *you* feel about it?"

"Deliriously pleased," she replied honestly. "Profoundly relieved. Terrified you'll take back your offer because I fail to say the right thing. We need you, sir. *I* need you."

He cleared his throat. "Advice only, mind you. I'll not usurp your authority, nor do I wish to take on your responsibilities."

"Oh, no. I'll do all the work. Really. You needn't put yourself out."

"Well, then." He gathered up the papers on his desk and stuffed them back into the leather folder. "Pull your chair next to mine, madam, and let us begin."

Chapter 10

Diana settled herself to his left, a little sideways on her chair because of the desk drawers directly in front of her, and smoothed her blue skirts over her knees.

She was, Alex realized, closer to him than she had been at any time since their wedding. He sucked in a deep breath, burningly aware of the soft, feminine scents hovering around her and the heat pulsing from her body. His bride. His wife.

What would she do, he wondered, if he pulled her onto his lap and kissed her? He had been unable to think of anything else for the last several minutes, while she nattered on about hand creams and private industries and Michaelmas Fairs.

She looked over at him expectantly. "Well, sir, how are we to proceed?"

Quite evidently *her* mind was entirely on the business at hand. Resigning himself, he arranged paper, pens, and ink in front of them. "Since I know no other way to go about it, we shall approach this as a military exercise. You have already chosen a target and recruited the soldiers, so let's begin by aligning them for battle."

At the top of a sheet of paper he wrote, in large letters, *Diana's Regiment*.

She laughed, the sound clear and musical. Like wind chimes in a Spanish courtyard, he thought, immediately distracted again. Had he ever heard her laugh before? Not in such a fashion, he was sure. He had given her few enough reasons to do so.

"I am to command a whole *regiment*? Does that make me a general, sir?"

"A mere colonel, I'm sorry to say." He regathered his wits.

"The first thing you must do is look over your troops and select those qualified to become officers." He drew a series of boxes. "We'll not assign ranks as yet, or set up a chain of command. For now, we shall list only their names and their skills."

"Now? But I cannot simply choose the leaders off the top of my head. I must think on it."

"To be sure. I mean only to show you how to begin. Later, when you have taken a decision about someone, go to this chart and fill in a box."

"I see." Her brow knitted. "Then we should start with Miss Wigglesworth, I suppose."

He wrote her name in the topmost box. "And what can she do, Colonel?"

She laughed again. "I shall have difficulty answering to that, especially when it comes from you."

"It will *only* come from me, unless you inform the ladies that they have enlisted in an army. I'm not persuaded they would be pleased to know it. Keep in mind that this chart is no more than a device to help you become better organized. Later, when you have mentally divided your regiment into battalions and companies, you will know who to put in charge. Understood? Now tell me about Miss Wigglesworth."

Diana propped her elbows on the desk. "Well, she is an excellent gardener. Mostly flowers, but she also grows herbs for the kitchen. She embroiders. She is an expert in the stillroom. She has a talent for nursing. Oh, she can do a great many things."

He had stopped writing after *embroiders*. "This is all too vague. What specifically qualifies her as an officer?"

"Hmm. Primarily, she lives here. She is always close to hand, and we deal well together. Moreover, she is practical by nature, which I am not. She sees when something must be accomplished long before I do. And she fears no one, while I fear anything that moves. Quite simply, I need her."

In the box he inscribed, *Colonel's Prop.*

As she leaned forward to read the words, her long hair brushed his sleeve and trailed over his wrist. He felt the touch resonate throughout his body.

"Infamous!" she exclaimed. "*Prop* indeed."

"That is what you just described to me. Mind you, half of what you said was twaddle. If necessary, you would get on perfectly well without her. But she has the experience of many years for you to draw upon, and you would be a fool not to take advantage of it." He scratched out *Prop* and wrote *Adviser.* "How's that?"

"Better." She gave him an impudent grin. "And I've thought of another reason to promote her. She is a gentlewoman, which sets her apart from the others. They defer to her. And they respect her as well, for more significant reasons than her birth. Whenever one of them is creating a problem, and I'm sorry to say there are more than a few troublemakers in the ranks, Miss Wigglesworth quickly sets the miscreant in order again."

Second-in-Command, he penned. "I'll leave you to fill in the rest. Decide how best she can serve, and be precise. Otherwise you are like to waste her time and talents."

She nibbled at her lower lip. "This isn't easy, is it?"

"You don't know the half of it," he murmured, wrenching his gaze from her mouth. The full, beautifully shaped lips. The— What the devil were they called? Small. White and even.

Teeth!

Damn. He couldn't think straight. His body, mounting an insurrection of its own, was drawing all the blood from his head and dispatching it in a southerly direction.

"I think I get the point," she said, her whole attention focused on the chart. "But I need more practice. Can we do another?"

"Another what?"

"Another officer, of course." She drummed her fingers on the blotter. "But you don't know the regiment ladies. Drat. You won't be able to tell if I get it wrong."

Alex chose a box near the bottom on the page and scribbled *Sergeant Alexander Valliant.* "We'll do me," he said.

She leaned closer to see. "Sergeant? *You?* Surely not!"

"Ah, but the sergeants are the ones who know everything, Colonel Diana. We gentlemen buy colors and swoop in, more ignorant than dishrags, good at riding and shooting and not very much else. The sergeants endure us, and teach us about war, and eventually we learn enough to lead them. I have always aspired to be a sergeant. In your regiment, it is the only rank I'll accept."

"Oh, very well, since this is purely an exercise. But I've no idea what the duties of a sergeant can be. What do we write in your box, sir?"

He had a sudden, intense desire to know what she expected of him. What she wanted him to do. She wouldn't write what he longed to hear, that was certain. But for a few minutes she would be thinking about him, which was more attention that he'd got from her since Gretna Green.

"Here." He gave her a blank sheet of paper and handed her his pen. "You put down what you think I can do to help. If in doubt, put down what you *hope* I can do. I'll write my own evaluation, and then we'll compare notes. Agreed?"

Her brow wrinkled. "I am to devise a list of your duties?"

"Precisely. And remember, sergeants are remarkably versatile. Use me however you will."

She bent over her paper with the concentration of a child trying to inscribe her name for the first time. Her knuckles were white as she clutched the pen tightly, the feather brushing at her chin the way his fingers wanted to do. Finally she wrote something.

He tried to see what it was.

"Oh no," she said, making a barrier with her shoulder and a curtain of her hair. "No fair peeking until I'm done."

Locating another pen, he dipped it in the inkwell and swiftly scrawled a few words. Then he leaned against the arm of his chair, pretending to be thinking, and simply gazed at her.

In the candlelight, her heavy auburn hair was molten copper. Unable to see her face, he traced the shape of her arm resting on the table. The shadows at the curl of her elbow and wrist became dark, seductive caves. The fine texture of her milky skin, so different from his own tanned and weathered body, entranced him. The pale golden hairs on her forearm were a forest he longed to roam for hours. Months. Years.

Even his too-long-banked sexual urgency melted in the softer heat of his desire to explore, with something close to worship, the seductive mystery of this woman. Sweet Diana. Brave and fearful Diana, who had no idea the power she wielded over him. She had only to look at him to bring him to his knees. And at the same time he knew that she was far too young and gentle for a rough-and-tumble soldier like Alex Valliant.

But he wanted her anyway. His very toenails ached from wanting her. He had restless dreams about her at night and erotic fantasies about her when awake. She was his wife. With a word or a gesture, he could have her. He was entitled.

Wasn't he? Why then could he not bring himself to say the words? Make the gesture? Did he fear to take a woman so precious as Diana to his bed?

Lost in thought, she brushed a shock of hair behind her ear. For once she had forgot to keep him to her left side, where he could not look too closely at the spiderweb scar on her right cheek. Now, the ridges of it etched out by candlelight, he could see clearly what she always tried to conceal.

She thought the scar made her ugly, he knew. Most probably it was the first thing anyone noticed when meeting her. She would be aware of that, and watchful for any sign of repulsion.

He wondered how she would react, could she see *his* scars. But they were invisible, thank the Lord, except to him, and he could not fail to be aware of them at every moment. They never stopped bleeding. They existed, he often thought, to keep him in mind of what he most wanted to forget.

He must make sure that Diana never saw them.

"I'm done," she announced, setting down her pen. "And were Sergeant Valliant to actually take up all these duties, he would be a busy man indeed."

Alex snapped to attention, curious to know what she would have him do. "Well, let me hear what they are, Colonel Diana. I hope they do not involve the testing of hand creams."

Her gaze went immediately to his hands. "Eau de Veau might do those calluses some good, I must say. But no, that is not on my list." She raised her sheet of paper and began to read. "Seek out suppliers of necessary materials and negotiate their purchase at favorable rates. Coordinate distribution of same to the respective manufacturers. Assist Mr. Beadle with construction and engineering. Arrange transportation for the troops, especially in bad weather, when they are required to attend classes or engage in group projects. Take note of particular abilities and recommend privates for promotion. Put down quarrels—a stern look will generally suffice. Be alert to profitable enterprises no one else has thought of."

She lowered the paper and smiled at him. "Above all else, advise hapless colonel how to go on."

Her smile caught at his heart, a piece of him he had thought long since turned to stone. "A formidable list indeed, madam," he said evenly. "Can you clarify 'construction and engineering'?"

"Not very well," she replied after some thought. "The soldiers, many of them, are billeted in unsuitable quarters. Am I using the correct terms? Anyway, Mr. Beadle has taken it on himself to repair leaky roofs, shore up disintegrating walls, and hammer down loose floorboards. The farm animals require decent lodging as well. And if we restore a few old boats fallen out of use, fish can be caught to supplement the army's rations. Also, much land that would otherwise be planted is too often flooded by runoff from the hills. If we found a way to divert the water—"

She threw up her hands. "Oh, I don't know what I'm talking about. I see the problems, but I've no idea how to solve them."

Awestruck, he regarded her with considerable respect. And annoyance, because she was so naive as to credit that miracles could be worked by a few country women and old Mr. Beadle and a weary, disillusioned soldier. She would do well to confine her ambitions to perfumed creams and small-town fairs.

But he'd no more squelch her enthusiasm than snuff out the last candle in a world already too dark by far. "One problem at a time, madam. It's well to have great dreams, but wise to build up to them in small ways. As you have already determined, I am sure. The Michaelmas Fair is a good beginning, but channeling water from the fells will have to wait."

"Yes." She sank back on her chair with a sigh. "I do get carried away. Half the regiment thinks me Bedlam-bait when I rattle on about grandiose schemes and impossible goals while they worry about feeding their children."

"If they are penniless, how the devil are you financing the projects you've already begun?"

"Oh, they give what they can—milk and eggs and wool, that sort of thing. For the rest, I've been selling a few bracelets and rings and earbobs. I've no need of them, after all. But the regiment mustn't know of it. The ladies do not wish for charity, I promise you, nor would they learn independence if they thought I would always be there to support them. You needn't think I'll come asking you for funds, sir, on my account or on theirs."

She was referring to their quarrel about her inheritance, of course, which he would as soon forget ever happened. He'd behaved like the backside of a mule. He had never considered her wishes and feelings. Females came equipped with a damnable lot of feelings, he was discovering, and he had not the least notion how to deal with them.

"You haven't showed me *your* list," she said, reaching for the sheet of paper on his side of the desk.

He took hold of her hand. "Leave it be. There's nothing on it."

"No fair, sir. We had an agreement. Let me see what you wrote."

Releasing her, he watched her turn the paper over and scan the five words he had scribbled there. *Whatever is asked of me.*

"I don't understand," she said, frowning at him. "What does this mean?"

"What it says," he replied tersely. "I was to list what I was willing to do, or capable of doing, for the regiment. There is my answer."

"Oh."

"Mind you, I'd no idea you had it in mind to divert rivers." He mustered a smile. "But I should have guessed. You are a remarkable young woman, Diana. You never fail to astonish me."

"Oh," she said again. She seemed unable to say anything else, but tears had gathered in her lovely hazel eyes.

He regarded them with something close to fear. "Colonels do not weep," he informed her sternly. "Nothing will be accomplished if you indulge your female sensibilities."

She wiped her eyes with the back of her hand. "That is your opinion, sir, but I cannot agree. All good things come from caring enough to make them happen. And men have sensibilities as well, even if they are not accompanied by tears. You have a devotion to honor and duty, do you not? And how does that differ from my own desire to be honorable and to make myself useful?"

It differed, he was sure. How, he could not say, but if females were so much like males, he would be able to understand them. Stood to reason.

She folded the paper where he had inscribed his commitment to the regiment and slipped it into her pocket. "You needn't answer, sir, but I hope you will think on it. And you may be certain that I shall call on you for help, if you truly meant what you wrote. No engineering projects, though. I shall confine my requests to reasonable duties."

"And I shall try not to disappoint you," he said, his mouth dry. *If* he meant what he wrote? How could she doubt it? He watched her stand, shake out her skirts, and move to the door. She was leaving, and he wanted to stop her, but his tongue was stuck behind his teeth.

She turned, with the grace of motion that never failed to entrance him. "I am most grateful, Alex. I know you do not care to hear words of apology or of gratitude, but sometimes they must be said. I'll not rabbit on about it, but I trust you know what is in my heart."

He nodded.

"Well then. I'll leave you in peace. You must be hungry, though," she added, her hand now on the door latch. "Shall I send a supper tray to you here, or would you prefer to eat in the dining room?"

He stood, willing his tongue loose, not sure he dared to say what he wanted. But he wanted it too much not to say it. "Come to bed with me, Diana."

Her hand dropped to her side. For the barest moment she held in place, her head bowed, and then she turned to face him again.

"Certainly," she said.

He felt as if a blanket of snow had fallen over him. *Certainly?* She'd have given the same answer if he'd said he preferred to take supper in the dining room. Asked her to pour him a glass of brandy. Pass him the saltcellar.

For an infinite time they gazed at each other in silence. Her face, which had been so bright with enthusiasm when she spoke of her plans to save half the world—or at least the part of it immediately surrounding Coniston Water—was totally without expression now.

Well, perhaps not quite. He would not have called it resignation. He would definitely not term it repugnance, or reluctance, or anything approaching an unwillingness to do his bidding. A maelstrom of female sensibilities was concealed by her passive acceptance. He'd have bet on it. But he was certain of only one thing, and it froze him past his rampaging desire to make love to her.

She would go to his bed because she was grateful to him. She would lay herself down under him because he had promised to help her, and she reckoned he was due some form of repayment for his efforts on her behalf. Oh, he doubted that was her conscious intention—he'd learned more respect for her than that— but it was true nonetheless.

"Shall we go, sir?" she asked quietly.

He shook his head. "*You* go, Diana. I spoke on impulse. It has been a long day, what with the journey to Lancaster, and I am somewhat tired."

"Are you certain? If you imagine I do not wish to—that is, I am not at all unwilling."

"I know," he said, the arid taste of dry sand on his tongue. "But now is not the time."

"As you wish," she said at length, turning back to the door. As she moved into the passageway, she cast him a look over her shoulder. "May I ask if there will ever *be* a time, Alex?"

He longed to ask if she would ever *want* him. If she ever felt the slightest spark of sexual desire for him. But he had discovered that she was painfully honest, and what would he do if she said "no"?

"Soon enough," he said more harshly than he intended. "Good night, Diana."

Chapter 11

Diana scratched item seven from her task list and moved on to number eight, which took her from the root cellar to the kitchen. She had it to herself, because on Wednesdays Mrs. Cleese always visited her sister.

Miss Wigglesworth and five of the regiment ladies were gathered in the parlor, assembling the openwork squares each had embroidered into a tablecloth. Since Diana believed that the completion of a project ought to be celebrated, a tray of cakes and sweets was waiting for them in the larder.

On that thought she put down her spoon and went to filch a macaroon for herself. Then she dragged the heavy ceramic pot from beneath an iron plate warmer, raised the lid, and set to work.

Her list of tasks grew longer by the day, but she took pride every time she could mark one of them accomplished. Indeed, she had never felt such a sense of purpose, and no longer minded very much when one of her efforts went awry.

"Here you are." Alex came through the door, his arms wrapped around a good-sized box. He set it on the pinewood kitchen table and gave her one of his faint half smiles. "I am pleased to report a large discount for buying in quantity, and the glazier has agreed to accept the return of unused merchandise."

He looked rather pleased with himself, she thought, putting down her spoon and crossing to where he stood. Alex had taken up his regimental duties as purchase officer with astounding diligence. She expected that merchants were somewhat intimidated by his commanding presence, but he was also willing to ride great distances in search of better materials and better prices.

"It will be a fortnight before the small jars are ready," he said, "but Mr. Dodd has adjusted his bill to reflect the delay."

"But we don't even require them yet, Alex. Seven or eight weeks would be soon enough."

"Nevertheless, he has failed to honor his contract. In future, when you require prompt delivery, he will be careful to provide it."

Laughing, Diana gestured to the box. "May I see what you've brought?"

He pried the lid from the box, brushed aside the packing straw, and handed her a square bottle about eight inches high. "The others are of similar shape, some larger and some smaller. Ten boxes in all. Will they do?"

"Oh, very well indeed. I'm so glad you suggested the square bottles, Alex. They will attract far more attention than the usual sort. Miss Gladys Yoodle is persuaded that we ought to tie colorful ribbons around the necks. What do you think?"

"I have no opinion on the subject of ribbons, madam, but every penny spent on packaging cuts into your profits. The bottles were not inexpensive, and we've yet to purchase the corks."

"Well, no ribbons then. We shall rely on the hand-painted labels, which the Yoodle sisters are producing for us."

His brow knitted. "Perhaps I am mistaken, but were not the Yoodle females in company with Mrs. Alcorn and her scandalmongers?"

"I fear so. They are gently born and would naturally prefer to move in the highest level of Coniston society, but they're also poor as church mice. When they asked to join us, I hadn't the heart to refuse them, and I must say that their labels are quite splendid. Come have a look."

She went to a cupboard and drew out a small stack of cards. "These are only samples, because we don't yet know how many we'll need of each one. Oh. Remind me to ask you about glue. And you see, they have inscribed the names of the different wines and painted a picture of what each is made from." She handed him the labels one by one. "So far we have rhubarb wine, cowslip wine, rose hip wine, elderberry wine, nettle wine, burnet wine, parsnip wine, dandeli—"

"Parsnip?"

"Parsnip wine, or so Mrs. Pottle informs me, will grow hair on an egg. She also says that it is delicious, but I shall have to take her word for that. In addition to our wines, we have orgeat, ratafia, and several varieties of cordial."

"What is that brew you were stirring when I arrived?"

"Ratafia." She led him to the ceramic pot. "It must be stirred every day."

He leaned over and took a sniff. "Good Lord, Diana. What the devil is in there?"

"Well, brandy for the most part, along with almonds, spices, and grated rind from lemons and oranges."

"That doesn't sound too bad—for a ladies' drink. May I taste it?"

"Not yet, I'm afraid. In another three weeks I'll add melted sugar, and then it will be ready to sample. Mind you, this is my first try at making ratafia, and the ingredients were frightfully expensive." She gave him a sideways glance. "Should I end up with a disaster, which is not at all unlikely, I shall feel responsible to pay for them myself."

"That is your decision, of course. But has the regiment become a guild of tapsters? I cannot help but notice that you are primarily engaged in the production of spirits."

"Oh, indeed we are. I have great confidence in the selling power of spirits, especially when they are sold in pretty bottles to give them a bit of cachet. Ladies will flock to them, Miss Wigglesworth assures me, and gentlemen can always be persuaded to buy intoxicants."

When he chuckled she rushed ahead, hoping the subject would hold him in the room a few more minutes. "The wines cost very little to produce, you know. The primary ingredients—rhubarb, dandelions, nettle tops, and the like—are available in our gardens or can be gathered in the fields. We have only to add water, sugar, yeast, and sometimes a bit of lemon juice. What's more, a number of the ladies already know how to make wines and cordials. They have their own special receipts and mean to show up all the others."

"Rivalries provide an excellent incentive, I agree." Seeming to lose interest, he gave her back the labels and headed for the door. "I am neglecting Mr. Beadle and Carver, who are waiting for instructions. Where do you wish the boxes to be stowed?"

"In the breakfast room, I suppose, stacked in a corner." She followed him down the passageway, digging into herself for a paring of courage. "Alex?"

He stopped immediately and turned to face her. "Yes?"

"Have you made plans for this afternoon?"

"None of importance." He clasped his hands behind his back, regarding her with a wary expression. "I had thought to help Mr. Beadle repair Mrs. Hinshaw's roof, but I'd more likely be in his way. Have you another errand for me?"

She hesitated. He did not look at all forthcoming, and perhaps this was not the best time to ask him. But with Alex, there never seemed to be a best time. "N-not precisely an errand," she ventured in a meek voice. "You see, this is the first free afternoon I've had in a long while, and I'd like very much to visit a farm where I once stayed for a few weeks. While there I learned a great deal, but I've many questions to ask the lady who took me in."

In the dim passageway, his eyes were an impenetrable midnight blue. She had no idea what he was thinking—not that she ever did. When he made no effort to enlighten her, there was nothing for it but to plunge ahead. "It's rather a long ride from here, sir. The farm, I mean. I had hoped you might be willing to accompany me."

"Certainly. When do you wish to leave?"

The immediate capitulation rocked her back on her heels. "Well . . . ah, right away, if you don't mind. First I must make sandwiches for Mr. Beadle and put on my riding habit. But I'll hurry."

She fled to the kitchen before he could change his mind.

An entire afternoon with Alex! Diana unwrapped cheesecloth from a joint of cold roast beef and took up a knife.

In the last three weeks, ever since the night he appointed himself her sergeant-of-all-purposes, she had rarely set eyes on him. When he wasn't gone to Kendal or Lancaster to procure supplies, he spent most of his time with Mr. Beadle, the only other male member of the regiment. More often than not they were employed elsewhere, after which they took supper together at one of the local pub houses. She often heard Alex return to Lakeview long after she'd retired to bed, his gait unsteady and his hand fumbling on the door latch of the adjoining room.

She could never sleep until he was come home. She listened for his arrival and for every sound he made until he went silent. And always she tossed and turned for an hour more, wondering what would have happened if she'd plucked up the courage to go to the connecting door, and open it, and go through it to his bed.

She wondered, but it never occurred to her to actually do so. By the end of a day spent teaching and putting down squabbles and making decisions when she hadn't the fuzziest notion what she was about, her allotment of courage was all used up. There was none to spare for her husband. None for their decidedly unconventional marriage. Not so much as a grain for her own unfathomable longings.

He knew perfectly well that he could bed her anytime he wished. She had taken vows to that effect. Gracious, she had twice offered herself in the most straightforward way she could—only to be rejected.

She hacked through a loaf of bread. What did he *want* of her, for pity's sake? When she said she was willing, he didn't believe her. Or she wasn't willing *enough*, by some incomprehensible standard of his own. Exactly how willing was she supposed to be?

It was plain as a pikestaff that *he* was the one with reservations. A man who wouldn't take "yes" for an answer must have been hoping for a "no." She understood his reluctance well enough—how could she not?—and would never blame him for it. But after all, they could consummate their marriage in the dark. It wasn't as if he'd have to *look* at her.

She slapped slices of beef between slabs of bread, added two cucumber pickles and several hard-boiled eggs, and wrapped the lot in a length of brown paper.

Leaving the parcel in the breakfast room for Mr. Beadle to find, she sped upstairs to change into the hunter-green riding habit she had worn on the journey to Gretna. Perhaps it would remind Alex what had happened when they got there. Colonel Valliant had taken himself—for better or worse—a wife.

He was waiting for her in front of the house, wearing a dark blue riding coat and a wide-brimmed beaver hat. "It looks to rain this afternoon, I'm sorry to say. Do you still wish to make the journey?"

"Oh, indeed. It rains most every day. Haven't you noticed?" She lifted her veil to glance up at the dark clouds scudding across a sky that had been clear only a few minutes earlier. "Never say you mind getting a bit wet, Colonel?"

Grinning, he tossed her onto the saddle and slipped her foot in the stirrup. "Where are we off to?"

"South, to the Rusland Valley." She watched him mount his restive horse with practiced ease. "When we get to the road, shall we have a run?"

He touched his hat. "After you, madam."

The rain set in as they were picking their way single file along a grass-floored track that led through holly groves and stands of silver beeches. Wind shuddered through the leaves, and fat drops of rain splatted on her bonnet and shoulders.

Alex pulled up to ride beside her. "Within a few minutes we are in for a deluge. Is there shelter close to hand?"

"None that I know of, but I've come this way only once before. I believe the farm to be no more than three miles from here, though, and the nearest village is Colton, which we passed some time ago." She gave him a hopeful smile. "We might as well go on, don't you think?"

With a shrug he dropped back, and they proceeded at a slow pace over the marshy ground. The storm blew in not long after, announcing itself with a crack of thunder that bounced off the surrounding hills. Rain hissed through the trees. When they emerged from the woodlands to open ground, they were pelted in earnest. The rain quickly soaked through Diana's riding habit and streamed down into her half boots. She could scarcely see through the sodden veil, but when she tossed it over the brim of her bonnet, the wind soon carried it down again.

The landscape became a patchwork of hillside pastures fenced in by low graystone walls. Inside them, sheep and cattle huddled with their backsides to the fierce wind.

"Over there!" Alex shouted, moving past her. "Wait here."

Confused, she reined in and saw him wrestle open a low wooden gate just ahead and to her right.

"Come now," he called.

She guided Sparkles through the narrow opening onto a rock-strewn field. The path, if there was one, could not be distinguished in the downpour. She waited for Alex, who seemed to know where he was going, and a few moments later he took the reins from her hands and led her up an increasingly steep hill.

At the top, on a ledge about thirty feet wide, a wattle-and-daub hut nestled against the cliff that rose straight up behind it. Rained poured down the sloping slate roof and puddled around the building, very much like a moat. There was a thatched canopy jutting out to one side of the hut, supported by wooden posts, and Alex drew the horses underneath it.

Diana slid from her saddle and splashed through the ankle-deep water to the door of the hut. It was unlatched, and she soon found herself inside what looked to be a storage shed for hay. Bales were stacked to the low ceiling against three of the walls, leaving only a small space where a herdsman had stashed a few tools and a rolled-up pallet. Two square blocks of hay, hip-high and likely used as a makeshift bed, made up the only furniture.

She removed her limp bonnet and gloves and shook her drenched skirts. So much for her lovely afternoon with Alex, she thought sourly, wrenching pins from her dripping wet hair and combing it out with her fingers.

But on the other hand, perhaps this was an unexpected opportunity, one she had scarcely dared to hope for. Until the storm subsided, she would have him alone in a confined space. A very dim space as well, for the only light came through the door she had left cracked open for him.

If he couldn't see her, she wouldn't be so terribly self-conscious. Well, not so much as usual. At least she would not be blisteringly aware of his height and his strength and his splendid good looks, which generally rendered her tongue-tied.

Perhaps, just perhaps, they could have a real conversation. Not one concerning the regiment's business, which was the only thing they ever seemed to discuss, but a conversation about them. More specifically, about *him*. She knew virtually nothing about the man she'd married, and thought it long past time he told her what he'd been doing for the four-and-thirty years before they met.

He appeared in the doorway, filling it as he stomped his feet and brushed water from his hat. "A snug enough cubbyhole. Have you got yourself oriented, madam? Unless I close this door, the hut will soon be as wet as we are."

She sank down on one of the blocks of hay and waved a hand. "Do come in, Alex."

He pulled the door shut, sealing off the light, and she heard the creak of wood. He was leaning against the door now, she guessed. When her eyes adjusted to the dark, she affirmed that he was. The barest trace of light, slicing through a narrow crack between the bottom of the door and the floorboards, was broken at the two spots where his boots were planted. She imagined him standing as he so often did, arms folded across his chest, watching and waiting.

If only she'd had time to prepare for this opportunity. Here they were, and she could not think of a single way to inaugurate a conversation. The silence grew like an inflated balloon. He would be content to wait forever, she expected, before saying a word.

"The storm will pass quickly," she said too brightly. "Don't you think?"

"In my experience, lakeland storms rise swiftly at this time of the year and soon blow through. With any luck, we can be on our way within the hour."

Again silence enveloped them. So much for the weather as a topic of conversation. And as she had resolved not to mention the regiment, what remained? Her toes curled inside her half boots, making a squishy sound.

It dawned on her that he was angry. He had not said so, but of course, he wouldn't. Nor could he be pleased to spend his afternoon in a pitch-black hay shed on her account. Possibly it would clear the air if she addressed the subject.

"I'm sorry for bringing you out in the rain," she said, taking care that her voice did not squeak. "When you indicated that we ought to stay at home, I should have heeded your advice."

He made a low noise in his throat. "I gave no advice. I simply asked a question. It occurs to me, madam, that I ought to levy a fine for each time you torment me with one of your needless apologies. Have I not made it clear that I don't want to hear them?"

"Perfectly clear, sir." Heat rose up the back of her neck. Why must he behave in such an off-putting manner? He was no wetter than she, and they'd soon be dry again. He could have said no when she asked him to ride out with her, but he had accepted straightaway. And what was the good of her sitting here on a bale of hay and him standing there against the door without a word passing between them? If he was angry with her for no good reason, she might as well give him a *real* reason.

Even though he could not see her, she deliberately sat straighter on the hay bale. "I believe, sir, that this would be an excellent time for us to come to know each other somewhat better than we do. We have been married for seven weeks now, but we remain strangers in almost every way." She took a deep breath and went on before he could stop her. "Naturally I'd be glad to tell you what little there is to know about me, although it would make a tedious story for a rainy day. The interesting bits, what few there are, you have already heard. They are, after all, the reasons you married me. For the rest, you cannot wish to hear about life at Miss Wetherwood's Academy for Young Ladies, nor how I went on as a pampered only child in my parents' home before being sent off to school."

"To the contrary," he said while she was seizing her next quick breath. "I would very much like for you to tell me about yourself. I would be interested even were I not a captive audience."

She let the faint joke pass her by. Another time she might have given him what he said he wanted, but she knew it was only an evasion, his wish to listen to a schoolgirl's stories. And she was too fired up to let him have his way, as he always did simply because she never dared to defy him.

Not until now.

Before her patched-together courage fractured, she closed her eyes and clenched her hands and jumped into deep waters.

"I wish to hear about *you*, Alex. It's my turn now. You have lived nearly twice as long as I, and you have gone to war, and you have seen and done a thousand things to my every one. Tell me of—oh, I don't know. What it was like to be in Spain."

"Hot."

"That is hardly a sufficient response, sir."

"Hot and dusty, then. I've no intention of discussing the war with you, madam. There is nothing of it that I care to recall."

This was much like drawing teeth, she supposed, never having seen it done. But she would keep pulling and wrenching, because she meant to have at least one tooth from him before the day was out. "Were you ever wounded?"

He made a low noise in his throat, rather like a snarl. "No. Not to any degree. Few soldiers escape the odd scratch. Now leave it be, Diana. I won't be subjected to an inquisition."

"We are having a *conversation*, sir. That requires you to participate. And since you have spent the better part of your life in the army, I cannot help wishing to hear about it. Surely you were not always engaged in combat. There must have been times that were not so very unpleasant. Can you not speak to me of those?"

"They would be incomprehensible to a female," he said after a lengthy hesitation. "We found ways to amuse ourselves, of course. Sports, wagering, drinking—the usual pastimes of men in the company of other men. For the rest, you may imagine long days of tedium and routine, broken occasionally by short periods of extreme horror. We marched a great deal. When encamped, the companies spent most of their time in training, preparing themselves to form squares against a cavalry charge,

111

load quickly and fire, use bayonets to advantage, that sort of thing. They must learn to react automatically, because in the noise and smoke and chaos of a battle, there is no opportunity to stop and think what to do."

"Did you train with them?" she asked, wondering what he meant by forming squares.

"At times I supervised, but the sergeant majors were primarily reponsible for drilling the troops. The Forty-fourth is a foot regiment, but like most superior officers, I went into combat on horseback. Officers ride as much to be seen as for any other reason, I have always thought, but there were occasions when I was in the thick of it and fought from the saddle. When horses were shot from under me—three at Salamanca alone—I had occasion to wield my saber from the ground."

"*Three?* But when you lose one, where does another horse come from? Do you have spares?"

"I traveled with a string of horses, yes. But they were never to hand when most I needed them. If grounded, one waits for a riderless horse to come by, and leaps on its back, and gets on with the fighting."

"Oh my."

"And that, madam, is all I have to say about the war." His voice was hard as granite. "I have done as you asked. I have *participated*. You must content yourself with what you have already heard."

Very little that signified, she realized, although she had been fascinated nevertheless. But he'd told her nothing about *himself*. Nothing that helped her to know him, certainly. She would have to leave the subject of the war now, if she hoped to make any progress, but what else was there? His childhood was too remote, although one day she meant to quiz him about it. She wanted desperately to know about the women in his life, for there must have been some, but even the rush of courage that had brought her this far would not permit her to broach such a dangerous topic.

What of his travels after the war? She remembered how anxiously Lord Kendal had watched for one of his brother's rare letters in the post. Months went by between them, and in the interim, no one could be sure where Alex was or if he was still alive.

"No more conversation about the war," she agreed. For now, she added silently. "But I should like to hear about what you did when it was over. You traveled extensively, I am told, all the way to South America. That must have been quite an adventure. But I've wondered why you went there instead of coming home."

"That is none of your concern, madam. And you needn't pry any further, because I'll not address the subject now or in the future. Understood?"

"No," she replied, clutching the bale of hay with both hands. He had never before spoken to her in precisely that tone. She could not have explained it, but in the darkness, she imagined ghosts hovering in the air. There was the faintest odor of blood, and the sound of iron walls dropping between them. "I *don't* understand, Alex. Why can you not speak of it?"

"Are you altogether certain you wish to know? Perhaps I have done unspeakable things."

"Rubbish!" she fired back immediately. "You could no more be wicked or dishonorable than I could fly to the moon. But I do believe you are troubled by something that happened in Spain, or possibly in the American War. It haunts you even yet, does it not? I can feel its presence here and now, Alex. You wear it around you like a shroud."

"Bloody hell, woman! You have no idea what you are talking about. All soldiers are haunted by what they have seen and done. It comes with the profession. And you may be sure that the last thing they want is to revisit the past and reopen old wounds to satisfy the pernicious curiosity of a green girl."

"I am not being fanciful," she said as calmly as she could manage. "As well you are aware. Nor am I the only one to recognize that you bear the weight of—well, whatever it is you are keeping to yourself. When I knew you even less well than I know you now, Lady Kendal advised me that—"

Something, probably his fist, slammed into the door. "You *dare* to discuss my affairs with members of my family? That is betrayal of the highest order, madam. Do so again and I cannot answer for what I will do in return. Meantime, we are finished here. Rain or no rain, we proceed now or return to Lakeview. And whichever direction we take, I'll hear not another word from you about matters that are none of your damn business!"

With that, he flung open the door and was gone.

Chapter 12

She was taking him to a bloody damned pig farm!

There was no mistaking the odor that hung thickly in the damp air as they came through a narrow fold in the hills. He had smelled it often enough in Portugal and Spain, a noxious brew of wet bristles, offal, and mud.

Diana was riding a considerable distance ahead, her posture straight as a rifle barrel, never looking back to see if he was still following her. Perhaps she hoped that he was not. Since leaving the cottage, she had spoken only once, a cool "Thank you" when he helped her mount, and she'd ridden off at a fast clip before he'd managed to swing onto his horse.

How was this quarrel *his* fault? he wanted to know. And who the devil was that prying, prodding female he'd been marooned with in the hut? Not his sweet-natured wife. Not shy, couldn't-say-boo-to-a-goose Diana, who melted into a puddle if he looked at her the wrong way.

What had possessed her to confront him all of a sudden? Demand that he tell her things she had no business knowing? He'd thought he had safely married a woman who would leave him be.

Well, she'd certainly done *that*.

Leave the *past* be, he meant. Take him as he was and never question how he got that way. How the devil could he answer her, even if he were willing to try? He'd spent more than two aimless years roaming the Americas in search of—well, he couldn't have said what, but all he'd got for his pains was a bout of dysentery that almost did him in.

As he'd told Diana, what did any of it matter now? Knowing why things had fallen out as they had, or what he could have done differently, changed nothing. He wanted only to forget. He never would, he was all but certain, but dear God, he wanted to. Moving on would help, he kept hoping. A purpose in life would help. Diana in his bed would definitely help.

But from out of nowhere she'd asserted herself, as she had never before done with him in such a fashion. He supposed that no harm had come of it. She had learned nothing, and he had set her right. It would be a long time before she tried such a thing again, and if she did, he was now firmly on his guard. Hell, it took only a raised eyebrow to set her shivering in her slippers. Oh yes, she would behave.

So why did he have the distinct feeling that this battle had only just begun?

The musky odor of wet animals grew keener. Directly ahead he saw smoke wafting from the chimney of a neat, two-story stone cottage set a little apart from half a dozen low farm buildings and a good-sized barn.

Diana was already off her horse and embracing a tall, full-bosomed woman of about his own years. She wore a mobcap over lush chestnut hair, a homespun gray dress with the skirt tied into a knot about her knees, and rubber work boots. A rake lay fallen at her feet, close by a repellent heap of straw and dung.

As he rode up, an ugly mongrel, all teeth and wet fur standing on end, rushed from the barn to bark at Thunder and spring about his hooves in a doggy game of tag.

Swearing under his breath, Alex quickly dismounted and planted himself between the dog and his horse.

"Alicia! *Come!*"

Bowing its head, the dog slunk to the farm woman's side and nosed repentantly at her boot. She scratched behind the floppy ears. "Good girl."

To Alex's profound disgust, Diana dropped to one knee in the mud and opened her arms. Yipping deliriously, the dog flung itself at her, licking her face and wagging a stubby tail so hard it ought to have broken off.

The woman approached him with open friendliness, a wide smile on her lips, one hand outstretched. With little choice he took it, meaning to bring it to his lips in a formal salute, but she grasped his hand in a firm grip and shook it vigorously.

"You are Kit's brother," she said. "The military one. He told me about you. And I am Helen Pratt, but I answer only to Nell." She made a sweeping gesture. "Welcome to Pratt's Piggery, sir, a thriving little establishment if I do say so myself."

"Honored to meet you," he said, somewhat taken aback.

"You must be uncomfortable in those wet clothes. Remove your coat, Colonel, and I'll hang it to dry." When he hesitated, she clicked her tongue. "Surely we needn't stand on ceremony in a barnyard."

"No. I suppose not." He peeled off his sodden riding coat and passed it to her. It wouldn't dry anytime soon, but perhaps the sun, just breaking through the clouds, would have some effect on his shirt. The soaked cambric adhered to his flesh like a second skin.

Nell regarded his shoulders and chest with a look of unconcealed admiration. "My, my. Diana did very well for herself, I must say. But then, the same could be said about you. She's as good-hearted as they come. In the short time she stayed here, I grew extremely fond of her."

Alex glanced over his shoulder at Diana, who was now surrounded by ducks and geese, all of them clamoring for her attention. She was *petting* them, by Jupiter. The dog, shunted aside by the aggressive birds, crouched at the perimeter of the circle and whimpered forlornly.

He knew precisely how that dog felt.

Nell cleared her throat. "Colonel, where I mean to hang your coat is t'other side of the house. Will you you join me for a few moments? There is something I wish to ask you."

"Certainly." He followed her to where a length of thin rope was suspended between two birches. "How may I be of service?"

"Well, sir, it happens that my Eddie was in the army as well. He died at Fuentes de Onoro." She carefully stretched his coat over the rope line. "Were you there?"

"I was."

She turned to him with an assessing gaze. "This will strike you as an odd request, I am sure, but I have always wanted to know what it was like. You see, Eddie took the king's shilling only a year after we were wed, and I saw him no more than a handful of times after that. He wrote nearly every day, though. Packets of his long letters would arrive twenty and thirty at a time, and in them he shared with me even the most insignificant of his experiences. I marched with him and fought with him and scavenged meals with him all the way to Fuentes de Onoro. And then I had only one letter, from his colonel in the Fifty-second, informing me that he had died heroically in battle."

Alex reflected on the scores of letters he had written under similar circumstances. Instant death. No pain. The fallen soldier had sacrificed himself to save his comrades. Would live in memory as one of England's finest and all that rot, when the poor sod was probably shredded by grapeshot without knowing what had hit him.

"I am acquainted with many officers of the Fifty-second," he said in a guarded tone. "Indeed, they are my particular friends. Whichever of them sent you the letter was doubtless giving no more than the plain truth of it. Eddie Pratt died a hero, although that can be little consolation now. Nor can I think how I might add to what you already know. In my experience it is always a mistake to dwell on the past, especially when it concerns matters of war and death."

She gave him an understanding smile. "I am sure of it, Colonel. Nevertheless, I want you to describe what happened there. Not the gruesome parts, of course. I'd not dream of asking you to call them again to mind. But I need to see all the rest. The countryside. The town. Where Eddie would have been and what he'd have been doing in the hours before battle. It's important to me, Colonel Valliant. I was with him nearly all the way to Fuentes de Onoro, and then he vanished. I lost him too soon. But if you will sketch for me his last few days and hours, I will then be able to join him there in spirit."

He must have been scowling, because she looked suddenly apologetic. "Although this seems exceedingly peculiar, I assure you that I am quite sound of mind. But I live my days and nights on a pig farm, sir, with only my memories for company. And the one memory I most long to have is the one you can supply me."

After all the battles that followed Fuentes de Onoro, he could scarcely recall details of the engagement with Massena save that it had lasted four interminable days. He remembered well enough the maze of cottages and alleys that swept down from a high plateau to the River Dos Casos, and the courtyard where he'd been pinned under his fallen horse for several hours, and—

She put a work-roughened hand on his forearm. "Never you mind. It was wrong of me to presume on you when I've no more than the briefest acquaintance with your wife. And Kit, of course, although I know him somewhat better. He is wed now as well, I understand. I've not met his Lucy, but Diana informs me that she is just the one to bring him to respectability."

"I cannot say," he said, wildly uneasy in the presence of a female so quick to share confidences with a stranger. He liked Nell, certainly. One could scarcely help liking her. But why was it that women were so prodigiously bent on cutting up a man's peace? He'd been too long in the company of men to have any knack for dealing with females. Somewhere along the way he'd picked up a notion of what they were supposed to be like, but the ones he'd met since returning to England defied his every expectation.

"I confess I'll miss the rogue," Nell said, leading him back to the farmyard. "He'd sometimes go to ground here when the excisemen were on his trail, and he never arrived without several bottles of excellent French wine. We had quite the time of it, we did."

They came around the corner, and Alex was stunned to see Diana whirling in a sort of dance and flapping her skirts up and down. She stopped the moment she saw them, but not before he'd got a comprehensive look at her shapely calves and creamy thighs.

Blushing furiously, she smoothed her wet skirt with both hands. "I was trying to dry out," she explained weakly.

"Come inside, love, and change into one of my dresses." Nell led Diana toward the house, flashing Alex a knowing look over her shoulder.

When they were gone, Alex let out the air he'd been holding. In those few seconds, he had seen more of his wife than in all the forty-eight days since the wedding. His reaction was predictably immediate and uncontrollable.

Nell had been aware of it, that was evident, but he couldn't be sure about Diana. Probably not, though. She never appeared to notice anything about him, save how he could be of use to the regiment. Where she was concerned, he might as well have been a packhorse.

Oh, she would come to his bed if he gave the order or made the request. She had said so often enough, in that calm, bloodless, I'll-do-my-duty tone of voice. And while he was heaving on top of her, she'd no doubt be calculating how many bottle labels would be required for the parsnip wine. Her detached resignation slapped cold water on his desire whenever it heated him to the point of asking. It stopped him short when he was all but ready to beg. He wanted her, by God, but not unless she wanted him as well.

Nell bustled from the house, a notebook and pencil in one hand and a cup in the other. She pressed the heavy ceramic mug into his hand. "Tea. It's left over from breakfast, I'm afraid, but it will warm you up. Diana will be out shortly. I told her to dry her hair by the kitchen fire." She cast him a sly look. "I understand, Colonel Valliant, that you are about to go into the pig business."

He choked on a swallow of tea.

"First you've heard of it, I expect," she said with a grin. "Or perhaps I mistook Diana's meaning. But she intends to learn all there is to know about raising pigs—within the next hour, it seems—and during the fortnight she was here, she did develop an inordinate fondness for the beasts. Mind you, that is not the proper state of mind for a swine seller. Pigs are well enough, I suppose, and they are certainly profitable, but it's a mistake to feel affection for any creature you mean to sell for slaughter."

He went cold, remembering how it was to give an order dispatching men to almost certain death. To lead them there and escape untouched, as he invariably did, while his fellows were cut down all around him. He almost never let himself recall those events. But she had spoken of Fuentes de Onoro, and asked him to think back on it, and now he couldn't stop himself. Nothing out of the ordinary had happened there, not to him, but now that the floodgates were open, battle after battle began to replay in his head.

"To be sure," Nell said, "she'd barely escaped a Bow Street Runner, and she'd been hiding for weeks with nothing whatever to do because it was far too dangerous for her to venture outside. When Kit brought her here, the poor child was boiling over with energy. She fed all the animals, mucked out the sties, and left me practically nothing to do. First holiday I'd had in years. For Diana, working on a pig farm was far better entertainment than hunkering down in a cave with constables and Runners poking about overhead."

That got his attention. "She was living in a bloody *cave*?"

Nell tilted her head, regarding him with curious eyes. "Diana has told you nothing of this? My, my. You should ask her about her adventures, Colonel. She has quite a tale to tell."

He produced a noncommittal grunt just as Diana emerged from the house.

She was wearing a woolen dress the color of wheat, far too large for her and shapeless as a sack. But he had seen something of what lay underneath, and thought of her legs, and was forced to turn his back to her.

She paid him no mind, to his great relief. And even greater regret, were he to be perfectly honest about it.

Nell and Diana had vanished into the barn before he rallied himself. For the next hour he trailed behind them, ignored, while they prattled about pig houses and farrowing rails and mast, whatever the devil *that* was. He learned what pigs ate, which was apparently everything, how fast they grew, and the best treatments for various porcine ailments.

All the while, he watched Diana. He had never before seen her eyes so bright. She laughed when Nell told her that pigs were fond of drinking spirits, and her mouth dropped when she discovered they were excellent swimmers. She asked scores of questions and took meticulous notes, her body practically vibrating with unmistakable passion.

For pigs.

She was all on fire—just as he'd always wanted her to be— for bloody damned *pigs*!

Next came herding techniques. After releasing several swine

from their stalls, Nell gave Diana a small sack of beans and showed her how to recognize the Leader Pig. That was an easy task, since a formidable-looking porker immediately began nosing at her skirts in search of food.

Diana headed for the barn door, dropping beans one by one in front of the Leader. It gobbled them up posthaste, but the others trotted along as well, evidently hoping for a stray bean to come their way. Very soon Diana had got them all to the courtyard, where she was quickly surrounded by eager pigs.

"What am I to do now?" she asked, giggling like a schoolgirl.

"A handful of beans directly center," Nell instructed. "Then extricate yourself."

Diana did as she was told, clambering over the pigs when they circled, snouts to the beans and curly-tailed rumps sticking out like spokes on a wheel.

"They will remain in that position for quite some time," Nell said. "Long after the beans are gone, they refuse to stray from the last place they found food."

"But why?" Diana regarded the ring of swine with a frown. "I thought pigs were supposed to be smart."

"So they are, but at times they think with their stomachs." Nell tossed a grin at Alex. "Creatures often do their thinking with irrational bits of their anatomies. You must learn, Diana, to exploit that particular weakness whenever you come upon it."

Alex gritted his teeth.

"One final lesson," Nell said, reaching into her pocket for a length of twine. "When you cannot get a stubborn pig to go in the direction you wish, you persuade it that you are aiming in the opposite direction." She expertly separated one pig from the circle, tied the string around a hind leg, and gave the other end to Diana. "Return him to the barn, my dear."

Looking puzzled, Diana moved to the front of the pig and tugged on the string. The pig speedily backed up, went off balance, and plopped onto the ground.

"Remember what I said," Nell advised. "You want to lead him into the barn, so that is precisely what you are trying to do. It won't work, I promise you."

"Oh!" Laughing, Diana made her way to the pig's backside. "I take your point." This time she pulled the string directly away from where she wanted to go, and the pig lumbered to its trotters, heading forward. To the barn, as Nell had predicted, and intent on getting there in a hurry. Diana, towed helplessly behind, vanished through the doors.

"She learns quickly," Nell said with a sly wink.

He nodded curtly, rather sure Nell Pratt had been educating his wife in matters that had nothing to do with pigs.

Diana soon emerged from the barn, beaming with satisfaction. "Right into the stall he went, bless his heart. I can't remember when I've had so much fun. Did you see that, Alex? Who would have thought pigs to be so biddable?"

"Biddable?" He gave her a black look. "You employed treachery, madam."

"It was wonderfully effective, though, and I've no objection to treachery in a good cause. Kit used it to advantage against my uncle, and now I have used it against a pig. Although come to think of it, my uncle *is* a pig."

Her eyes had gone bleak of a sudden, reminding Alex that his resourceful wife bore the scars of her uncle's fury. Never conscious of her scar until she put him in mind of it, he sometimes forgot that she was unceasingly in mind of it. Casting about for something to say, he found only a terse, "Some pigs are better than others."

But her face lit up again, and she came to him and gazed hopefully into his eyes. "Might we choose one of the better ones, Alex, and take it home with us?"

"Now? *Today?*"

"Oh, yes. We ought to get started right away, don't you think? And if we don't select a pig while we are here, we'll only have to come all the way back to get one."

After seeing her brightness snuffed, even for that brief moment while she was thinking of her uncle, he could not say no to her. Not to anything she asked of him. "Are we to tie a string around its leg," he said with a forced smile, "and pull it backward the whole distance to Lakeview?"

"That won't be necessary," Nell said, visibly enjoying his discomfiture. "Why don't you retrieve your coat, Colonel Valliant, while Diana decides which pig she prefers? And if you take your time about it, I'll have everything ready to go when you return."

He understood well enough that the ladies wanted to exchange confidences out of his earshot, and he was acutely aware that they would likely be talking about him. "As you say, ma'am," he agreed with a stiff bow before retreating in the direction of the clothesline.

He paced for twenty minutes behind the house, pocket watch in hand to check the time. Twenty minutes was all he was willing to allot for pig selection and the dissection of his character, which was doubtless their prime order of business.

Nell was attaching an oval-shaped wicker cage to his horse when he returned to the barnyard. Inside the openwork container was a wriggling, squealing piglet.

"I trust you can mount in spite of this," Nell said, fastening the last tie and tugging at the cage to make sure it was firmly affixed behind the saddle.

He gave her a sour look.

Diana finished rolling her wet clothes into a bundle. "If you don't mean to wear your coat, sir, I'll add it to this lot."

He passed it over, and when she had stuffed the clothing into a sack and secured it to her mare, he helped her onto the saddle. "You will be chilled on the ride home, madam. We'll not reach Lakeview before dark."

"Nell has gone to fetch me a woolen cloak," she said, "and you are to have a blanket. But what think you of our pig, sir? Is he not a handsome fellow?"

He was spared having to answer by Nell, who tossed a blanket over his shoulders. "Diana chose well," she said. "Now off with you both while the light holds."

Mounting effortlessly, still mildly insulted she had implied that he couldn't, Alex looked down into her gold-specked brown eyes. Quite a woman, Nell Pratt. And she had sheltered Diana, befriending her when most she needed a friend.

"Regarding the matter we discussed earlier," he said in a stilted voice, "I have had a change of mind. If you still wish it, and when time permits, I'll call on you again."

Nell's smile all but knocked him off the horse. "Thank

you, Colonel Valliant. I knew I could not have mistaken your character."

He could not help but smile back. "It will be my pleasure, ma'am. And it will be soon, I promise you."

"Excellent. But for now, sir, your wife is leaving without you."

He looked up to see Diana disappearing around a curve some distance away. And without so much as a good-bye to Nell, which was unlike her, or a sign to him that she was going. What in blazes had set her off *this* time?

Not wanting to appear in a great hurry, he guided Thunder along the path at an easy trot. Trotting, he quickly discovered, did not agree with the pig, which expressed its displeasure in no uncertain terms. Alex supposed it could not be comfortable, trapped in a cage and bouncing about atop Thunder's flanks, but he wished to hell it would shut up.

He slowed and the level of noise decreased, but that meant it was half an hour before he caught up with Diana. She had put on her soggy bonnet and lowered the veil.

They rode side by side for a time, not speaking, and the silence was so tense that even the pig joined in.

Finally Diana looked over at him. "I know that you dislike it, sir, but I feel that I must apologize to you for my behavior in the hay shed. I had no right to quiz you in such a fashion, let alone continue to do so when you told me quite plainly to stop."

She must have been rehearsing that little speech, he thought. It clipped along like hoofbeats on a flagstone courtyard. And unlike her usual meek apologies, it had sounded not in the least repentant.

"The incident is forgot," he assured her. "You mustn't refine on it. I was out of temper."

Nodding, she picked up her pace and rode ahead of him for what seemed an eternity. They were leaving Nell's house, he thought, the same way they got there—at odds. Diana, javelin-straight in the saddle, was leading the way while he straggled behind, wanting to close the distance between them and unable to think how to do it. Telling her things she had no right to know was not an option, even if he wanted to take her into his confidence.

125

Sometimes, primarily when he'd had overmuch to drink, he wanted to do precisely that. He'd spent too many long nights in the taproom of the Black Bull with only Mr. Beadle for company, staggering home in the wee hours several sheets to the wind. He'd stumbled to his empty bed and collapsed there, wondering if he ought to have gone instead to the room next to his where Diana lay. But there'd been little he could do in his inebriated state, even if she'd welcomed him with open arms, and he soon fell fast asleep.

Nevertheless, he had actually considered telling her. That was progress of a sort.

The track widened, and she dropped back again to ride alongside him, her veil fluttering in the late-afternoon breeze. "I have to know, Alex," she said. "You have every right, I'm sure, and I'll not make any objections. But she *is* my friend, and you must see how difficult this will be."

"How difficult *what* will be?" Damn, but he hated that veil. He could not see her eyes. "I've no idea what you mean."

"Of course you do. I may be a virgin, sir—well, I *am* one— but that doesn't make me altogether stupid. If you intend to take Nell as your mistress, just say so."

"As my—?" He reached over and snatched the hat from her head. "What in bloody blazes gave you such a ridiculous idea?"

She was white as milk, but she raised her chin and regarded him with disdain. "What you said to her. 'If you wish it.' 'I'll call on you.' " She gulped. " 'It will be my pleasure.' "

If she weren't trembling so, he'd have broken down in laughter. From her perspective, his conversation with Nell must have sounded decidedly odd. Even provocative, come to think of it. Dear Lord.

He schooled his voice to a calm tone. "Do you really imagine, Diana, that I'd have arranged an assignation with another woman in your presence? You have a poor opinion of me, I must say."

"Well, I'm not sure I really thought it." Her hands clenched on the pommel of the sidesaddle. "But then I couldn't stop thinking *about* it, so I made up my mind to ask you straight out."

He knew her well enough by now to understand what it had

cost her, that direct question. And he was astonishingly pleased that she cared he might take a mistress, although he certainly never would.

"I regret the misunderstanding," he said slowly, casting about for an explanation that would reassure her. "Nell had asked me to tell her about the battle at Fuentes de Onoro, where her husband died. And as you might expect, I declined. But when we were about to depart, I heard myself agree to do so, and because I hadn't intended to say any such thing, my words were not well chosen. It was all perfectly harmless."

Color flamed on Diana's cheeks. "Oh, my. Oh, do forgive me, Alex. How foolish of me to—"

"*Stop* that!"

She froze in alarm.

"I was talking to the pig," he said between clenched teeth. "Sorry. But what the devil is he *doing* back there?"

"Well, he's got his front trotters through the openings in his cage, and they are having at your . . . your—" She erupted in laughter.

He scrunched forward on the saddle, to no avail. "I have tried to cooperate, madam, and if you insist on turning Lakeview into a pig farm, I'll not prevent you. But in future, you will import your stock without my direct assistance. Understood?"

"C-certainly," she replied, still laughing. "But only this one pig, I promise you, is destined for Lakeview. If there are to be any pig farms, they will be established elsewhere. I am hoping that a few members of the regiment, those with little productive land, will take up the profession, but Nell was of the opinion that the very idea of raising pigs would meet with resistance unless you and I showed the others how easy it is."

"How can we raise pigs with just one? Even swine require a pair for mating purposes."

"Yes." She blushed again. "We will only demonstrate the care and feeding of a weaner. Most anyone can rear a weaner. Indeed, I want every member of the regiment not living in town to have one."

"And you believe they will follow our example?" he asked dubiously.

"Oh, yes. And just imagine, Alex. Come winter, we shall have a lovely supply of ham and bacon and sausages."

Winter, he thought as the pig squealed and prodded, could not come soon enough.

"And he'll find most of his own food," Diana continued blithely. "He's a clever little thing, our piglet, with a spirited nature and remarkable vigor."

Oh, indeed. A pattern-card of pighood. The absolute cynosure of swinedom.

"I think he should have a name, Alex. What shall we call him?"

He cast her a dark look. "Dinner."

Chapter 13

Dinner, Alex couldn't help but notice, seemed to spend most of his time in the house.

Mr. Beadle had constructed a pen behind the stable to lodge him, but the determined young pig was not so easily contained. Every night he contrived to escape and take up a position by the front door, waiting for someone to open it. Then he shot inside like a bullet, aiming directly for the kitchen.

There was little point trying to catch him, Alex had learned after several attempts. And since no one else was keen to evict him, he'd resigned himself to a piglet running tame in his house.

The regiment ladies took special delight in the pig's company, slipping him morsels from the refreshment trays or bringing him treats from their own kitchens. When there was no food in the offing, the pig trotted briskly behind Diana as she went about her tasks, grunting with pleasure whenever she paused to scratch the top of his head. In the evenings, while she worked at the writing table or sat reading a book, Dinner was invited to stretch out on her lap for a snooze.

This particular weaner would never live up to his name, Alex was certain. If Diana had her way about it, Dinner would enjoy a long and pampered life as a member of the Valliant household.

Not unexpectedly, he had joined Alex that morning for breakfast, poised beside the chair like an alert puppy, his bright piggy eyes focused expectantly on the fork as it moved from the plate to Alex's mouth. Now and again the flat disk of his snout nudged Alex's boot, reminding him—as if he could fail to be aware of it—that a poor starving pig waited expectantly for a handout.

Trying to eat in the face of such intense regard grew increasingly irksome. Alex finally abandoned the effort, set his plate on the floor, and left the room, taking his cup of coffee with him to drink in peace.

He wandered in the direction of the entrance hall, where Diana was greeting the ladies who were arriving for a lesson in pencil making. That was one of her favorite projects, and she had high hopes for its success. A fortnight ago he'd accompanied her to Keswick, where the graphite was mined, and on the way he had learned considerably more than a man really needed to know about pencils.

Much of the assembly work, Diana informed him, was contracted out to independent laborers. They required little space, which meant that her ladies could set up shop in their own homes. But first they must be taught the skills, so she planned to hire an instructor and hoped that Alex wouldn't mind if he stayed at Lakeview while the classes were in progress.

Having accepted a pig into his home, he could scarcely object to a pencil maker. Bemused, he had followed her through the streets of Keswick as she popped in and out of shops and small factories, asking questions, collecting names and information, and evaluating suppliers of cedarwood, blacklead, and glue.

None of those encounters began well. Without exception the men in the shops and factories listened politely to what she said, and then promptly turned to him. Business was not the province of females, their expressions said clearly, and when it came to actual discussion of terms, she must naturally step aside.

His heart ached for her. He wanted to step in, take over, and spare her the humiliation. But she would resent him if he seized command, so he pasted a look of profound stupidity on his face and pretended to be a servant. When someone addressed him, he mumbled, "Dunno what you be talkin' about," and slumped off to the nearest corner.

Left a mere female to deal with, the shopkeepers and manufacturers dismissed her out of hand. All the air seemed to go out of her then. But she straightened her spine, turned on her heel, and flounced away with Alex slouching after her, his hands itching to pummel the louts. When they reached the pavement she marched to the next shop and tried again.

As the day wore on, he suffered for her until he could scarcely draw breath. Unused to playing a passive role, he had to force himself minute by minute to hold back, look stupid, and bank his rage. She was unaware of his presence, he suspected, all her energy and will concentrated on the task at hand. Like a race-horse or a soldier in the heat of battle, she permitted nothing to distract her.

Only once, as they emerged from the office of Keswick's most prominent pencil wholesaler, did she speak to him. "I should very much like," she said solemnly, "to carve out the entrails of that pompous windbag and feed them to Dinner."

"No discriminating pig would have them," he replied, pleased to hear her laugh from under that damnable veil. She had kept it pinned back on the ride to Keswick, but the moment they came in sight of the town, down it came and down it stayed.

In every other way she was uncommonly brave that day, and eventually her persistence won out. When they finally set out for home, she had found her teacher, struck bargains for the necessary materials, and negotiated a contract with a whole-saler for several thousand pencils to be supplied by her regi-ment within six months. All on her own.

He was so proud of her that his tongue twisted into knots. And just as well, for she never stopped chattering all the way back to Lakeview. With an acerbic wit he'd not seen in her be-fore, Diana skewered the pretentious merchants with devas-tating accuracy. Success had freed her of her inhibitions, and she glowed with triumph.

He fell in love with her that day in Keswick. Or he admitted to himself that he had loved her for a considerable time, as-suming love consisted of respect, desire, and a red-hot cannon-ball lodged in his chest.

The classes had been going on for the better part of a week now, and Mr. Filbert, a shy, thin man with gold-rimmed spec-tacles balanced precariously on his narrow nose, reported that all five students were making excellent progress.

Hoping for a word with Diana if he could catch her alone,

Alex waited in the shadows, aware that his presence always made the ladies uncomfortable. Gradually they filtered into the parlor where their tools and supplies were laid out, and soon after, Dinner trotted by. Alex watched the upturned comma of his tail vanish around the doorframe, and heard the women greet him with enthusiasm.

Mr. Beadle came through the door just then and immediately began speaking to Diana with unusually rapid gestures. Whatever he was saying appeared to distress her.

Alex set his cup on a pier table and went to join them. "Is something amiss, my dear?"

"Mrs. Derwent isn't coming to class today," she said in a worried voice. "When Mr. Beadle stopped by to give her a lift, Mr. Derwent said that his wife was needed at home."

Mr. Beadle made another series of agitated gestures, from which Alex divined that Mrs. Derwent would not be returning at all, by order of her husband.

"But she has done so well!" Diana exclaimed. "Better than any of the others. And Mr. Filbert says that the final two lessons are the most important. She mustn't miss them."

"It's unfortunate, certainly. But if Mr. Derwent refuses to let her continue, there is nothing to be done about it."

"Rubbish. I shall go directly there and speak with him. Will you be so kind as to accompany me, Mr. Beadle?"

Shaking his head, Mr. Beadle pulled a stubby pencil and a scrap of paper from his pocket, went to the pier table, and scrawled a few words.

Diana leaned over to read them. "Oh dear God." She clutched at the table for support.

Grim-faced, Mr. Beadle handed the note to Alex.

Window. Saw her face. Beaten.

Alex crushed the paper in his fist and crossed to the door. "I'll deal with this. Mr. Beadle, come with me to the stable, if you will. I require directions to the cottage."

Diana hurried after them. "I'm coming with you."

He turned and placed his hands on her shoulders. "Indeed you are not, madam. I'll hear no discussion on the subject."

"But what if I'm needed? She could be badly hurt."

"You may safely rely on me to do whatever is necessary.

Now, go back to the house, and carry on as if nothing has occurred."

She released a long sigh. "Oh, very well. I'm sure you are right. But, Alex, please take care. I know that you mean to punish him—I can see it in your eyes—but he will almost certainly take it out on her."

"Understood." He brushed a kiss against her hair. "She will come to no further harm."

While his horse was being saddled, Alex memorized the rough map Mr. Beadle scratched for him in the dirt with a stick. And the journey, taken at a gallop, put him within minutes at the narrow track that led from the road to the Derwents' cottage. A low, white-walled building with a slate roof, it was set at the base of a sloping hill patched with spinneys of oak and hazel. Just beyond a small, scraggly garden, one thin brown and white cow stood dejectedly in a crude paddock.

Alex dismounted and went the rest of the way on foot, leading his horse and making no great hurry of it. The curtains were drawn shut, he saw as he drew nearer the cottage. Except for the raspy call of rooks in the trees, the landscape was eerily silent and motionless, as if it were holding its breath.

The door opened and a man emerged, slamming it behind him. Not overly tall, with beefy arms and a barrel-shaped torso, he had a ruddy face under a thick shock of salt-and-pepper hair. Standing with his arms folded across his chest, he looked strong, angry, and defiant.

"Go away," he shouted when Alex continued moving in his direction. "This is my land. You're not welcome here."

"I didn't expect to be." Without halting, he looped the reins over a bush.

Derwent visibly dug in his heels, his hands clenching and unclenching. Sweat beaded on his forehead. "That's far enough."

Alex stopped precisely ten feet away, an unthreatening distance but close enough to read his opponent's face. He regarded Derwent steadily, unsurprised to see the man's eyes shift away. In his experience, most bullies were cowards at heart. "I am Colonel Alexander Valliant," he said evenly. "I wish to speak with your wife."

"Can't. She's sick."

"So I understand. Nevertheless, I *will* speak with her."

"You got no right! I say who comes into m'house. You try it and I'll set the constable on you."

"Do that. I'm sure he'll be interested to see what it is you are hiding in there."

"Ain't hiding nuthing." Derwent glanced over his shoulder at the door. "M'wife be sick, that's all. She don't want to see no-body. Told me so."

Alex closed the distance between them, wondering if this oaf had any idea how close he was to being soundly thrashed. "Move aside, Derwent."

For several tense moments Derwent stood his ground. Alex had begun to hope he'd be forced to go through him when he sidled out of the way, leaving clear the path to the door.

The room Alex entered was low-ceilinged and sparsely furnished, lit only by a pair of candles set above the hearth. A thin shaft of sunlight sliced through a gap in the curtains to his right, and he moved to it, making sure that his face was illuminated. "Mrs. Derwent?"

"Over here, sir," came a faltering voice from the farthest corner. She was huddled on a low wooden chair, arms clutched around her waist. "You had best go away, sir. Mr. Derwent won't like it that you be talking to me."

"He has already said so." Alex gentled his voice, which sounded harsh and strained even to his own ears. Lord knew what she must be thinking to hear it. "You needn't worry, ma'am. All will be well."

A choked sound, wordless and agonized, carried to his ears.

Her fear—of him and of what might happen when he was gone—curled around him like acrid smoke. He was far out of his depth here. Perhaps he should have brought Diana with him after all. She would know what to say, and how to comfort and reassure this woman. It had been a mistake to come here alone.

"I'm a soldier," he said, fumbling ahead as best he could. "Most of my life has been spent among men very much like myself, more given to action than to words. If I am blunt, ma'am, it's not because I mean to be unkind. I know no other way to proceed."

"I understand," she said after a moment. "But you cannot help me, sir. Nor should you try. We are nothing to you."

"To the contrary. You mean a great deal to my wife, which makes you my concern. May I see your face, Mrs. Derwent?"

The figure on the chair shuddered, and he thought she would deny him. But to his astonishment, she came to her feet and crossed slowly to the hearth. Taking a candle, she clutched it between both hands and held it so that the flame danced just below her chin.

He moved closer, careful to maintain an impassive expression. Pity was the last thing any wounded creature so brave as this one would accept. Even so, his knees went weak when he saw the bruises on her face. One eye was nearly swollen shut. Her lips, puffed and cracked, trembled as he gazed at her. Light brown hair streaked with gray hung in tangled damp strings around her shoulders.

"Has he beaten you before?" Alex asked softly. "Tell me the truth."

"No. Not like this. Not so bad."

"But he's struck you?"

"Yes. A slap, sometimes. The back of his hand sometimes. He never used his fists afore."

Alex took the candle and returned it to the hearth. "He'll never do so again, I promise you."

"He's not a bad man," she said urgently. "We did well enough for more'n twenty years, when he was working at the slate quarry. But a load of rock fell on his leg and broke it in three places. He was fit enough when it healed, saving for a limp, but they wouldn't hire him back. Things went hard for him after that. There be no jobs hereabouts except at the quarry, and mining slate is all he knows how to do."

"I see." Alex rubbed his chin. Plainly Derwent objected to his wife taking up a job while he remained unemployed. "What do you do for money, Mrs. Derwent?"

"We have none," she said simply. "Everything we could sell is long gone. The parish helps, and sometimes Mr. Derwent finds a bit of work mending fences or the like. He never stops looking for work. He's a proud man, sir. He wants to make his own way."

135

That struck home. She might have been talking about him, Alex thought, except that Derwent was a desperate man while Alex Valliant had the safe cushion of his aristocratic family to fall back on. Not to mention a wealthy wife, whose fortune he had already spurned. Would he turn it away with such disdain, he wondered, should his own efforts come to nothing?

In any event, there was no excuse, not *any*, for what Derwent had done to his wife. It was unforgivable. But it would be forgiven, he knew, gazing at Mrs. Derwent with better understanding than he'd brought with him into the cottage.

"My wife tells me, ma'am, that you are by far the best pencil maker in Mr. Filbert's class. She also says that you can't afford to miss the final two lessons, although today's class is half the way through by now. But someone will catch you up tomorrow. I'll instruct Mr. Beadle to come by an hour before the usual time."

"I—" She plucked at her apron. "Mr. Derwent will never permit it."

"Leave him to me. And pardon me, for I should have asked this beforehand. Do you feel well enough to attend the class?"

Her hand went to her swollen cheek. "I doubt that I can do the work, sir, with only one eye to see with."

"But you can observe the others, and hear Mr. Filbert explain the procedures. Would you like me to have the apothecary stop in?"

"Oh, sir, don't you understand? The shame of it. I don't want anyone to see my face. I don't want anyone to *know*."

Damn. How could he have failed to consider that? He nodded. "Perhaps other arrangements can be made. I'll ask Mr. Filbert to remain at Lakeview another day or two, and Mr. Beadle can bring him here to give you private lessons. Would that be acceptable?"

Hope lit her battered face. "Do you think he might?"

"Yes, indeed." Alex would pay him whatever he asked. "No one need hear of this, Mrs. Derwent. But Mrs. Valliant will insist on dispatching a servant with food and whatever else she reckons you might need, so I beg you to indulge her. She'll also wish to come herself, perhaps tomorrow if you've no objection."

"Whatever you say, sir." Mrs. Derwent sank onto a ladder-back chair, looking overwhelmed. "You are very kind. It's no wonder Mrs. Valliant thinks you put the moon in the sky. But I don't know how we are ever to repay you."

Diana thought *what*? He returned his attention to Mrs. Derwent, who was regarding him curiously.

"Repay? Ah, yes. What say you give me the first pencil from your workshop, and one every month after that for so long as you continue to produce them. A man is always in need of a good pencil. And now, if you will excuse me, I require a few words with Mr. Derwent." Taking her hand, he bowed and touched his lips to her wrist. "Never fear. We shall come to a peaceful understanding."

He left the cottage, blinking against the bright midmorning sunshine and looking around for Derwent. He was slatting stones at one of the paddock fence posts. Splinters flew as a rock slammed into the post and bounced away. When he saw Alex striding in his direction, he picked up another stone, this one large and sharp-edged, and planted his worn boots some distance apart.

Battle stance, Alex thought, coming directly up to him. "I will say this only once, Derwent. Raise a hand to your wife again, and you will answer to me. Is that understood?"

Scarred knuckles whitened as Derwent clenched the jagged rock. "I don't got to do what you tell me. Even a plain man knows his rights. If my wife don't obey me, I can make her. It's the law. And you can't stop me."

"I can," Alex said, holding his gaze. "I will."

For several tense moments, he thought he might actually have to fight the man. And for all his promises to Diana and Mrs. Derwent, he was looking forward to it with considerable pleasure.

But Derwent's bravado soon crumpled. Indeed, he appeared to sink into the ground. His gaze fell, and the ruddy color in his cheeks leached away. The rock dropped from his hand.

Alex almost felt sorry for him. Derwent was far from the only man who had done a great wrong, never expecting to, surprised to find that he had. In that way, if in no other, they were meeting on level ground. They had each betrayed the trust of those who depended on them. It was a bond of sorts—a bond of shame and regret. He would not strike a fellow sinner.

"If you imagine the law gives you the right to brutalize your wife," he said evenly, "you are very much mistaken. But we'll let that pass. You will not make the same mistake again."

Derwent wiped his nose with his sleeve. "I never meant it. All to a sudden I was fistin' her, but it was like sommat else doin' it, not me. I dunno who I come to be now. We was always bacon and eggs, me 'n Molly, afore I lost m' job. Even when the babies died we stuck together. She had three boys 'n a girl, but they was sickly. John made it all the way to seven years, but then the fever got 'im."

"And now it's only the two of you," Alex said, his stomach knotting up. Four children buried. Dear God.

"Since twenty years ago. We've 'ad cross words, but we always made it up. Then Mrs. Valliant come and took her away. Suddenlike, Molly were never to home. All the time goin' off to the fancy house 'n comin' back with fancy things like I don't got the money to buy for 'er." He scuffed his toe in the dust. "I thought if she got work makin' perfumes and pencils, she'd go away and not never come back. Mebbe she oughter go. She'd be well rid of me."

"So far as I can tell, she would not agree," Alex said. "It was always her intention to work here at the cottage, once she had learned a trade."

"Women wasn't meant to take up a trade. Don't matter where, they oughtn't be doin' it. Ain't natural for a wife to do the providin' for a family."

"It's somewhat unusual, to be sure. Before making the acquaintance of my own wife, I thought much as you do about what females were meant to be in this world. But the world is changing, Derwent. At the least, it is rarely as we wish it to be. I think you ought to give your wife permission to make her pencils. It is what she wants, and after what you did to her, you have an obligation to make amends. Don't you agree?"

"Rather do it some other way," he grumbled. "But she can go on about the pencils if that's what pleases her. I won't make no more trouble about it."

"Had you considered the possibility of helping her? She could show you how it's done."

Derwent held out his gnarled, stubby-fingered hands, bent nearly shapeless after punishing years in the slate quarry.

"I see," Alex said, embarrassed for failing to notice earlier. "Well, pencil making is clearly out of the question. Shall we take a walk together?" He clasped his hands behind his back and set out for the hill that rose up behind the cottage. "Do you own this property?"

"From here down to the lake, and more'n half a mile t'other direction, but that's all hills 'n trees. No good for sheep. Narrow, too, mebbe three hunert yards across at widest point. Water runs off them hills and goes to the lake, leaving nuthin' but mud in between. Can't grow a crop in mud. It's no use to anybody."

"As it happens, mud is practically a requirement for the scheme I have in mind," Alex said, giving him a wry smile. "Tell me, Mr. Derwent. What do you know about pigs?"

Chapter 14

Alex was eating his breakfast in company with a fat and greedy Dinner when Diana came into the room.

"Mr. Beadle is nowhere to be found," she said, her voice edged with concern. "He didn't pass by this morning at his usual time, and he failed to pick up Mrs. Truscott and bring her to the embroidery class."

"More than likely his pony has gone lame," Alex said. "Or his cart suffered a broken wheel. Such things happen, my dear."

"They've never happened before. You are the one who spends time with him. Have you any idea where he lives?"

He put aside his fork and set the plate on the floor for Dinner to clean. "I've seen where he turns off the main road when we leave the pub house. You want me to go in search of him, I gather?"

She did, and she meant to accompany him. Half an hour later they made the turn onto a narrow track that led through a series of increasingly high hills. They followed it for a considerable time, into a part of the country Alex had never seen before. They were going the right direction, he was certain, because the ground was worn into two grooves that matched the wheels on Mr. Beadle's cart. But when they had passed through a copse of ragged oaks, he saw that the ground was now unbroken.

Telling Diana to wait, he went back through the trees to a spot where the terrain was exceptionally rocky and made a careful search. After a considerable time he detected a break in the woods, all but invisible unless one happened to be looking for it. Low-hanging branches shadowed the path, and he was forced to duck as he followed it a short distance. When the trees and undergrowth thinned, he was startled to come upon a tall wrought-iron gate set between a narrow gap with steep cliffs rising on both sides of it.

"What in heaven's name is *that*?" Diana asked, drawing up beside him.

He should have known she would follow. "It's not locked," he said, bending from the saddle to raise the crossbar. "Mr. Beadle appears ready to welcome visitors, if they can find him."

They rode side by side for another quarter mile, passing a small tarn that gathered water from a stream flowing down from the hills. Alongside it the track widened, and once again they saw the imprint of the wagon wheels. The high cliffs cut off most of the early morning light, and Alex felt as if they had entered a tunnel. It twisted and turned as they moved deeper into the fells above Coniston Water, the beat of the horses' hooves on marshy turf and water rushing over pebbles the only sounds to be heard.

"This is positively eerie," Diana whispered. "Can he really live in such a place?"

"Look there," Alex said as they came around a sharp curve. The cliffs melted into soft hills, still steep but now covered with grass, and one more turn carried them into a lush dale several hundred yards wide. The stream hugged one side of it, and at the other to their right, an enormous building rose up like something from a dream.

Diana gasped.

They both reined in, equally stunned.

It was part castle, with towers and turrets and arrow slits set high in the walls. Part church as well, with spires and Gothic arches and stained glass in some of the windows scattered helter-skelter as if put there on impulse. Tiled mosaics decorated otherwise bare stretches of stone and mortar. Fantastical figures, animals and human faces and cherubs, were molded at every corner, and there were many corners. Seashells and carved wood had been fitted into the walls. Every kind of ornament was to be found. Finials protruded from the parapets. Ceramic gutter spouts shaped like open mouths hung wherever water might gather. And directly in front of them, set in a stone arch, two thick oak doors stood wide open.

Alex had seen many wonders on his travels—palaces and

Inca temples and great cathedrals—but nothing quite like this. He dismounted, tethered both horses to a small marble obelisk near the doors, and helped Diana from the saddle.

Her eyes were round with astonishment. "What in heaven's name have we come upon, Alex?"

"Mr. Beadle's cottage, I expect." He felt as amazed as she looked. "Shall we see if he's to home?"

They knocked at the open doors, calling his name, but no one responded. No lights were to be seen. A cavern lay straight ahead, unbroken by windows.

Diana tugged him inside, and he soon saw that all the beauty was to be found on the exterior. A short wide passageway quickly came to an end, and beyond was a seemingly endless series of rooms, most of them tiny, connected to one another at random.

They found themselves in a labyrinth. Whichever path they followed, opening doors to go from one room to another, they eventually came to a dead end. It was pitch-dark when they wound themselves near the center of the edifice, and brightly lit when they stumbled upon a room that boasted windows.

Now and again, fanciful carvings were etched into the walls and doors. Other times they passed bare stone and openings that had no doors set in them. Once they found themselves back where they had started, sunlight pouring through the wide arch of the main entrance.

"We went to the right before," Alex said. "Let's try the left this time."

They came through a number of rooms they'd been in before, or so he believed. They all looked pretty much alike. But by turning left whenever possible, they eventually arrived at a tall, narrow oak door inset with bits of colored glass. On either side, like sentries, two brightly painted plaster angels had been affixed to the walls.

Alex, sensing they had come to where they were supposed to be, rapped on the door.

Again there was no response.

He raised the wooden latch, which was carved in the shape of a serpent, and stepped inside an enormous room with a vaulted ceiling. On the opposite wall were a number of small windows,

142

zigzagging high and low. The morning sun had yet to reach them, so the room was a patchwork of pale light and shadows. It was bare of furniture, he saw, save for a narrow bed with a brass-work headboard. It was nearly center of the room, resting on a colorful handwoven carpet.

On the bed, unaware of them, Mr. Beadle lay on his back with a blanket covering him to his waist.

Diana grasped Alex's arm. "Oh dear God. What—?"

"Wait here." He went to the bed and looked down at two closed, sunken eyes and an ashen face. Mr. Beadle was struggling to breathe, wincing with each raspy gulp of air. Alex pulled off his gloves and put two fingers against Mr. Beadle's bony wrist. His skin was clammy. His pulse was irregular and weak.

Diana came to Alex's side. "Is he very bad?" she asked in a whisper.

Mr. Beadle's eyes flickered open. For a few moments he gazed blankly at the stone ceiling, his breath more labored than before.

"It will help if we raise him up," Alex said. "See if you can find pillows or blankets to put at his back."

"I'll hold him." She brushed the sparse, damp hair from Mr. Beadle's forehead. "Lift him for a moment, please."

While Alex held Mr. Beadle, Diana slipped onto the bed and wrapped her arms around him so that he was sitting with his back against her breasts. After only a short time, his breathing grew noticeably easier. Traces of color appeared on his cheeks and lips, and he gave a choked cough.

Alex passed Diana his handkerchief. "I'll see if there is water to be had. Will you be all right for a few minutes?"

She nodded, her attention focused on Mr. Beadle's face.

There was no distinct order in the house, as he had already learned. Alex wandered through a score of empty rooms before locating the primitive kitchen. It was sparsely equipped with a water pump, a scatter of dishes and pots on a small table, and a banked fire in the hearth. He filled a kettle with water, took the lone cup from the table, and made his way through the tangle of rooms in what he hoped was the right direction.

143

The chill of death hung in the air. He felt it as he had countless times before, that hushed twilight when flesh and spirit cling fiercely to life while death wrestles with them to claim its own.

His heart clenched. In the few weeks since they met, the peculiar old man had become a friend of sorts. They'd spent considerable time together, working in companionable silence, sometimes sharing a meal and tankers of ale at the Black Bull. It was a relaxing, undemanding comradeship between two men with nothing to say to each other, although Alex had always sensed that Mr. Beadle understood far more than he let on.

Recognizing a gargoyle he'd passed on the way to the kitchen, he took only one more wrong turn before arriving where he'd left Diana. She looked up with a faint smile when he entered the room.

"I think he's feeling better, Alex. Perhaps he can swallow a little water."

Dropping to one knee beside the cot, Alex filled the cup and raised it to Mr. Beadle's lips. This is futile, he was thinking just as a pair of faded brown eyes flickered open.

They took several moments to focus. Then, holding Alex's gaze steadily, Mr. Beadle sipped the water. When he was done, he sagged back against Diana's hold with a sigh.

"Th-thank you," he murmured.

Astonished, Alex nearly dropped the cup.

Mr. Beadle's white lips curved with amusement. "I d-didn't mean to startle you. B-but there's so little time. How does it go? I must s-speak now, or forever hold my peace."

Diana's eyes were round as dinner plates. "What can we do to help you, sir? Should Alex go for a physician, or—"

"No need. No n-need. This has happened before, you s-see, only not so bad. But I've been told what to expect, and here it is. Weak heart, I'm afraid. N-nothing to be done now."

When Diana looked poised to object, Alex shook his head in warning. He had seen it before, this last surge of energy and coherence before the body closed down. He'd sat with dying men and listened to them—sometimes for hours—because they must be allowed to say what they needed to say.

"Do you l-like my castle?" Mr. Beadle asked, a secret smile

in his eyes. "I hoped you would c-come here one day and see it. No one else ever has, you know."

"It is altogether splendid," Diana said. "I cannot imagine how you built such a wonder all by yourself."

Good girl, Alex thought.

"And you want to know why," Mr. Beadle said, resting his head against her shoulder. "There's no sense to it, most folk would say. N-not you, though. I saw it first time we met, the ambition to make something beautiful. 'Tis better your way, to do so with people, but I could work only with mortar and stones."

"But that's not at all the case, sir. You have helped us enormously."

"I have tried. Think of me when the regiment goes to the Michaelmas Fair. God willing, I shall contrive to be there with you in spirit." He coughed, and Alex gave him another drink of water. "Forgive me. You must look to the future, but my thoughts carry me into the past. And have you observed that my stammer has all but left me now? 'Tis proof that I have one foot in heaven. Or my tongue, at the very least. When a boy, I could not put three words together before everyone around me lost patience, and who could blame them? Often I became stuck on a single syllable, unable to leave it however much I tried. Had I addressed you then, you'd have heard Mrs. Va-Va-Va-Va-Va until I fled in shame."

"I'd have followed you, sir, to hear what you wished to say."

"I am sure of it. But my schoolfellows were less k-kind, in the way of boys who mock anyone chancing to be different. On my tenth birthday I resolved never to speak again in company, and I have kept to that vow these four-and-fifty years. That same day I left school, and my family as well, and apprenticed myself to a carpenter."

He fell silent then, and Diana shot Alex an anxious look.

"Will you tell us about your castle?" he asked softly.

"What?" Mr. Beadle murmured, as if awakened from a deep slumber. His brow furrowed with concentration. "Ah, yes. You see, one of the bullies—worse than all the others—lived in a large house that I passed each day on my way to school. It was unjust, I thought, for the likes of him to live in such a fine house, so I resolved to build an even finer one for myself. It was not long after that I came upon this dale, and for many years I scavenged stones and t-tools and hid them here, awaiting the time I had saved enough money to purchase the land. When it was mine, I moved here and began to build. The castle will never be finished, of course. It was never meant to be. Were I to live a thousand years, I'd continue building, because it gives me pleasure." He smiled. "I call it Beadle's Folly."

A tear streaked down Diana's cheek. "I am sure it is the finest house in all of Lancashire," she said.

"There can be no other like it, that is true. As I laid stone upon stone I spoke to each one, telling it precisely where it fit and how important it was—even if it was a very little piece of rock in a p-place where it would never be seen. The stones were patient. They didn't mind that I stammered. And over the years, what with p-practicing every night, I learned to talk in almost a normal fashion."

His voice was growing perceptibly weaker, and his skin had taken on a faint bluish tone. Alex, keeping a close watch, reckoned it would not be much longer now. He wondered if Diana had been misled by what had taken place in the last few minutes. There was no hope, none at all. She ought to be warned, and prepared for what was to come. But how could he tell her while Mr. Beadle remained conscious to hear him?

"Why did you never speak with us?" she asked gently.

Mr. Beadle raised a trembling hand to cover her hand, the one that rested over his failing heart. "I had t-taken a vow. 'Twas only a foolish promise to myself, but I was ever a p-proud and stubborn man." He gave a ragged sigh. "If you will forgive me, perhaps God will grant His mercy as well."

"You may be sure of it." She brushed a kiss against his temple. "I love you dearly, Mr. Beadle. And I shall never forget you, or what you have taught me today."

"S-sleepy," he murmured, his eyes drifting closed. "But all is well. Ready." He raised his hand, making a vague gesture. "In th-there."

His hand fell onto his lap. He slumped against Diana, his head on her shoulder, his face turned in to her neck like a child gone to sleep in the arms of his mother. He still breathed, Alex saw, but he would not wake again.

Diana looked up, a question in her shimmering eyes.

"I don't know," he said, coming to his feet. "A few minutes, perhaps, but it could as easily be hours. You cannot remain any longer in that cramped position, Diana. Let us lower him onto the bed."

"No, please. He can stay as he is. I'm perfectly fine."

Alex rubbed his forehead. "He won't know the difference, my dear."

"You can't be sure of that. How can any of us guess what he knows and what he feels at such a time as this? He is *dying*, Alex. And he has had little enough of love in this world. Before he leaves it, I mean to give him all the love that I can."

Alex managed to nod before turning away, his eyes burning. This young girl, holding an old man in her arms and waiting for Death to take him from her, rendered him mute. He went to one of the windows, a small square with cast-off fragments of glass leaded together into a pane, and leaned his shoulder against the casement.

Bright morning sunshine poured over the grassy hillside and danced on the swiftly flowing stream that sliced through the narrow valley. Mosses and wildflowers huddled among the stones alongside the beck, and in the distance he saw a pair of small roe deer pick their way down the steep hill for a drink.

Diana had begun to sing. Soft and clear, the words of an old hymn floated in the air, and then another hymn, and another. She sang ballads, too, about knights and princesses in their castles, long intricate tales of honor and love—and death. She sang of it fearlessly, unafraid to draw it into the room.

After a while, Alex turned to look at her.

Still cradling the old man in her arms, she stroked the back of his head and gazed down at him with loving attentiveness, as if they were the only two people left in the world. From a score of arrow-slit windows set high in the walls, thin shafts of golden light poured over them from all directions, transforming the shabby brown blanket wrapped around Mr. Beadle to molten bronze. Diana's hair shone like a torch.

This was, Alex thought, the way every man would choose to die. He could ask no more than to be wrapped in the arms of a comforting woman, his last sight that of her beautiful face, her soft skin the last touch he feels, her fragrance in his nostrils, her soothing voice singing him to sleep.

An intruder in their intimate communion, he put his back to them and gazed out the window, seeing nothing. Mindless and empty of soul, he waited—as they all waited—for the arrival of one last visitor to Mr. Beadle's castle.

At some point, minutes or hours later, he became aware that Diana was no longer singing. The room was achingly still. He turned. She was looking at him, tears streaming down her face.

"I think he's gone, Alex."

He went to the cot. Mr. Beadle's brown eyes, open and fixed, stared past him into eternity.

Taking hold of his shoulders, Alex held him while Diana stood, staggering as blood rushed into her cramped legs. She grabbed Alex's forearm for a moment, using it to steady herself, and then moved out of the way.

He lowered Mr. Beadle's head onto the flat pillow and straightened the blanket over his lean body. "Good night, sweet prince," he murmured, using his thumbs to press the eyelids closed.

Diana came to stand beside him, wordless with grief. He opened his arms and she fell into them, burying her head against his shoulder and weeping soundlessly while he rubbed her back. It must surely pain her after so long a time supporting Mr. Beadle's weight.

Finally she gazed up at him from swollen eyes. "I've never seen anyone die before."

"And I've seen a great many. He felt no pain, my dear. You may be sure of it."

"I scarcely knew when it happened. He grew colder and colder, and after a while the sound of his breathing became a whisper, like feathers brushing together, and then I couldn't hear it at all."

Lifting her chin with the back of his hand, he gazed into her luminous eyes. "Because you came when most he needed you, he was able to tell you his story. He was proud that you had seen his castle and marveled at it. You gave him joy, Diana. Remember only that."

"Yes, I know he would not wish us to grieve for him. But I

can't help being a little weepy. He was such a loyal, generous friend. All the regiment ladies will miss him enormously. Well, perhaps not Mrs. Myrtle. For some reason, they never scratched along together."

"Is Mrs. Myrtle the one with saggy jowls? Looks like a basset hound and never stops talking?"

"Indeed she is. I'd have cashiered the old battle-ax long since, but we needed her horse and wagon to carry all the things that wouldn't fit into Mr. Beadle's pony cart. Besides, she makes the best jams and jellies in Lancashire." Diana chuckled. "This is a sorry discussion to be having, Alex."

"But one Mr. Beadle would appreciate." He drew her away from the cot. "I think we should be going now. The authorities will have to be notified, and there are arrangements to be made for his burial."

"I've been thinking on that. What do you suppose he meant at the end? He said, 'All is well. Ready.' Then he pointed—I could not tell where—and said, 'In there.' It must have meant something."

"Only that he was ready to die, I expect." Alex started for the door. "Come along now. We've much to do."

She held back, looking around the room. "He was trying to tell us . . . oh, I don't know what. But it was important. I'm sure of it."

Swallowing his impatience, Alex watched her go to one of several doors set into the walls of Mr. Beadle's bedchamber. It must have led to the privy, because she quickly pulled it closed again, her nose wrinkling as if she'd smelled an unpleasant odor, and went to a door set in the opposite wall.

"Come see this, Alex!"

He halted just inside the small room, looking around in amazement. The first thing he saw, directly center, was a plain wooden coffin with a shovel laid across the top. The coffin was recently constructed, he could tell by the tools and shavings and sawed-off planks piled at its side. Mr. Beadle, always precise in his habits, must have been too weak to clean up the mess.

Near the room's only window, he saw a chair and a small table with a number of items strewn across the top. Diana was standing next to it, holding a sheet of paper to the light, her head tilted as she read what was inscribed on it.

"He wrote a will, Alex. It's barely legible, though. Can you make out what he was trying to say?"

Alex took the paper and scanned the short paragraphs, scrawled in pencil by a shaky hand. It was a will, sure enough, and the provisions were few and simple. He translated them for Diana.

The parcel of land, the castle, the pony and cart, all his tools, and any other property of value were given to the regiment, to be sold or used however would best profit the new owners. His pocket watch, handed down through several generations of Beadles, was for Colonel Valliant. Mrs. Valliant was to have his mother's lace handkerchief and wedding ring. The hand-carved birds on the desk went to Miss Wigglesworth. There were several other tokens designated for regiment ladies he held in special regard.

His signature, unlike the rest, was written in bold, steady letters.

And there was a postscript, which made Alex laugh. The large cork on the desk, the one carved into the shape of a snarling dog, was Mr. Beadle's gift to Mrs. Myrtle. He hoped that some kindly soul would stuff it in her mouth.

"Oh my," Diana said when Alex was finished. Then, like him, she dissolved in laughter.

"A gallant gentleman, Mr. Beadle," Alex said when he recovered his voice. "He took his leave with one final jest. To be sure, he has been playing his games with us all along, pretending to be mute and forcing us to communicate with him by means of finger signs and gestures. When we tried to speak his language, *we* were the ones who stammered. He must have enjoyed that."

"Yes, indeed. How we underestimated him, though." Her expression grew sad again. "I should very much like to have known him better, Alex. If he had known I cared about him, if I had made the effort to convince him that I did, perhaps—"

"Hush, Diana. This serves no purpose. You were acquainted with Mr. Beadle for—what? Two or three months? Do you truly imagine you could have changed his life in so short a time? He was thrice your age and more, long set in his ways, with no apparent wish to alter them. Would he be glad to think his legacy to you is one of regret? Honor his memory, my dear, but let him go in peace."

"You are right, I suppose." She emitted a grudging sigh. "And we did arrive in time. He was not left to die all alone."

Alex folded the will and put it in his pocket. "I'm not sure what is likely to become of his property, given that the will was not witnessed, but we shall make every effort to see his wishes carried out. Kendal will be the best judge how to proceed. For now, madam, please let us go."

"You go," she said. "Do whatever has to be done and fetch whoever has to be fetched. I'll wait with Mr. Beadle until they come."

Recognizing that mutinous glint in her eyes, he braced himself for battle. "You cannot stay here alone, Diana. I'll not permit it."

"And I won't leave him here by himself. It's out of the question. Animals might come down from the hills and get at him."

He reminded himself that she was overset and mourning a friend. "We'll secure the doors," he said in a calm voice, "and check all the windows before we leave."

"Well and good. But this is an odd sort of dwelling. He built rooms and left them empty when he moved on to build others. What if there are rats? Can you say there are none? And I've seen any number of spiders already."

The man is *dead*, Alex thought, his frustration mounting. Worms would be at Mr. Beadle soon enough. Visions of twisted bodies scattered across the arid Spanish landscape rushed by him. Bodies piled high in the breach at Badajoz. Bodies tossed into a common pit with lime shoveled over them, left behind as the army marched to the next deadly objective. Sweat broke out on his forehead. He closed his eyes, willing the ghosts away.

"This once," he said, forcing the words past a clogged throat, "you must obey me."

"I'm sorry, sir." She wrapped her arms around her waist, looking only a little more determined than frightened. "Even if it makes you angry, I will not go."

"How then if we put him on the pony cart and take him out with us?"

"We'd only have to bring him back again. Don't you see? He wanted to be buried here, on his own land. He left the coffin." She went to it and picked up the spade. "He left this as well, and we are meant to use it. What could be more clear?"

"You think we ought to plant him now and be done with it? Confound it, Diana, there are laws regarding the disposition of bodies. It's possible an inquest will be required."

"I care nothing for any of that. Mr. Beadle's last request must surely take precedence." Shovel in hand, she marched to the door. "If you won't dig his grave, Alex, *I* will."

No longer surprised to find himself outmatched, he snatched the shovel away and ordered her to select a burial site.

As if by instinct, she went directly to a spot overlooking the castle, a small piece of nearly level ground where a low hill folded into a steeper one. They'd have the devil of a time carting Mr. Beadle such a distance, Alex thought, but he peeled off his coat and set to work.

It was damnably *hot* work under the noonday sun. The rocky ground resisted him at every dig of the spade, but he carefully set aside the rocks he dug up. Later, he would pile them atop the grave to keep it free of predators.

Diana had returned to the castle. To defend Mr. Beadle from the rats, he presumed, driving into the soil with a too familiar motion. Even colonels dug their share of graves when the army was on the move. He had done so, at any rate, rather than leave a single man of the 44th to the scavengers.

When the hole was chest high, he struck a shelf of limestone and knew he could go no deeper. Another few minutes of work leveled the grave, and by the time he climbed out, he had devised a plan to bring Mr. Beadle up the hill.

Two long poles were located near the scaffolding on the other side of the castle where Mr. Beadle had been constructing a round tower. Alex attached a blanket to them. With Diana's help, he lifted Mr. Beadle into the coffin, nailed it shut, and set it on the blanket. He'd thought to use the pony, but it proved impossible to secure the poles to the animal without causing it discomfort. In the end, he took hold of one pole while Diana grappled the other, and together they towed the coffin from the castle, along the narrow track alongside the beck, and finally up the steep slope to where the grave lay open.

Carefully they tilted the poles, and the coffin slid down into the shallow grave, the sound of it like a long sweet sigh in the still afternoon.

Stooping, Diana took a handful of dirt and sprinkled it over the coffin. "Good-bye, Mr. Beadle," she whispered. "And thank you. You have taught me that all things are possible."

Chapter 15

When Alex had broached the idea of a picnic with Mrs. Jellicoe, one of the few regiment ladies who did not walk in fear of him, she had leapt on it immediately. A celebration was certainly in order, she'd informed him. Only a handful of women would be going to the Michaelmas Fair, which had left the others feeling a bit let down.

They planned a gala event to include the regiment, any menfolk still in residence with their families, and a great number of children. Alex had been given little to do, practically speaking. He'd provided barrels of ice for lemonade, kegs of ale, and brought in ponies for the children to ride. The ladies had supplied enough food to feed three regiments, and the Yoodle sisters had been charged with creating a gift for Diana.

That had been his idea as well. He had even sketched out the design, and naturally he purchased the materials. Shortly before the picnic had got under way, Alice Yoodle, fluttering with excitement, had showed him the results. It was, he'd assured her sincerely, a masterpiece.

Alex asked only for the sight he was now gazing upon— Diana, moving from group to group, *not* wearing her veiled bonnet and clearly enjoying herself. He was standing apart from the others, leaning against an oak tree about halfway up a grassy hillside. It was a good spot from which to observe the grand presentation, which looked about to begin.

Mr. Pottle, who had lost an arm at Waterloo, blew a discordant tattoo on his battered cornet. The picnickers gathered around, and Mrs. Jellicoe led Diana to a knoll where everyone could see her.

"I won't make no speeches," Mrs. Jellicoe shouted.

The crowd cheered its approval.

"Oh, stubble it, you lot! We've all of us worked hard, and day after tomorrow, we'll finally get paid for what we done."

More cheers and a few catcalls. Alex began to regret supplying such a large quantity of ale.

"Most of us got regular work now," Mrs. Jellicoe persisted. "Some is raising pigs and some is making pencils and some is doin' other things. But we'd all be in the same dark place we was if Mrs. Valliant hadn't put her spurs to us. She don't want our thanks, but we mean to give it anyway. Come up here, Yoodles, and show what you made for her."

The Yoodle sisters, rigged out in all their finery, made a procession of it as they mounted the knoll. The crowd fell silent as Gladys Yoodle, her arms full of something shiny and colorful, curtsied to Diana and put something into her hand. It was the end of a thin rope, Alex thought, not expecting this development. Slowly Miss Yoodle retreated down the hill, and as she did, the rope unraveled to disclose dozens of fluttering triangular flags—red and yellow and green—attached to it.

"These will wave atop our booth at the fair," Mrs. Jellicoe announced to oohs and aahs from the crowd. "And from every booth at every fair we go to from here on out."

Alice Yoodle stepped forward then, her face more crimson than the scarlet flags rippling from her sister's rope. Gently, she set the folded bundle she carried into Diana's arms.

Alex suddenly wanted to be standing closer, where he could better see his wife's face as Mrs. Jellicoe helped her unfold the banner. Together they held it up. A hush fell over the crowd.

Against a background of white satin, a golden bolt of lightning streaked from corner to corner, cutting the banner into two triangles. In the upper triangle was a blue castle—a tribute to Mr. Beadle—and in the lower triangle, by Alex's command, a green bow and arrow, the symbol of Diana the Huntress. At the very bottom corner, invisible unless one came very close, Alice Yoodle had embroidered a small pink piglet.

"The Regimental Colors," Mrs. Jellicoe announced with evident pride.

The audience broke into wild applause, giving three cheers for Diana and three more for themselves. Then a fiddler struck up a tune and people began to dance, mothers with children or with their husbands, children with other children, and spinster ladies with whoever was to hand.

Alex turned away and wiped his sleeve over his eyes, which had unaccountably watered at the sight. He wished Diana were with him now. Wished she did not belong more to these people than to him. It was a selfish wish, but dammit, he needed her more than they did.

When he looked back again, done with his repugnant bout of self-pity, he saw that someone had tied the rope of pennants between two trees. Someone else had mounted the banner atop a tall pole, which someone had thought to provide. All these splendid people, doing wonderful things while he stood alone and useless.

Perhaps he wasn't fully recovered after all. But when was it he had started feeling sorry for himself? It was so out of character, at least out of the character he'd always assumed he possessed, that he could not begin to explain it. Still, he was most assuredly envious of the regiment ladies who absorbed so much of Diana's attention. And were he perfectly honest with himself, he'd sometimes been jealous of Dinner. A *pig*, for pity's sake. How low could a man sink?

Diana had separated herself from the others and was making her way up the hill to where he stood, her face flushed with pleasure. "You arranged all this," she said. "I knew it the moment I saw the pig on the banner."

He shrugged. "I made a few suggestions, no more than that. The ladies did all the work."

"Very well, sir, have it your way. But we both know better, don't we?" She came to his side and gazed down at the rollicking dancers. "I still cannot believe that we've done it. Look at them, Alex. They have accomplished so much in only a few months. I am so very proud of them."

"Reserve more than a little of that pride for yourself, madam. This was all very much your doing."

"I regret to inform you, sir, that I am *insufferably* proud of myself. True, I ruined two entire batches of ratafia, created rosewater that smells like vinegar, and produced a freckle cream that turns one's skin alarming yellow. But so long as I didn't actually *do* anything, I did very well indeed."

"Admirably." He watched her pluck a sprig of heather and thread it behind her ear. "You have a gift for leadership, Colonel Valliant."

"If you continue in this fashion," she said with a laugh, "you will make me quite full of myself. Shall we walk up to where all those wildflowers are growing? They must be the last before autumn sets in. Oh my. Harebells! How lovely."

He trailed a little behind her as she went from flower to flower, collecting a bouquet and humming along with the distant music. How graceful she was, he thought. How unutterably lovely with her green skirts flowing around her legs and her glorious hair loose about her shoulders.

She looked over at him. "Tell me something, Alex. Do you believe in Destiny?"

"Only that which we create for ourselves." He saw a tiny frown come and go on her brow. "Did you wish me to say otherwise?"

"Not at all. I only wondered what you thought on the subject. Miss Wigglesworth is persuaded that we inevitably end up with what is best for us, no matter that we may have wanted something else entirely." She paused to look down the hill again. "I can scarcely credit that in two more days it will all be over."

"How so? When Michaelmas Fair is passed, will you not begin preparations for another fair? I'd have expected you to set to work the very next day."

"*They* will, I am sure. But it is time for me to withdraw and leave them to proceed on their own. Oh, the natural leaders among them will provide direction and order, but I should not want them to become dependent upon anyone—least of all me."

"Understandable. But I fail to see why you must entirely separate yourself from their enterprises. Unless that is your wish, of course."

"It's they who wish it, Alex." She went to a patch of daisies, adding a few to her bouquet. "I know they are fond of me, and of you as well. But most of them were greatly relieved when the classes at Lakeview drew to an end. They felt out of place in the home of an aristocrat, and so they were. Surely you have been aware of their discomfort?"

He'd assumed they were only uncomfortable in *his* company. "How does it signify?" he asked. "You are perfectly at ease with them. You even left off wearing that pernicious veil in their presence."

"I fairly well had to, after all but setting it on fire a dozen times while working near the fireplace. But that is nothing to the point. The regiment will march on without me, Alex. I am firmly resolved to sell out."

"By all means, madam, if you think it best. But I cannot imagine you content to remain idly at Lakeview while others continue on with what you began."

"Nor can I," she said, her expression becoming somber. "It would be intolerable. Will you sit with me for a few minutes, sir? There is something I have long wished to discuss with you."

The blow was so unexpected that it rocked him on his heels. She meant to leave him!

What else could it be? Staying, she had said, would be *intolerable.* And he'd told her that he would not prevent her, should she ever decide to go. Not that he imagined she actually would, of course. How could the shy, naive girl he had married get on in the world by herself?

Now he knew. She would go on very well indeed. He had seen the proof of it.

She went gracefully to her knees beside him and sat back on her heels, flowers spilling over her skirts. When he continued to stand there like a post, she selected a daisy and held it out to him. "Please, Alex?"

His legs melting under him, he sagged to the ground and drew up his knees, folding his arms across them.

She put the daisy into his hand. "I have been thinking on this for a considerable time, but feared to address the subject because I expect you will disapprove. Still, I don't believe I shall ever feel braver than I do today, so I may as well leap into the fire. You see, during the last few months I have learned a number of things about myself. Not all of them to my credit, certainly, but I don't appear to be quite so helpless as I used to think I was. Well, as I *was*, actually."

Say it and be done! he thought, cold needles digging into his spine.

"The thing is," she said, "I require something useful to do. And while I've no idea as yet what that will turn out to be, I'm fairly sure I cannot do it here."

His hand fisted, crushing the flower she had given him. "You wish to leave, then."

"Well, yes." She looked surprised that he had grasped the obvious. "This is a small community, and you have met what passes for gentry in Coniston. What's more, Mrs. Alcorn has done everything in her power to set them against me. And Lakeview is a very small estate. I know you mean to develop the land, but Mr. Beadle once told me it was good only for sheep, and truly, I cannot see myself as a shepherdess. If you *want* to run sheep, then of course you must, although—"

"Enough!" The thin thread of his control had snapped. "Will you come to the point, madam?"

She paled. "Yes. I'm sorry. I invariably dither when I'm nervous. And now I'm doing it again. Oh, drat." Her hands twisted on her lap. "Alex, would you mind terribly much if we didn't remain at Lakeview? If we moved somewhere else?"

All the breath rushed out of him. We. She had said *we*! "To where?" he managed to ask, not that it mattered. So long as she stayed with him, the moon would suit him sublimely.

"I haven't thought so far ahead," she admitted. "We should make that decision together, don't you agree?"

We again. That was rapidly becoming his favorite word. "I've no objection," he said, knowing he sounded curt. Relief had clogged his brain and stiffened his tongue. "Lakeview will have to be sold, of course. And there's no telling how long it will take, given the poor condition of the house and the relative worthlessness of the land. I don't expect we'll be able to relocate for a considerable time."

"Why so?" She plucked the petals from a harebell. "We needn't remain there while it's on the market. And truly, Alex, I don't think you should sell it at all. The house was willed you by your grandmother, was it not? It ought to remain in the family.

Miss Wigglesworth could live there as caretaker. I know she'd like to continue working with the regiment, at least for a while."

He finally began to see where she was headed. Damn! A few moments ago, when he thought he had already lost her, he'd have severed both his legs to get her back again. The last thing in creation he wanted to do was stand against her now. But if they were to stay together, it had to be on his terms. He would not live on her money. He *could* not.

"Unless I sell Lakeview," he said, "I cannot provide you another home."

She met his gaze steadily. "You would have me always dependent on you, then?"

"Yes." He sensed the ground crumbling under his feet. "Financially, I mean."

"Might I ask to what purpose?"

"We have had this conversation before, madam. You understand well enough."

"I'm afraid that I do. But let me ask you this, Alex. Why should the fortune I brought to the marriage, the fortune you now control, sit idly in the three percents when we could make such good use of it? Why must we scrape by on an officer's half pay when we could build something together and pass it on to our children? Wouldn't you rather give them a flourishing estate or a thriving business than a bank account?"

"Business? You would have me go into *trade*?"

"I would see you occupied, sir. It matters not what you do, so long as it gives you pleasure and a sense of accomplishment. You can no more be idle than I. And as there is no war for you to fight, you must find another way to use your abilities and challenge your spirit. Taking root at Lakeview simply because you own it is no solution. You did not even buy the house yourself. You did not earn it. It was *given* you."

He was sinking rapidly, clinging to the shreds of his pride with his fingernails. And she met him with equal pride, even though her hands were trembling and she had gone alarmingly pale. Despite the strength she had discovered in herself, the confidence that had begun to grow in her, Diana remained inordinately fearful. But she defied him anyway, this astonishing young woman he had taken to wife.

At the protracted silence, her gaze lowered. "It appears that I have your answer, sir. And I must accept it, because I took a vow to obey you. But while I cannot promise I won't keep trying to change your mind, I *will* try very hard not to be a nagging wife. That's the best I can do, I'm afraid." She stood, flowers tumbling from her skirts. "Shall we return to the picnic?"

"Wait." He clambered to unsteady feet. Courage and fear were so carefully balanced in her now that he could crush her in an instant. He didn't want that much power over her. He wondered what she would do if she realized how much power she wielded over him. Hesitantly he placed a hand on her shoulder, searching for words to bridge the chasm he had opened between them. "Diana."

She gazed up at him, her beautiful eyes shimmering with tears. Sunlight washed over her face and lit her hair to fire. And he knew, there *were* no words, and bent his head to touch his lips to hers.

It was the lightest of kisses. He expected her to end it, to turn her head or step away. But she swayed into him, soft and supple and yielding, her arms at her sides and her breasts against his chest and her mouth against his mouth.

Wrapping his arms around her, he deepened the kiss. He felt her welcome it, felt his body surge with desire for her.

She raised a hand and threaded her fingers through his hair, drawing him even closer. He tasted her desire then, all the lush feminine sensuality banked inside her until this moment now suddenly ablaze. And like to incinerate them both, he thought dizzily, unless one of them put a stop to it before he carried her down onto the grass and made love to her in full view of the regiment. And the children. *Damn.*

Willing control into flesh that was all but beyond it, he lifted his head, seized a ragged breath, and gently set her away.

She gave him a stunned, heartbroken look. "D-did I do it wrong?" she asked into the shivering silence. "I've not been kissed before. I'm s-sure I could learn to do it better."

"I—" He made a vague gesture in the direction of the picnickers.

"Oh." Her face brightened. "Too many witnesses. Is that why you stopped?"

He nodded.

"Thank heavens. I have waited so long for you to kiss me. I thought you never would. Except for when I was afraid you would, and then not like it, and never want do it again."

"You needn't ever worry about that," he assured her, aching to do it again this very moment. He held her gaze. "I want to do a great deal more, Diana."

Her lips curved. "Yes, please."

Just like that. Yes. Well, she always said yes. She had said it on their wedding night. But she had never said *please*. And when he kissed her, she had opened herself to him and passion had flowed out from her. Hot waves of passion. He felt them even now, although she was standing an arm's length away and touching him only with her smile.

"Tonight, then," he said.

"Tonight." She glanced up at the sky. "Go away, sun. Will this day *never* end?"

Bewildered, he watched her scoop up handfuls of flowers and toss them over his head. A sprig of heather slid down his forehead and came to rest on his nose. He examined it cross-eyed. Was he dreaming all this? She was dancing around him, scattering flowers and laughing. Were they both gone mad?

"Cheer up, sir." She plucked the heather from his nose. "I'm the one supposed to be skittish and shy. To look at your face, one would think *you* were the virgin here."

He cleared his throat. "I had not expected you to be so . . . so eager, madam."

"Well, I am. And I have been for a good long time. I'm very much afraid that you have married a wanton, sir." She fluttered her lashes. "Will that be a problem, do you suppose?"

By Jove, she was *flirting* with him. No. *Flirting* was not the word. His shy schoolgirl bride was openly seducing him. She was a sliver away from *ravishing* him.

He must have died and gone to heaven.

She tilted her head. "Do you know, not counting when you kiss me, I like it above all things when you smile. And I wish you would not measure out your kisses and your smiles like a miser, Alex. I want lots and lots of both." Laughing, she twirled away again. "Gracious, just listen to me. I cannot believe I am saying such things. I must be a good deal braver than I ever imagined."

He could not mistake the low note of fear in her voice. The vulnerability. She had daringly offered herself, all of herself, while he continued to stand like a granite monolith. And still, as always, she took care to keep her scarred cheek turned away from him. Dear God.

He must find a way to make her understand that he never saw it when he looked at her. Well, yes, he did. But it was part of her, as lovely in his eyes as all the rest of her. In a way, it had given her into his hands. Without the scar, she would have felt free to dance in London ballrooms instead of here, on this hillside, with only a tongue-tied soldier to watch her with painful longing. She would have found a better man than Alex Valliant to marry.

He treasured that scar. He wished desperately that she did not regard it with such shame, but she did. She thought herself no longer beautiful and would go on thinking so, he feared, for a very long time. His eyes burned. Catching her hand as she danced playfully by him, he drew her close for another deep, breathtaking kiss.

Tonight, he thought. Tonight he would tell her what he had known since they went together to Keswick, and what had probably been true since a long time before that. Tonight, when he made her his wife in more than name, he would tell her that he loved her.

Chapter 16

Coniston Water lay smooth and still, the color of molten brass as the setting sun hovered over the western fells. Fingers of light painted the cloud-streaked sky pink and amber and gold.

Diana's heart was singing as she rode beside Alex on the way home. Although they hadn't spoken since leaving the picnic, she felt him reaching out to her. Their silent understanding curled her toes and set the ends of her hair on fire.

The last two hours had seemed to her an eternity. They had rejoined the others, taking care to single out each member of the regiment for special attention. Although Diana never said so, she was bidding them farewell. And she had wondered, as she chatted with Annie Jellicoe and Meggie Doyle and all the loyal soldiers, if they had seen her with Alex on the hillside. If they had seen her kissing him.

Well, what if they had? He was her husband, after all, and had been so for nearly five months. They could not possibly imagine it was the first time he had ever kissed her. But she'd felt the heat of embarrassment in her cheeks, and a greater heat elsewhere in her body, as she'd sampled the homemade wines and eaten lightly from the lavish picnic baskets.

When Alex had finally taken her arm and led her to where their horses were tethered and lifted her onto the saddle, she had felt as if her life were about to begin.

"What the devil is that?" Alex said when they made the turn from the road.

She looked where he was pointing and saw a carriage drawn up in front of the Lakeview stable, the crest of the Earl of Kendal emblazoned on its lacquered doors. "Oh, dear," she said, giving him a rueful smile. "It appears that we have guests."

They had left their horses at the stable and were approaching the front door when it sprang open and Kit Valliant stepped out, his arm wrapped around his wife's slender waist.

He gave Alex a reproachful look. "Past time you ambled home, old lad. Lucy and I had about decided you were avoiding us."

"Need I point out that you were not expected?" Alex went to him and shook his hand. "It's been a long time, Kit."

"Six years, I do believe. But as you see, I'm still a handsome devil. And Kendal tells me you've had the uncommon good sense to marry yon fair lady. Hullo, Diana." He gave her an exaggerated wink. "I was of a mind to marry her myself, but Lucy wouldn't let me. Snapped a shackle on m'leg while I wasn't looking."

"Twaddle." Lucy separated herself from her incorrigible spouse and curtsied to Alex. "I am pleased to meet you, sir."

He bowed. "And I am in your debt, madam. You are responsible, I am told, for rescuing Diana from her guardian."

"Ahem." Kit looked offended. "I played no small part in that adventure."

Laughing, Diana swept them all into the downstairs parlor. Of all the days for her two best friends to drop out of the blue! But here they were, and she expected that the brothers would like some private time to become reacquainted. "Shall I make us a pot of tea?" she offered with a nod at Lucy, who took her meaning instantly.

"May I join you?" she asked, already on her way to the door.

"Uh-oh." Kit waggled his brows at Alex. "The ladies want to be alone. Think they mean to talk about us?"

"Only when we have exhausted every subject of real interest," Lucy informed him as she flounced from the room.

"I think we've been insulted, old man." Kit flopped onto a wingback chair. "Any chance the Lakeview cellar runs to a decent bottle of wine?"

"I may have just the thing," Alex said. "Diana, you know the one I mean."

She was rather afraid that she did.

Lucy was waiting for her a short distance down the passageway, her gray eyes alight with curiosity. "My heavens," she said, pulling Diana into a warm hug. "I have come home to find that we are *sisters*! Kendal told us how it all came about, of course, but I must have the story from you. Men invariably leave out the best parts."

She would be leaving them out as well, Diana was fairly certain. Not even to Lucy could she open her heart on the subject of her marriage. "Of course," she said, detaching herself before sentiment got the better of her. "I'm so glad you are home. I have missed you prodigiously."

"And I have worried about you constantly. But to no purpose, it seems. How extraordinary that Alex should return to England precisely when you found yourself in need of him."

"Yes. A remarkable coincidence, although Miss Wigglesworth insists on calling it Destiny. But never mind all that. I wish to hear about your wedding trip."

"No, no. I shall leave Kit to tell the tale. He is far more entertaining. I do have news to share, though, probably the same news he is giving Alex at this very moment." Smiling, she patted her stomach.

"Oh, Lucy!" Diana stepped back for a better look. "But are you certain? You are slim as a whippet. How can you tell?"

"The signs are unmistakable. I lose my breakfast every morning, I've missed my courses three times, and blessed be heaven, my breasts are expanding. Needless to say, Kit is especially pleased with that development. Mind you, when first I suspected, I dared not believe it for the longest time. He so wants children, and I knew how disappointed he would be if I told him and then proved to be wrong. But now a physician has confirmed the pregnancy, and Kit is strutting around like the veriest rooster."

"I'm so pleased for you both," Diana said sincerely. And more than a little envious, although she could hardly say so.

Lucy regarded her searchingly. "You asked how I could tell. Does that mean you have been experiencing—"

"Nothing of the sort! No indeed. I was merely curious. I assure you that I have experienced nothing whatever." Heat rose to her face as she realized what she had just said.

166

Lucy appeared to take no notice. "He is astoundingly handsome, your Alex. I was quite taken aback when I saw him."

"Yes. I feel much that way each time I see him. But to be perfectly honest, I could wish he were not so . . . well-favored. It makes it all the more difficult."

"Because of this." Lucy brushed her fingertip against Diana's scar. "Will you ever understand that it is of no consequence?"

"Understanding, I have learned, has very little to do with how I feel." She sighed. "I do try, you know. I tell myself a thousand times a day that it doesn't matter. Sometimes I can forget it ten whole minutes at a stretch. But the moment I go into company, the instant someone stares at me or makes an effort *not* to stare, I become a giant scar atop a pair of quaking legs. And if I am standing near to Alex, the effect is multiplied beyond accounting. How could so handsome a man have married such an antidote? they are thinking. I know they are. How could they not?"

"The real question," Lucy said reprovingly, "is why do you care what they think? You tie yourself in knots, Diana, worrying over the possible thoughts and impressions of people who mean absolutely nothing to you. Clearly Alex takes no mind of your scar, and surely his is the only opinion that signifies."

"You are right, of course." She had nearly spoiled their reunion by raising a subject better left alone. "Pay me no mind, Lucy. I grow braver day by day. I shall come about."

"Yes, my sweet, I am sure of it. Now, where is the kitchen?"

Mrs. Cleese threw up her hands when they appeared at the door. "What am I to do?" she exclaimed. "Guests for dinner and no one to help. I cannot prepare a meal and set the table and serve the food all by myself!"

"It was unforgivable of us to descend on you in such a fashion," Lucy said. "You must not put yourself out on our account. Cold meats, cheese, bread, whatever you can toss together will suit us perfectly well."

Diana knew she ought to take charge of her own kitchen and servant, but Mrs. Cleese had always been so temperamental. She left it to Miss Wigglesworth, and now to Lucy, to put her cook in order. Feeling chickenhearted, she busied herself measuring tea and laying out cups and saucers.

Carver and Betsy arrived just when she was about to lift the heavy kettle from the hook over the fireplace. They were arm in arm, she noticed, although Carver quickly let go of the maid to help with the kettle.

Diana turned to Betsy, who looked a trifle starry-eyed. "We have company for the night," she said. "Lay a fire in the Blue Chamber, please, and put fresh linens on the bed. Well, you know what to do. And then you may retire, for I'll not be needing you this evening." Because I'll be spending the night with my husband, she thought with a shiver of anticipation. Sooner or later, they would contrive to be alone together.

While Carver finished preparing the tea tray, she went to the pantry in search of wine, really hoping she would not find the sort Alex had in mind. But there was one last bottle, so with some reluctance she carried it, along with a bottle of brandy for Alex, to the parlor. Lucy brought glasses, and Carver followed with the tray.

"They have dissected us into little pieces," Kit told Alex mournfully as the ladies entered the room. "They have measured out our faults, plucked our imperfections to the bone, and concluded that we are worthless fellows."

"Indeed we have," Lucy affirmed. "And you may as well know, Kit, that Alex came off significantly better than you did."

"I am delighted to hear it," Alex said, taking the wine bottle from Diana's hand. "And not in the least surprised."

She watched in some dismay as he removed the cork.

"I don't suppose," Lucy said, "that you gentlemen came around to discussing your beloved wives?"

"Only to praise your charms," Kit shot back with a grin. "And you may as well know, Lucy mine, that Diana came off a great deal better than you did."

Laughing, Lucy drew up a tapestry stool and sat at his knee. "But it is so much easier for Diana to be charming, my love, for she hasn't to put up with the likes of you."

Kit ruffled her short, pearl-colored hair. "I was just about to explain to Alex how it is we are here. He is far too civil to ask, of course, even though he has given me the distinct impression that he wishes us to the devil."

"You are not so dull-witted as I have always believed," Alex said, handing his brother a glass of yellowish wine. "Since Diana and I are expected at Candale tomorrow morning, I wonder than you did not wait to greet us there."

Kit swirled the wine in his glass before taking a sniff. His nose wrinkled. He sniffed again.

Diana watched apprehensively. Kit was inordinately fond of good wine, she knew. He had been smuggling a load of French contraband across Morecambe Bay when robbers accosted him, put a bullet in his shoulder, and made off with the booty. His compatriots had fled, leaving him to bleed to death or drown. He was alive only because Lucy had seen the encounter and brought him to shore.

Destiny. A miracle. Or amazingly good luck. Who could say, except that the results were unquestionably for the best. She glanced at Alex, who looked singularly pleased when Kit raised the glass to his lips and drank.

"B-bloody hell!" he sputtered. "What in Lucifer *is* this swill?"

"Vintage parsnip," Alex said with satisfaction. "I knew you'd like it."

"*Parsnip?* Good Lord." Kit took another sip. "Not bad, really. Not what I was expecting at first taste, but it has a kick to it."

Alex chuckled. "Look to your chest, halfling. Diana assures me that parsnip wine will grow hair."

"I've hair aplenty, thank you very much." Kit drained the glass and held it out for a refill.

Lucy rolled her eyes. *Men!* her expression said.

Evidently Kit would down the entire bottle of parsnip wine before admitting he disliked it. But brothers, Diana thought, must always be rivals of a sort. She'd too little experience with men to know how they behaved on a regular basis, but these two appeared to be enjoying their squabble. She was glad of it. Alex was overly somber by nature, and Kit could wring laughter from a stone. Already he had got Alex to play something of a practical joke on him.

"As I was saying," Kit remarked pointedly, "we didn't set out to call on you. But it seemed foolish not to drop by when we were so close. Who was to guess you'd be off at a picnic?"

"We were close," Lucy explained, "because we had decided to have a look at Kit's cottage in Hawkshead and see if it would suit us. I don't wish to remain overlong at Candale."

"She's scared of Kendal," Kit said, grinning.

Diana knew precisely how she felt. Lord Kendal was invariably kind, but one always felt the need to walk on tiptoes in his presence. She certainly did. Until this very afternoon, when Alex kissed her, she had felt much the same in *his* company.

"Nonsense!" Lucy slapped Kit's knee. "Deranged creature that I am, I simply want a home of my own. The cottage is small and somewhat drafty, but it will do well enough for now."

Alex poured himself a glass of brandy. "As it happens," he said with a darting glance at Diana, "Lakeview will soon be in need of tenants. You might consider taking residence here."

Diana's heart jumped about in her chest. Gracious! Alex was telling her, in sideways fashion, that he had agreed to move elsewhere. She had forgot, when he kissed her, what they had been discussing beforehand. But he remembered, and now he was giving her his answer.

"You're not staying here?" Kit's brows shot up. "Why ever not? Where will you live?"

"Slow down, Kit. We're not gone yet." Alex smiled at Diana. "We mean to look for a house with more land attached. I have some thought to raising horses, and since I married an excellent horsewoman, it seems the logical thing to do. But no decisions have been made, except that we will move from here. You are welcome to Lakeview, rent-free, so long as you allow Miss Wigglesworth to remain if she wishes to."

"No rent? Did you hear that, Lucy? I won't have to sell you to the Gypsies after all."

Before Lucy could respond, Betsy appeared to announce that supper was laid out. They trooped to the dining room then, and later returned to the parlor for tea, Kit regaling them all the while with improbable stories about the wedding trip. There were a great many of them, since he and Lucy had traveled the better part of a year. Once the children started popping out, he explained with a grin at his wife, there would be no more gallivanting about.

Alex sat close by Diana on a sofa, not touching her, although it felt as if he were. She listened to Kit, and laughed in all the right places, but her mind was far away. Well, not too far. Only up the stairs, in Alex's bedchamber, and she could hardly wait for the rest of her to join it there.

Finally Lucy gave a pointed yawn and tugged at Kit's sleeve. "That's enough, my love. You've started telling tales about places we never even went to. And we must all make an early start of it in the morning."

"Oh, right. The fair." Kit stood, stretching broadly. "Well, we'll toddle off now. Where to?"

Diana jumped to her feet. "I'll show you the way. Alex, will you extinguish the lights? I told the servants they could retire early, since they were half asleep anyway after the picnic."

"Go along," he said, his eyes heated. "I'll join you in a few minutes."

"Lucifer! I nearly forgot. Alex, when we were in London a fortnight ago, I ran into a friend of yours." Kit looked over at Lucy. "What was his name, moonbeam?"

"Are you speaking of Lord Blair?"

"That's the fellow. It seems he's about to tie the knot, poor sod, and is relying on Colonel Valliant to stand at his side and hold him steady. The wedding is—let me think. Well, I've got it written down somewhere. I'll give you the particulars when we get to Candale. No more than a week from now, I'm fairly sure, and he said all the chaps will be there. I presume you know who he means."

"Yes," Alex said shortly. "I know."

Diana looked at him with alarm. The color had washed from his face, and he'd gone stiff as a board. The others seemed unaware of it, but she knew that something terrible had just occurred. He had gone away from them, and from her, as surely as if he'd taken himself to the far side of the moon.

Kit was already at the door, his arm around Lucy's waist. "Coming, Diana?"

"Y-yes." With one last glance at Alex, who was staring fixedly into nowhere, she led them upstairs. Miss Wigglesworth must have stolen in and gone to her bed, because her snore could be heard as they passed her room.

Kit raised an eyebrow. "I hope we're not right next door."

"No. Clear the way down." She showed Kit and Lucy to the Blue Bedchamber, assured herself that Betsy had arranged everything they required to be comfortable, and bid them good night.

Once in the passageway again, she couldn't decide where she ought to go. Downstairs, to find out from Alex what had overset him? To his bedroom, to wait for him? Or to hers, hoping he would come and get her?

Fear made her weak as she stood indecisively for several moments. She could hear Kit and Lucy bantering as they readied themselves for bed, and the distant rumble of Miss Wigglesworth's snore. Finally she went to her own room and sank down on the edge of the bed. It had all gone terribly wrong, and she had no idea why. Something to do with Lord Blair, of course, but how could an invitation to a wedding be of such grave consequence?

Wild thoughts skipped about in her head. Could Alex have once been in love with Lord Blair's wife-to-be? She had no reason to think so, but it was the only explanation that made the slightest sense. Well, unless he had some other quarrel with Blair, or with the "chaps."

After what seemed a long time, she heard a light tap on her door. He stepped inside without waiting for her to admit him, his face still shadowed and his eyes distant. He leaned against the closed door and folded his arms.

"I'm sorry, Diana," he said.

She knew what he meant, of course. Her eyes blurred with tears. "Will you tell me why?"

"No."

Well, she had expected that, too. But he had spoken gently this time, unlike the other occasions when he'd fended off her questions. "Very well, sir. I'll not ask you again."

"It has nothing to do with you, I promise. Nothing to do with *us*." He swiped his fingers through his hair. "It is not even of any great import, except that it has stirred up memories that would come between us when nothing should. I want you to have all my attention, Diana, when we make love. You would not have it tonight."

"Yes. I know." She pulled herself from the bed and went to

172

him, hearing the regret in his voice. Seeing the sorrow in his eyes just before he opened his arms to embrace her.

"Soon," he whispered, his breath soft against her cheek. "When the fair is over, when I have come to my senses again, we shall take up where we left off this afternoon. I want nothing more, I swear, than to be with you."

She lifted her gaze. "We may become lovers, Alex. I want that as well. But we will never truly be together while you keep so much of yourself hidden from me. Will it always be this way?"

"I honestly don't know," he said after a moment. "But I will try to give you what you want. Not now, certainly, and perhaps not very soon. As for tonight, I shall do far better left to myself."

He was too much alone, she thought. But neither could she force her company on him. "After the fair, then." She stood on tiptoe and brushed a kiss on his cold cheek. "When I am rid of my ladies, we shall contrive together to rid you of your ghosts."

He gave her a faint smile as he opened the door. "I have seen you work miracles, Diana. Perhaps you can work another."

Chapter 17

Late the next morning, on the very fringes of town, Diana watched the finishing touches being applied to the regiment's booth.

She had been warned not to expect a prime location, for those were reserved far in advance by merchants who made the round of markets and fairs in northern England. Local merchants were given second priority, and apparently every decent spot had long since been spoken for. Market square and all the nearby streets were filled, and as one of the last to apply for a site, she had been relegated clear the other side of the River Kent, hard by one of Kendal's arched stone bridges.

The four ladies chosen to work in the booth on fair day were gathered around her, waiting to unpack the boxes and arrange the merchandise. Alex, wearing shirt, trousers, and boots, was atop a ladder, tying the rope of triangular pennants to the roof.

"They have certainly stashed us in the back of beyond," she said, trying to keep the disappointment from her voice. "Except for that pie seller, we are the only ones this side of the river."

"It's not so bad," Mrs. Jellicoe said bracingly. "I've been watching, and there be considerable traffic over that bridge. We wasn't like to be noticed until his lordship sent over the tent, but now everybody looks in this direction."

A blue and white pavilion tent had been erected over the squat little booth that had been sitting there when first the ladies arrived. Now only the front of the booth, with its wooden counter for displaying goods, was visible. The tent covered the rest and extended a good way beyond, creating a rather striking edifice.

"Perhaps it is all for the best," Diana conceded, holding the hem of her veil between thumb and forefinger against the morning breeze. "Were we crowded in among the others on market square, we'd not make so impressive an appearance."

"And when we're done workin' this afternoon," Mrs. Pottle said, "we mean to go around spreadin' the word where we are. See?" She handed Diana a small card.

Recognizing the work of the Yoodle sisters, Diana read the words inscribed in elegant print and embellished with bright flowers. *Gifts. Wines. Cordials. Jams and Jellies. Fine Foods. Embroidered Linens. Creams. Ointments. Fragrances.*

"We have two hundred cards," Mrs. Jellicoe informed her. "When we come on a likely customer, we'll give over a card and say where our booth is. It was Meggie Doyle's idea."

"And such a fine one!" Diana exclaimed, more than a little impressed with Mrs. Doyle's transformation from bitter abandoned wife to entrepreneur.

Glancing over at the bridge, she saw Kit and Lucy coming across it arm in arm. Lucy, anticipating the new wardrobe she would soon require, had gone in search of a mantua maker, and naturally Kit had accompanied her.

"He sticks to me like a plaster," Lucy had confided shortly before they left. "Kit is under the misapprehension that because I am with child, I am consequently frail and helpless."

She certainly looked the picture of good health, cheeks glowing and a decided bounce in her step. As Kit led her to where Diana was standing, the women of the regiment silently melted away.

"Look what I found!" Kit proclaimed with a broad gesture in the direction of a short, thin man wearing baggy trousers and an oversized coat. "Mrs. Valliant, may I present Felix the Magnificent?"

With his wizened face and bright round eyes, Felix the Magnificent put Diana strongly in mind of a monkey. "How do you do?" she said politely.

"More to the point," Kit said, "*what* does he do? Show her, my good man."

Looking befuddled, Felix raised his arms and snatched at the air as if trying to catch flies. Suddenly a red ball appeared in his left hand, and then a blue one in his right. He tossed them up and snatched at the air again, producing two more balls. Green and yellow, they joined the others midair, arcing up and down as he caught them and sent them flying again. From nowhere, a fifth ball appeared, and then a sixth. He juggled them low and high, behind his back and between his legs, an expression of surprised panic on his face as if he couldn't figure out how it was all being accomplished.

Then one by one the balls disappeared. Felix stared down at his empty hands, looking sorrowful.

Diana applauded with enthusiasm, and from some distance behind her she heard the regiment ladies clapping as well. "You truly *are* magnificent," she told him. "The juggling is splendid, of course, but however do you make those balls appear and vanish?"

In reply he plucked an orange from behind her shoulder. It must have displeased him. He tried again with his other hand and came up with an egg. Then he slammed his hands together and when he opened them, the egg and the orange were gone.

Kit smiled benevolently. "I have persuaded Mr. Magnificent that his talents will not be appreciated in the center of town, where there is precious little space for him to work or attract an audience. So, Felix, what think you? Is not this the ideal spot to ply your trade?"

The juggler bounded up a good yard or more, clicking his heels together.

"I'll take that as a *yes*," Kit said, laughing. "Seven o'clock, then, and don't be late."

Four balls reappeared in his hands as Felix left, juggling all the way across the bridge.

Diana saw people point to him and follow along to watch him perform. "Kit," she said under her breath, not wanting the regiment ladies to hear, "you *hired* that man to draw a crowd."

"So what if I did?" He gave a negligent shrug. "Felix will have himself a very good day, what with wages from me and what he'll earn passing the hat. I shouldn't be at all surprised if a number of street performers play here tomorrow. They're a close-knit lot, I have discovered. We met while Lucy was being measured for her new clothes."

"Madame Gloriette tossed him out on his ear," Lucy said with a grin. "He was getting on her nerves."

"If that old fussock is French, I am Marie Antoinette. Under all those *'très biens,'* the woman had a Yorkshire accent thick as bacon fat."

"It was excessively kind of you," Diana said, putting a hand on his arm. "I'll not even tell you that you ought not have done it, because I am so very glad that you did."

"Can't let Alex be the only one of use," Kit said, a tinge of color on his cheeks. "I must say, though, that if he leans over any farther, he's going to fall directly into that tent."

Diana glanced up, horrified to see Alex balanced precariously on the ladder, tying her regimental banner to a pole he'd affixed to the top of the booth. A brisk wind had sprung up, and he was having considerable difficulty holding on to the flag while he secured the ties. Mr. Pottle stood below him, clutching the ladder with his one arm to hold it in place.

After several breathless moments of watching Alex teeter a dozen feet above ground, Diana had to close her eyes. She heard Lucy gasp and closed them even tighter. If Alex plunged to his death on account of the regiment, she didn't want to see it.

"You can look now," Kit said. "And breathe again, if you've a mind to. He's on his way down."

Alex had both feet on the ground when she dared to open her eyes. He was gazing up at the tent.

Blue and white silk billowed in the wind. Pennants of red and yellow and green fluttered in a cheerful dance. And streaming out only to snap back with a crisp sound, the regimental flag flew proudly against the clear morning sky.

Tears welled in Diana's eyes, blurring her vision. Within a few hours, everything she had worked for would come to the test. What the members of the regiment earned tomorrow would see them through the harsh Lakeland winter. The money would feed their children, buy coals for their fires, and put warm blankets on their beds. It would pay for the materials they needed to produce goods to be sold at the first spring fair. It would give them the confidence to keep working. It would give them hope.

The women bustled forward, Mrs. Jellicoe and Mrs. Pottle,

Mrs. Renfrew and Mrs. Truscott, to help unload the flatbed wagon. A few passersby had stopped to look at the tent. She heard them inquire of the women what was to be sold there and promise to return on the morrow.

One gentleman insisted on taking a bottle of burnet wine immediately. He remembered seeing his mother make burnet wine when he was a child, but had never been granted the opportunity to taste it. Mrs. Jellicoe fished out a bottle, gave it him, and rushed to Diana with the coin he'd given her in return.

"A whole sovereign!" Mrs. Jellicoe's eyes were wide as serving platters. "He never even asked the price!"

"Our first sale," Diana said, fingers curling with pleasure. "Keep this coin aside, Mrs. Jellicoe. You'll want to show it when you tell the story to all the ladies who cannot be here with us for the fair. How I wish everyone could have come. After all their hard work, it's a shame they won't get to enjoy the excitement firsthand."

"Not this time. But in future, we'll be taking turns going to the fairs. 'Tis only fair." Laughing at her own joke, Mrs. Jellicoe hurried back to the wagon.

How she would miss them all, Diana thought with a pang of regret. Wherever she went, she would always be thinking of them and wondering how they were getting on.

Alex materialized at her side, wiping his forehead with a limp handkerchief. "It looks well, don't you think?"

"Altogether splendid. Thank you for putting up the flags, Alex. Are you finished now? Will you be coming with us to Candale?"

"There's still much to be done here, and I am required for the heavy lifting." He smiled. "But I'll be along directly the work is completed. Mr. Pottle has agreed to stay in the tent tonight and keep an eye on things, and the ladies have rooms at a nearby inn. There is nothing more for you to worry about."

"Don't dawdle," Kit told him. "Celia has planned a feast for the grand reunion of the Valliant clan. It will be the first time we are all of us together, and you know that females like to make a fuss about such trifles."

"I'll be there." Alex rushed over to the wagon and seized a

wooden box from Mrs. Truscott before it brought her to her knees.

While Kit and Lucy went to the carriage, which was drawn up a few yards away, Diana took one last look at the tent and especially at the banner, thinking of Mr. Beadle when she saw the blue castle. It was the exact color of the sky. She remembered his promise to be here in spirit, and perhaps he was. But who could ever really know?

She had just turned to the carriage when half a dozen street urchins, whooping and hollering, came over the bridge and spotted the tent. Apparently wanting a closer look, they galloped past her, and as they did, the wind lifted her veil and tossed it over her bonnet.

One of the boys, thin and dirty with hair the color of straw, pulled to a halt and pointed at her face. "Cor! Lookee that. It be a dragon woman."

The others, laughing and jeering, formed a circle and danced around her as if she were a Maypole. "Dragon!" they chanted. "Dragon!"

Hot with embarrassment, she couldn't bring herself to lower the veil. She doubted she could move at all. Others had clustered about to watch the boys make fun of her, and she stood silently, pretending not to care and willing herself not to cry. It seemed to go on for years, their singsong chants and her humiliation.

But it was probably only a matter of moments, because Alex came charging at the boys like an enraged lion. They scattered in all directions, their skinny legs pumping as they fled. Alex went for the leader, who dodged around the pie stall, keeping it between himself and his assailant. Kit came up behind him then, sending him off in the direction of the bridge.

Alex was on him before he reached it. Grabbing the boy by the collar of his shabby jacket, he lifted him high into the air. The boy flailed at him with legs and fists, catching him a glancing blow on the thigh. Alex swore and looked about to cuff him soundly.

"Don't hurt him!" Diana cried, rushing in their direction.

Alex glanced at her over his shoulder, receiving another kick

179

from the boy while he was distracted. "Keep away," he ordered Diana. "I mean it."

She stopped, and saw him set the boy on the ground and grapple him by the shoulders, turning him so that they were face-to-face. At one point, Alex shook him soundly.

Remembering to lower her veil, she waited in place. Of a sudden Lucy was by her side, taking her hand in a warm, reassuring grip. Kit was busy dispatching the curious onlookers.

And this was what it was like to go out in public, she thought. A chance gust of wind, nothing more, and she became the object of ridicule. She didn't blame the boys. Children who lived on the streets had no opportunity to learn manners. It was the whispers from the crowd she took to heart, the "Poor thing" and the "She'd be so pretty without that scar." "No wonder she wears a veil." "She oughtn't to show herself, looking like that."

But Kit had got rid of them all, and now the silence was even worse than what they had said. It gave her time to take their words to heart.

Alex came up to her, towing the ragged, red-faced urchin by one arm. He set him loose directly in front of her and stepped behind him in case he tried to scarper.

She looked down at the thatch of greasy yellow hair. The boy was staring at the ground, scuffing his worn shoes in the dirt.

"I be sorry," he said. "It were wrong of me."

"What else?" Alex demanded.

"I won't never do no such thing again. Not to nobody. Swear to God I won't."

Diana put a hand on his shoulder. "That's all right then. You can go along now."

He raised his eyes. "I really is sorry, ma'am. Really truly."

Alex stepped aside, and the boy ran off as if the devil were on his heels.

"Thank you, Alex," she said, keeping her voice steady. "I believe he has learned his lesson now." She turned to Kit. "Celia will be growing impatient. Shall we go before she comes looking for us?"

Everyone seemed to understand she wished the incident put behind her. Alex bowed, and Kit went to open the carriage door.

Lucy kept hold of her hand until she mounted the steps. But in that short time, Diana had come to a decision.

Never, not *ever* again, would she permit a stranger to see her face.

Chapter 18

Diana was dreaming of the glass spider when something woke her.

She opened her eyes and saw Alex leaning over the bed. He was wearing his dressing gown. In the flickering light of the candle he was holding, his face looked somber.

"A messenger has just arrived from town," he said. "There has been some sort of disturbance at the booth. He could give us no details, save that the constable thought we should be informed immediately."

She sat up, cold with dread. "What are we to do? Shall we go there?"

"Kendal has ordered the carriage brought around. You needn't come if you'd rather not, but I expected that you would wish to."

"Of course." She threw back the covers. "I'll dress straightaway."

"Come downstairs when you are ready, then." He brushed his fingers over her tangled hair. "And try not to worry, Diana. It may be nothing of consequence."

The sun had just appeared over the horizon, but already the road was choked with vehicles and pedestrians making their way to the fair. Alex guided his horse alongside the crested carriage and rapped on the window.

Kendal lowered the panel. "Problems ahead?"

"You'll make slow progress from here on out, I'm afraid. Kit and I are taking to the fields."

Diana's face appeared at the window. "Will you take me with you?"

He gestured to the driver, who brought the carriage to a halt. Diana bounded out and Alex scooped her onto the saddle in front of him.

She was a warm, silent presence in his arms as they rode behind Kit, following the roundabout route he had assured them was the swiftest way to town. "Don't think about it," Alex said after a time. "There's no use anticipating the worst."

"I know." She rested her head on his shoulder. "I am putting together my courage, is all. I mustn't fly to pieces in front of the others."

"You won't."

They didn't speak again until they came in sight of the tent. And then there was nothing to be said.

He heard the breath catch in her throat. For the barest moment she went limp in his arms. Then she drew herself up and raised her chin.

The tent looked as if a troop of cavalry had charged through it. One side had been trampled to the ground and the other listed at a sharp angle, a few colorful pennants fluttering bravely in the morning breeze. The wooden booth, still intact, was smeared with creams and jams. Broken glass covered the display counter.

Standing in front of it, as if they could not believe what they saw, three of the regiment ladies huddled together. A few curious fairgoers had gathered nearby, and others viewed the devastation from the bridge.

Not far from the riverbank, Mr. Pottle was sitting with his back against a tree. Beside him, Mrs. Pottle dabbed a wet handkerchief against his temple. A stocky man wearing a blue uniform appeared to be asking questions and taking notes.

The constable, Alex supposed. When he set Diana to the ground, she hurried to the women and embraced each of them in turn.

Alex tethered his horse and went to Mr. Pottle, who looked slightly dazed.

"It's me own fault," he said. "I nodded to sleep, and they was on me afore I knowed they be there."

Alex crouched next to him, noting the crimson lump just above his temple. "Can you tell me what happened?"

"Aye, the first part. I come awake when I heard a noise, and then I sees a knife cutting through the tent. *Whoosh!* it went. I were about to yell for help, but summum musta come in from behind me. Next thing, I was hit on me noggin."

"They tied him up," Mrs. Pottle said in a tight voice, "and put a gag in his mouth. Then they hauled him behind those bushes."

"I couldn't see nuthin' after that," Mr. Pottle said, "but I heared them breaking up all what was in the tent. They was laughin'. I guess I went fuzzy-headed then. Next I knowed, a man were leanin' over 'n askin' if I be hurt. Like I could answer 'im with a rag in me mouth."

"He thinks there were two of them," the constable put in. "Hooligans, I expect, out on a lark."

Alex very much doubted that. The destruction was too complete. He stood. "Lord Kendal will be here shortly, ma'am. He'll see the both of you cared for. For now, I wish to speak with the constable."

"I'm a Carlisle man, hired on for the fair," he said when Alex drew him to one side. "I'll give my report to the magistrate, but I can tell you that nothing will be done about it. Not today."

"Have you found any witnesses? This booth was not ransacked without a good deal of noise. Someone must have heard it."

"Happen so, if they were crossing the bridge just then." The constable made a sweeping gesture. "But there's nothing close by, no houses or shops. Only that pie stall, and nobody has come to open it."

"Understood. When Kendal arrives, you will take your orders from him. Meantime, station yourself by the bridge and keep the sightseers at a distance." Alex waited until the constable was in place, and then went in search of Diana.

She was standing alone amid the ruins of her dream, ankle-deep in shattered bottles and shredded tablecloths. The regimental banner—what remained of it—was clutched in her arms.

She looked up at him from wounded eyes. "Why ever would anyone do such a thing, Alex?"

He made his way across the fragments of glass and took her

in his arms. "I mean to find out," he said. "You may be sure that I will."

"They left nothing. Not one single bottle or jar. Not a scrap of lace or an embroidered napkin. They ruined *everything*. And how are we to tell all the others waiting for us to come back with our pockets full of money? I cannot bear to face them."

"There is no reason. The regiment will be paid."

"Yes. I'll pay them myself, if you will permit it. But they mustn't be told that I did. We'll pretend we caught the vandals and that they made resti . . . oh, I cannot think of the word."

"Restitution." He could scarcely breathe, the stench of wine and perfumed creams and pickled vegetables all but over-whelming. "Trust me to deal with this, Diana. And now, come away from here."

She let him lead her into the fresh air.

"Don't look back," he said, holding her close at his side. "What's done is done."

"I know." She sighed. "I shall remember the tent as I saw it yesterday, with the flags flying and all our beautiful things laid out. And Mrs. Jellicoe has the sovereign from our first sale. Our only sale, but it proves that we would have made a great suc-cess, don't you think?"

"Absolutely." Alex had never before felt so helpless. "You'll wish to have words with Mr. Pottle, I expect. He holds himself responsible for what happened."

"Gracious!" She looked at him with alarm. "How could he? Of course it's not his fault. I must speak with him directly."

She sped away, the frayed banner still clutched in her arms.

"Sir?"

Turning, Alex saw a familiar dirt-streaked face. "What is it?" he snapped.

"I saw the men what did this," the boy said in a nervous voice. "Thought you'd wanna know."

"You can be sure of it." Alex beckoned to Kit, who was standing with the women. "My brother may as well hear this at the same time. What's your name?"

"Jemmy Thacker. But it's a made-up name. I be a foundling."

"What have we here?" Kit said. "Not in trouble again, are you, lad?"

"He claims to be a witness," Alex said. "Go ahead, Jemmy. Start from the beginning."

"Well, I wuz sleepin' in there," he said, indicating the pie stall. "Weren't nobody to stop me, and it be better than the streets. Anyways, suddenlike there was noises. Woke me up, they did. I reckoned folks had got in a fight, but I were too scared to go see. Went on a long time, them noises. I could tell they wuz comin' from the tent. Then it got real quiet."

"You told me you *saw* the men."

"Don't bark at the lad, old thing." Kit put a hand on Alex's forearm. "He'll come to the point when he gets there."

Jemmy chewed at his lower lip. "I didn't see 'em *do* it. But I sneaked outside after it were quiet, and I saw 'em goin' over the bridge. There was two men, and I knows they wuz the ones 'cause they wuz carryin' some bottles. Square bottles, like I seen yesterday at the tent. Afore I said those bad things," he added, flushing.

"Never mind that. Would you recognize the men if you saw them again?"

"I 'spect so. Went after 'em to get a better look. But they took a turn, and when I come round it, they wuz gone."

Alex swallowed his disappointment. Even if he trolled Jemmy through the crowded streets for the rest of the day, there was little chance of spotting the vandals.

"I been lookin' for 'em ever since," Jemmy said. " 'Bout an hour ago I saw 'em come outer a posthouse the far side of town. Luck, it were. I wuz gonna give it up, and then there they wuz. So I followed 'em till they went inter a pub. Then I come here. Run all the way, I did."

"Excellent work, young man!" Kit clapped him on the back. "You have the makings of a Bow Street Runner. Let's go find them, shall we?"

"Hold on," Alex said. "Kendal is finally here, and we'd better tell him where we are going. Do you know the name of the pub, Jemmy?"

"Can't read," the boy muttered. "But the sign had a pitchur what looked like a cheese."

"Wait here with him, Kit."

Kendal was regarding the ruined tent with a grim expression

on his face. "It's true, then," he said. "I had hoped we were misinformed."

Alex quickly recounted what he had learned. "Kit and I are going after the two men. Will you see to Diana and the others?"

Kendal raised a brow. "I presume, Alex, that you mean only to apprehend the vandals. It would be most inadvisable to kill them."

"Not the way I see it. But I won't. You may tell that to Diana."

"Oyez, oyez, oyez!" the bailiff cried, clanging his handbell.

Above the din of the crowd, the official summons to the fair rang out from the market square. Alex and Kit, mired in a throng of fairgoers one street away, had lost sight of Jemmy.

"Where the devil is he?" Alex jumped onto the back of a stalled wagon heaped with cabbages and searched the crowd for a thatch of yellow hair. Finally he spotted Jemmy at the next corner, waving his arms.

At this rate, Alex thought as he led Kit to where he'd seen the boy, they would reach the pub house well after dark. Someone stumbled against his back, muttered an apology, and shoved past him.

". . . that no person pick any quarrel, matter, or course for any old grudge or malice," the bailiff shouted, "to make any perturbation or trouble!"

"He's charging us to keep the peace," Kit said with a short laugh. "Small chance of that, wouldn't you say?"

"None whatever. There's the brat. I think one of us had better hang on to him the rest of the way."

"Not far now," Jemmy said as Kit took his hand. "We'll go round the back where they don't be so many people."

The buildings they passed were each one shabbier than the one before as he guided them away from the market square and through a rabbit warren of narrow streets. Just the sort of place the men they were looking for would go to ground, Alex was thinking when Jemmy drew up across from a good-sized pub house.

"That be where they wuz," he said, pointing to the half-timbered building.

A weather-worn sign hung above the open door with "The Wheel of Cheese" crudely printed atop the picture of an orange cheese. To judge by the noise coming from inside, the pub was a popular gathering place. All the voices were male, and even at this early hour, most of them sounded well to let.

Alex had to dodge a pair of louts emerging from the pub as he led Jemmy inside. The taproom, its low ceiling blackened with smoke from the hearth fire, stank of ale, foul breath, and sweat. There were a few small round tables ringed with ladder-back chairs, all of them occupied, and a long wooden bar was elbow-to-elbow with roughly garbed men.

Jemmy plucked at his sleeve. "Them two," he said in a whisper. "That tall 'un near to the middle of the bar and the one next to 'im takin' a drink."

Alex saw a tankard at the mouth of a big-shouldered, barrel-shaped man with spiky black hair. To his left, a man about his own height was trying to get the barkeep's attention.

"Lucifer!" Kit indicated the black-haired man. "That's the fellow who shot me."

"Did he?" Alex regarded his brother with a frown. "When was that? And why is he not in gaol for it?"

"Long story, old lad. More to the point, the rascal works for Sir Basil Crawley. I expect we both know what that means."

"No great surprise," Alex said. "Jemmy, wait outside until we are done here."

"I wanna watch!" the boy protested, looking eager at the prospect of a fight.

"Go!"

Grumbling, Jemmy slouched away.

"This reckoning is long overdue," Kit said, striking out for the bar. "You take care of Longshanks. Blackie belongs to me."

Alex followed, halting directly behind his quarry. Kit did the same.

The men paid them no mind. They were tossing dice together, and a considerable amount of money was piled before each of them. Their pay for demolishing the tent, Alex surmised.

Kit tapped a finger on Blackie's shoulder. "Hullo there, darlin'."

"Huh?" The man turned, a scowl knitting his thick eyebrows. "Who the devil—?"

"Remember me?" Kit planted his right fist in Blackie's face, sending him halfway across the bar.

Alex seized the other man's wrist, wrenching it up behind his back, and grabbed the man's hair with his other hand. He smashed his face against the bar. "Make the slightest move," he cautioned, "and I'll break your arm."

Blackie pulled himself upright and launched himself at Kit, who ducked his swinging fist and sent a blow to his stomach. He doubled over, groaning. Chairs and tankards clattered to the floor as everyone scrambled out of the way.

"Come on, sweetheart," Kit coaxed, standing loose-limbed with his hands open at his sides. "You can do better than that."

Bellowing an oath, Blackie went at him with both fists flying. One caught Kit on the shoulder, but he grabbed hold of it and used Blackie's momentum to send him flying headfirst into the wall. He bounced off and landed on his backside.

The audience, clustered at the far side of the room, laughed and applauded.

Blood streamed from Blackie's nose and a cut over his eye.

Grinning, Kit tossed him a handkerchief. "On your feet, my good fellow. I can't hit you while you're down."

Blackie rocked to his knees, his sleeve pressed to his nostrils. " 'Nuff," he mumbled. "I'm done for."

"Pity. And here I was just getting started." With a dramatic sigh, Kit turned to Alex. "What of your little pussycat, Colonel? Any fight left in him?"

Alex looked down at the limp figure in his grasp. "None to speak of, I'm afraid. It appears we'll have to turn them over to the magistrate relatively intact."

"Knife!" someone shouted.

Kit hit the ground just before the blade could drive into his back. The blow met empty air, sending Blackie off balance and staggering forward. Kit rolled away and sprang to his feet.

The taproom grew hushed as the two men circled each other. Blackie, a malevolent sneer on his face, waved the long-bladed knife in mocking arcs. "We'll see who has the last laugh, boy."

Kit, his arms splayed and hands held shoulder-high, came

up against a fallen chair and hopped over it. Blackie used the opportunity to slash at him, but Kit darted out of reach. Again they moved in a circular pattern, face-to-face, but Blackie was slowly forcing him in the direction of the wall.

Alex knew better than to make a move. It would only break his brother's concentration. But his heart was pounding in his chest, and the man he was holding moaned as his grip tightened on the bent arm.

Still smiling, Kit came closer and closer to the wall with each turn of the circle. One more time around and he'd have no room to evade the knife. "Now or never, luvvie," he invited, drawing to a halt and beckoning with his forefinger. "Come and get me."

With a howl of rage Blackie charged at him. The knife slashed at Kit's throat.

And then it was skittering across the floor, landing against the bar where Alex was standing. He planted his foot on it and watched Kit pummel his adversary to the ground.

When Blackie lay unconscious, Kit brushed his hands together with evident satisfaction and gazed around at the stunned crowd, one brow raised. "Any of you chaps got a rope?"

The barkeep came to life. "I'll fetch one from the back room, sir."

"Make it two," Alex said, regarding his brother with some awe. "But first, pour the winner a stiff drink."

Leaning against the bar at Alex's side, Kit downed most of a large glass of whisky and poured the rest over his bruised knuckes. Wincing, he said, "And here I was thinking that the fight wouldn't get interesting."

"How the devil did you do that, Kit? I've never seen a move like it."

"A thing of beauty, what? Ran into a Chinese fellow once upon a time, me smuggling wine and him smuggling tea, both of us chased by a pair of excise cutters. Our boats were driven onto Jersey by a storm and we were stuck there for a considerable time. With nothing better to do, I taught him to deal seconds, and he taught me to fight with my feet. One quick twirl, foot lashes out, knife gone. Piece of cake."

It was nothing of the sort. Kit had been a blade's edge from a slit throat or a length of steel in his chest. And he knew it as well, however lightly he dismissed the affair.

"Oughtn't you let your sweetie come up for a bit of air?" Kit asked. "If you don't smother him, he might answer a few questions for us."

Alex had forgot he was still pressing Longshanks's face to the bar. He released the greasy hair and the thick wrist, turning the man so that his back was to the wooden railing. "You are in the employ of Sir Basil Crawley, I believe."

"Not me!" the man blubbered, pointing to the prone figure on the floor. "Him!"

The barkeep had returned with several lengths of hemp rope, and two men were cheerfully tying Blackie's hands behind his back. "Feet, too?" one of them called.

"Hobble him," Alex ordered, returning his attention to Longshanks. "What is your name?"

"Ned Tyler. The other 'un be Mick. Dunno the rest. Met 'im yesterday at the posthouse where I been stayin'. In the stable, mind ye. Couldn't pay fer a room. Come in for the fair, I did, lookin' for work. Mick said 'e'd pay me to 'elp him break up one o' the booths. Said 'is boss didn't want the folk what set it up to be sellin' their things." Sweat trickled down his battered face. "It were good money for an hour's work, so I done it."

"Otherwise," Kit said pleasantly, "you are no doubt an honest fellow with a wife and six children to feed."

"Four. An' one of 'em ailin'." He sniveled. "I'd have took an honest job, but there weren't none."

Alex, remembering the regiment ladies and their hard times, nearly tumbled to Ned's hard-luck story. Then his gaze fell on the dice the two men had been tossing, and the coins Ned was wagering between rounds of ale. Not a coin would have made it home to his family . . . assuming he had one.

Lord, he was going soft, to be so taken in. It was Diana's influence, he supposed, and the openhearted generosity he admired in her. Were she here, she'd sweep Ned under her wing and offer him a job at Lakeview, never mind that he'd probably loot the place first chance he got.

The taproom, which had erupted in noise once the fight was

over, suddenly went hushed again. Alex glanced over his shoulder and saw everyone facing the door.

Kendal turned his gaze slowly around the room. It paused a moment at the bound man laid out on the floor, moved to the barkeep standing with pieces of rope dangling from both hands, and finally settled on Kit and Alex. One brow arched in a query.

"About time you got here," Kit said. "You missed all the fun."

"Someone had to tend to business," Kendal replied, a look of resignation on his face as he moved past Mick and saw the damage Kit had done to him. "I've brought along a pair of constables, if you are quite finished beating up on the prisoners. May I presume they can be taken away now?"

Alex shoved Ned in the direction of the two men trailing behind Kendal. "They're all yours."

Mick, still dead to the world, had to be hauled out. Kit tossed coins to three fellows eager to do the job, and within a short time the taproom was virtually empty. Kendal's arrival appeared to have put a damper on things, because most of the patrons wandered off in search of another place to bend an elbow. The barkeep, looking distinctly unhappy, poured whiskey into three glasses at Alex's order before retreating to the back room.

"You *do* know how to nip a party," Kit said.

"And you continue to find unorthodox ways of entertaining yourself. What will your wife make of those battered knuckles, I wonder?"

"Oh, she'll kiss them and make them all better," Kit said with a laugh. "You don't know her. After my first encounter with Mick, she ordered me to chase him down and wring his neck. Bloodthirsty wench, my moonbeam."

Kendal shook his head. "This 'Mick' was the prone gentleman recently dragged away, I assume. How came you to know him?"

"Our paths crossed once or twice," Kit said negligently. "Three times, to be precise. The first is irrelevant. The second and third, he was in company with Basil Crawley."

"Ah. I'd assumed he was responsible for the destruction of the tent, but it's well to have proof. Can his thugs be persuaded to testify against him?"

"Mick went after Kit with a knife in front of a score of witnesses," Alex said. "He'll talk in exchange for deportment instead of the hanging he deserves."

"Thank you," Kit said sourly. "Jimmie wasn't supposed to hear of that."

"Sorry. I lack your talent for deception." Alex turned to Kendal. "The penalty for hiring vandals to demolish a booth cannot be of any account."

"Oh, I have a bit more than that to discuss with him. Not to put too fine a point on it, his business practices have not stood up to close scrutiny. I shall advise him of certain information in my possession and suggest that he depart Westmoreland with all possible speed."

"You'll let him go *free*?" Kit erupted. "I think not, Jimmie."

"I wish him gone," Kendal said coolly. "But he'll not escape punishment, you may be sure. Now, shall we drink up, gentlemen, and be on our way? Before the morning is out, I mean to pay a call on Sir Basil."

Alex picked up his glass. "Have you magically divined where he can be found?"

"Oh, at home, I should imagine. Perhaps Mick, if he has come to his senses, will enlighten us. And I must hire a mount, assuming that one is to be found in this hubbub. The carriage has taken Diana and the other ladies back to Candale."

"We'll go with you, of course."

"Not you, Alex. I'll take Kit along, but you would do better to see to your wife. She is putting a brave front on it, but I fear she has taken this incident rather hard."

"Yes." Alex thought of her standing in the ruined tent, her banner held tightly in her arms, trying not to weep. "I'll leave Crawley to you. But see to it he makes full restitution, James. Return with cash or the equivalent so that we can put it into Diana's hands."

"She will have it by this evening." Kendal raised his glass. "A toast, then. To Diana's Regiment."

When they had drunk, Kit swept the coins Mick and Ned Tyler had left on the bar and gave them to Alex. "A down payment, old thing. We'll come back with the rest if I have to sell Crawley's corpse to the knackers."

Alex followed his brothers from the dim taproom, watching them move purposefully through the crush of people and vanish around a corner. For a moment he was wild to go after them. He had missed too many last battles, fighting nearly to the end only to be elsewhere when the decisive action played out. It was the battles he hadn't fought that haunted him. He was never where he was supposed to be when it counted.

"Were a good fight!" Jemmy declared, appearing at his side. "I sneaked in to watch. When the black-haired bloke pulled out the steel, I thunk fer sure Mister Kit were a gonner. Right handy, he be. You never got much inter it, though."

"I'm sorry to have disappointed you," Alex said, "but my opponent was disinclined to joust. I daresay you expect a reward, Jemmy, and you shall have it after you have guided me back to where I left my horse."

"Don't want no reward, sir. I owed this 'un to the lady. 'Sides, I'm doin' well enough." He reached into his coat and came out with two pocket watches and several coins. "Filched these while ever'body wuz gawkin' at the fight. I ain't even got started at the market square. Good pluckin's to be 'ad there, what with folks all packed together pushin' and shovin'."

Good Lord. Alex glared down at the filthy face beaming up at him. "You're a bloody pickpocket?"

"A fella's gotta eat, sir. What I gets t'day will keep me fer a month. C'n we go now? I be glad to take you back where I found you, but then I's work t'do."

Alex took hold of his hand, letting Jemmy tow him through the winding backstreets of Kendal. He ought to turn the cheeky little felon over to the authorities, he supposed, but it was really out of the question. So was letting him ply his trade. One day the boy was certain to be caught, and fairly soon if he couldn't resist boasting of his successes.

"How old are you, Jemmy?"

"Dunno. I sez I be fourteen, but it's more like 'leven or twelve."

"And where do you live when you're not come to town for the fair?"

"Oh, I allus live in Kendal or nearabouts. Sometimes in a barn when it be too cold to sleep unner a tree or a wagon. I run off from the foundlin' home mebbe three years ago. There be a man there what likes to cane folks just fer breathin'. Reckoned I'd do better on the streets, 'n so I 'ave." They came alongside the River Kent and followed it a short way. Soon Alex saw the blue and white tent directly ahead. Several men surrounded it, shoveling broken glass onto the back of a wagon. Kendal, always thorough, must have hired them to clean up the mess.

Alex came to a decision, although he expected to wind up regretting it. When they arrived at the tree where Thunder was tethered, he turned Jemmy to face him and gazed intently into the boy's surprised blue eyes. "I want you to come with me, young man. You will have a warm place to sleep, regular meals, and a job that will pay steady wages. I've no use for a pickpocket, and devil knows what else you are capable of doing, but we'll find something. My wife has a talent for putting people to work. Are you interested?"

Jemmy gaped at him.

"I'm not promising a life of ease," Alex warned. "You'll have to work hard, obey orders, and keep out of trouble. Can you do that?"

"Mebbe." He looked worried. "Will the lady 'ave me, sir? After what I said to 'er?"

Diana would sweep the boy into her arms in a heartbeat. "She has a great regard for courage," Alex assured him. "If you are brave enough to leave what you know and make a new life for yourself, you will be most welcome."

He might as well have been addressing himself, Alex thought with sudden, painful insight. He had failed to do what he was demanding of this child. Mired in the failures of the past, he had lacked the will to strike out and make a new life, even when one was practically handed to him. Diana was a gift he'd accepted without giving of himself in return.

Well, he had given what he was willing to spare. He gave his time. His work. He supported the regiment. He was more than willing to kill on her behalf. But he withheld what she had asked of him, knowing all the while how hard it was for her to ask.

"You changed yer mind, sir?"

Alex, hot with shame, had forgot the boy. He put his hand on Jemmy's shoulder, gazing past him to the bridge where fairgoers were making their way across the river. A bright mound of color drew his attention. Flowers piled on the back of a wagon.

He located a guinea. "We'll set out in a minute. But first, see that flower seller? Go buy the best she has to offer—roses if there are any. I mean to give them to my wife."

Chapter 19

On her knees in the kitchen garden, Diana wrenched a stubborn weed from the base of a rosemary bush and tossed it into the basket at her side.

The Candale gardens, all of them, were far too well tended to suit her mood. For the past two hours she had been at pains to search out the occasional stray weed, and it had become something of a challenge to find one. When she succeeded, she felt a special satisfaction at ripping it out.

She had just pulled something she expected ought not to have been pulled when she heard Alex call her name. He was coming across the lawn, his arms filled with flowers.

"*There* you are!" he said. "I've been looking everywhere for you. What the deuce are you doing in the kitchen garden?"

Rising, she brushed soil from her skirts and stripped off her gardening gloves. "Taking out my temper on hapless plants, I'm afraid."

"Well, here are some more of them." He put the flowers into her hands. "Tear them to pieces if you must."

"They're lovely, Alex. Thank you." He looked—well, it was impossible to know. But there was something in his eyes she had not seen before. "I should put them into water, I suppose."

"Aren't you going to ask me what happened?"

"Yes. Certainly." She wasn't sure she wanted to hear it. The news could not be good if he'd brought hothouse roses to soften the blow. "Shall we go inside? You can tell me while I arrange the flowers."

"They are meant to be a gift," he said, walking beside her to the house. "I brought you another, too, but you won't like it half so well. Where the devil is everyone? It was all I could do to locate a servant."

"They've all been given a holiday to attend the fair, save for the babe's nursemaid and one or two others. Lady Kendal and Lucy have gone, too, and taken the regiment ladies with them. It was foolish for them to sit around here moping when they could be enjoying themselves. We have the house quite to ourselves."

"Excellent. I've had enough of crowds for one day." He opened the door for her. "Where does one go to arrange flowers?"

"If you will fetch some water, sir, I'll find a vase and scissors and meet you in the downstairs parlor."

He arrived a few minutes after she did, with water, two glasses, and a bottle of brandy. "Would you care for a drink?" he asked, still with that odd look in his eyes. When she declined, he poured one for himself and sat on a sofa near the table where she was clipping leaves from the bottoms of the rose stems. "May I tell you the news now? It's not all bad, I promise you."

"I have been afraid to hear it," she acknowledged. "Did you find the culprits?"

"Yes indeed. Jemmy led us straight to them. There was a bit of a scuffle, but no harm done except to a particularly loathsome specimen who once, or so I am informed, put a bullet in Kit."

She dropped the rose she had been holding and spun to look at him. "Sir Basil sent them? I should have guessed he was behind this."

"Ah. You know the fellow. Well, he is now in the hands of the magistrate, and we expect he'll be transported when next the assizes are held. As for his employer, my brothers have gone to deal with him. Kendal assures me that he will return this evening with full compensation for the regiment's losses."

She felt her blood drain to her toes. "It's all over, then? Sir Basil will not—"

"You are free of him, my dear. Destroying the booth was a petty act of vengeance by a desperate man. I would be very much surprised if Crawley spent another night in Westmoreland, and Kendal means to pursue him through the courts until he is hounded from England or thrown into Newgate. In either case, he'll make no more trouble for you. He knows that we'll kill him if he tries."

"Oh." Relief made her dizzy. She sank onto the sofa beside Alex, welcoming his arm when it went around her shoulders. "He was the spider," she murmured.

He drew her closer. "What spider?"

"The one in my dreams. The one that did this." She put her fingers to the scar. "It was my uncle who hit me, of course, but only because Sir Basil drove him past reason. And I have felt him lurking in every dark corner since first he set out to have me, waiting to strike."

"You must put him from your thoughts, Diana. And from your dreams as well, although I know how difficult that will be." He hesitated a moment. "I, too, have bad dreams."

She remembered watching him thrash about on her bed, tormented by nightmares, mumbling words she could not distinguish. He was a stranger then, but she had felt, during those long hours, a closeness to him that they had not shared since. Not even when they kissed at the picnic. His heart was open and raw that night, and at times she thought she could touch it. But morning came, and when next she saw him, he was wearing the armor that had kept him separate from her to this very moment. She nestled her head against his shoulder, accepting his comfort and wishing he would permit her to comfort him in return.

"The fair is over," he said after a while. "For us, in any case. And I promised you that when it was, we would take up again where we left off. I should like to do that now, Diana, if you are willing." His voice was strained. "And no, I don't mean that we should . . . that is, not right away. First I would like to explain, if I can, why it is I have been . . . why I *am* . . . well, what I am."

He took a drink of brandy. "Damn. I'm making even less sense than usual. But I'm no good at talking, Diana. You know that. Can you bear to hear me out?"

She lifted her head, breathless with astonishment. "Oh yes, Alex. Of course I will."

"Don't look at me, then. And don't say anything. Just let me get on about it as best I can. It's an ugly story, and one I am not proud of. Very much the contrary. But you must hear it, because you'll give me no peace until you do. And most like I'll have no peace until I tell it. Only the core of it today, though, because the whole of it would take too long."

"Whatever you wish to say, Alex." She leaned into him again and closed her eyes. "We have a lifetime for the rest."

"Thank you," he whispered against her hair. "The hope of that will see me through."

He spoke then, sometimes faltering, sometimes stopping for minutes at a time. Often she could not understand him. She knew nothing of military matters, and he used words she had never heard and described things she could not imagine.

Not battles, though . . . not at first. He said nothing of the war in Spain, beginning at the point when his regiment was ordered to America. It was clear he'd been reluctant to go, and had done so only because he would not abandon his men.

His disgust at the politicians who sent them there was bitterly apparent. "We were ordered to 'chastise the savages,' " he said at one point. "I could find no sense in it. Bonaparte was a tyrant, and we'd no choice but to put him down, but why the Americans? By running the blockades and keeping commerce open with the French, they had certainly made things more difficult for us. But the war didn't touch them. They were under no immediate threat, and failed to understand the consequences of what they were doing. I grant them foolish and shortsighted, even greedy to profit from the war, but never savages. Their actions did not merit the punishment we were directed to inflict on them."

He expelled a sigh. "I expect there were grievances on their part as well. And we certainly gave them more than enough reason to despise us in the months ahead."

He took up the story at the point they made land and set about a campaign of burning houses, farms—even whole towns—if the residents held out against them. He told of places she had never heard of—the Chesapeake Bay, the Potomac River, Bladensburg and Baltimore and Georgetown. He began describing battles then, in excruciating detail, and she felt perspiration running down his neck.

"In one Maryland township," he said, "a tiny, insignificant place, I disobeyed a direct order for the only time in my life. We had been sent to burn it to the ground. And so we did, torching even the chicken coops after making off with the birds for our suppers. It was the middle of the night, and all the occupants had fled long before we arrived. All but two, as it turned out. I was in company with a handful of men when we arrived at a pair of small houses standing side by side near to the church. A woman came out of one of them and leveled a rifle at me. Her name was Miss Kitty Knight. She said that with pride, and it is a name I shall never forget. Her neighbor in the other house was ill, she told us, too ill to be moved. If we fired her home down about her, we would first have to deal with Miss Knight. And she would shoot the first one of us to raise a torch.

"I've no doubt she was ready to put a bullet in me. But that wasn't the reason I ordered the men to move on, leaving both houses standing and the church as well. If we had come to making war on women, brave ones and sick ones alike, I wanted no part of it."

Diana pressed her nails into her palms, longing to assure him that he'd done the right thing. Perhaps he knew that he had. But it was nevertheless a violation of his duty, and it struck him to the heart.

Next he described the march into Washington and the burning of the president's house and the Capitol. His regiment had been left on the outskirts of the city to keep guard, but he had been summoned to join the officers who wandered through the buildings, sometimes taking souvenirs and even snatching food from President Madison's dinner table, which had been laid out for a meal just before word came that the British were almost at the door.

"When we had demolished the Capitol, even the Congressional Library, the decision was taken to go on to Baltimore. It was summer, hot and muggy. The Sickly Season, it was called. The whole area is one great marsh, and men were dropping by the hundreds with fever and dysentery. I went down, too, and was billeted in a farmhouse where an old lady and her daughter did all they could to keep me alive. It was a near-run thing. I'd little interest in making a recovery by that time, but they fought me like tigers, pushing food down my throat and cleaning up after me when I expelled it again."

He reached over and poured himself another drink. "Suffice it to say I had become useless to the army. Before heading on for Baltimore, my commanding officer advised me to take ship back to England as soon as I had recovered. But it was one thing to despise the war and another thing to flee it. I insisted on catching up with the regiment when I could, so General Ross gave me papers granting extended leave—no questions asked—for as long as I required it. That was an extraordinary gesture on his part. But I had chanced to spare his head from being lopped off by a saber some years earlier, and I suppose it was his way of repaying me. In any case, Diana, I am still on that leave. I have made no effort to take up my duties again."

She thought he was finished then, and almost spoke. But he must have sensed it, because he covered her hand with his.

"There's more," he said. "The worst is to come. I don't think I was malingering, but I have often wondered if that is true. It's certain that whenever I thought myself well enough to follow the army, I went down with another bout of fever. Two attempts were made to get me on ship for home, but I resisted them. For several months I remained in Maryland, but shortly before Christmas, I was well enough to travel. The army had gone south by then, in the direction of New Orleans, so I set out after them."

His hand tightened around hers. "Before I got there, word came that the battle was over. Jackson had routed our forces and driven them from Louisiana. But worst of all, to my mind, was that the Forty-fourth went down in shame. They had drawn the Forlorn Hope for the attack, and were assigned to march at the head of the column. The Americans had raised a parapet to hold them off, and the Forty-fourth was responsible for carrying the ladders and fascines needed to scale it. But the officer in charge mistook where they had been stored. He sent the men to the wrong place, and by the time they were redirected, it was too late. The column had been ordered to advance, and the Forty-fourth were coming up behind them. But they thought they were in front, you see, so when the shooting started, they shot back and took down the fellows in between, who were now being fired at from both sides. They panicked and broke ranks, as did the Forty-fourth, and the officers could not rally them."

He fell silent, his head thrown back against the sofa. "My brave lads," he murmured after a time. "For so many years they fought with honor, only to end in disgrace. And all because Mullins failed to do his duty. I should have been there. The fight may have been lost in any case, for it was ill planned from the first. But I'd damn well have known where to find those bloody ladders."

Diana felt tears streaming down her cheeks. He might not think she understood, but she did. He would rather have died in that battle than failed to be with his men when most they needed him. And the fact that it was in no way his fault changed nothing. He wasn't there. That was all that mattered to him.

"The greatest irony," he said, "was that a treaty had already been signed in Ghent and ratified in London. A ship was on its way to America with the news. Those men fought and died in a war that was over, Diana, and the ones that lived were left only with their shame. I felt it, too, need I tell you?

"Transports were departing from several ports, and when I had word of a convoy, I went to the docks with the intention of boarding the next vessel bound for England. I arrived too late. Of course, I might have sought out another port, and ought to have done. But there was a cargo ship about to depart for Cartagena, and for no reason I can explain to you, I bought passage and sailed with her. From Cartagena I went on to Rio de Janeiro and Buenos Aires, and from there around the horn to Chile and Peru."

Pursued by his ghosts, she had no doubt. The ones that haunted him still. She thought he was done now with his story, and thought it safe to open her eyes and look at him. He was staring into the distance at something she could not see.

"I didn't suppose it would signify to anyone," he said, "my futile, self-indulgent odyssey. With no more battles to be fought, who would miss one ineffectual half-pay officer? But I was wrong yet again. Bonaparte escaped Elba, and the most important battle of them all took place without me. Because I failed to ship home any one of the many times I had the chance, I was not at Waterloo."

"Where you might have found redemption," she said softly.

"Yes. Perhaps." His eyes came back into focus. He turned to her. "I believe that is all for now, Diana. You have been remarkably patient."

Not quite all, she thought, wondering if she dared to ask any of the questions burning on her tongue. She could not bear to leave the story where he'd left it, but neither did she wish to make him regret telling her by prodding him for more.

He put his handkerchief into her hand. "I have made you weep. You mustn't. Not on my account."

"Of course I must," she said, blotting her wet cheeks. "I am a weepy female, don't you know? Considering the buckets of tears I've shed for myself, I can certainly spare a few for my husband."

A smile flitted over his lips, faint but unmistakable. It gave her heart to continue. "Will you sell out now, Alex?"

"I suppose so. I've been putting it off because it means a trip to London. My separation from the army was somewhat out of the ordinary, and I expect I've got some explaining to do. One day I shall present myself at Horse Guards, hand over my orders from General Ross, and see what the officials can make of it all."

She tossed a mental coin, but heads or tails, she already knew what she must say to him. "Why not straightaway? You can settle things with the army and attend your friend's wedding as well. It's on for Saturday next, I believe."

His eyes darkened. "No."

"Tell me why, then. It was learning of it that sent you away from me. At the time, I could not imagine a reason for you to react as you did. But now I think it's to do with what you have said today. Was Lord Blair somehow involved with the battle in New Orleans? Or another incident in the American War?"

For a long time she thought he would not reply. But he shook his head with what looked like frustrated resignation.

"Will you ever leave me in peace, woman? But no, Blair was never in America. He was one of my particular friends on the Peninsula, as were the others he'll have roped in to play groomsmen. I cannot face them. Perhaps someday, but not yet. They will know, don't you see? They'll have heard what happened with the Forty-fourth, and that I wasn't there. Had I gone back when I should have done, things would be different. I might have stood with them at Waterloo and regained some small degree of the honor I had lost. But I took myself off to South America, no one advised of it, no reason for it, and stayed gone the better part of two years. There is no explaining that to them, Diana. I'll not even try."

She put a hand on his knee. "Honor can be won other places than on a battlefield, you know. And you have never lost yours, no matter what you think. It is so much a part of you that no one with the barest acquaintance could fail to recognize it. Your friends surely will not. But for your own sake, Alex, you must go to London and meet with them. And when you do, I believe with all my heart that you will be glad of it. Lord Blair would scarcely have invited you to his wedding, after all, if he shared the misguided opinion you have of yourself."

"Is there no mercy in you, Diana?" But his eyes were no longer so bleak. "Misguided, am I? Well, I shall need an escort then, to show me the way. Shall we strike a deal? I'll go to London, if you will come with me."

She hadn't expected that. The last thing in the world she wanted was to be paraded among strangers to be gawked at. Well, the second to last thing. What Alex needed was infinitely more important than her own sensibilities, and all he'd asked was that she accompany him to London. She needn't show herself, nor would he expect her to once they got there. Would he?

He was waiting for an answer, a challenge in his eyes. And a trace of fear, she thought, that she might let him down. "Yes, of course I'll go with you to London," she said, as if she had never questioned it. "Lancaster is the largest city I've ever set foot in until now, and I've always longed to travel."

"Well, then." He looked relieved, although he was trying hard not to show it. "You can purchase a fashionable new wardrobe while we're there, and I'll take you around to all the sights. We'll make a wedding trip of it, and go on to the seashore if you like, or anywhere else that takes your fancy. Perhaps we can look about for a property suitable to raising horses."

"Oh, yes! Let's do that, Alex. A new start for both of us." She flung herself onto his lap and wrapped her arms around him. "We shall dispatch my spider and your ghosts to the devil and get on with things. Except," she added in strictest honesty, "I still wish to hear about South America. Two years is an exceedingly long time to be wandering about all by yourself. Or were you?"

"By myself?" He chuckled. "Are you imagining a flock of señoritas at my heels? I assure you, Diana, that I was very much alone. Never more so. A man has no need of company, nor does he wish any, when he has gone in search of his soul."

She sat back, gazing into the deep blue of his eyes. "And did you find it? Your soul?"

"Not there." He brushed a finger across her lips. "Turned out it was waiting for me in a dark room at Lakeview with a skillet in its hand."

"Oh." Her heart made great leaps in her chest.

"Yes, madam," he said, a hesitant smile curving his lips. "I'm afraid that *you* are my soul, or the part of it that had gone missing. I cannot do without you now. You will have to stay close by me, and whack me to my senses again whenever I run astray. Like it or not, my brave and beautiful wife, you have drawn the Forlorn Hope."

She was weeping again, this time for joy. "The Bright Hope, Alex. I have drawn the Bright Hope."

Next she knew, he had swept her up and was carrying her out of the room, pausing only to take a rose from the vase and put it in her hand. But as he mounted the stairs, his intentions clearly all that she wanted them to be, a piping voice called to him from the entrance hall.

"What I s'posed to be doin' now, sir?"

Diana looked down to see the boy who had made fun of her.

"That's your other gift," Alex said with a rueful smile. "I thought you might not like it. But he was on his way to pick pockets at the fair, so I brought him here instead. He might make a decent stableboy."

"Oh yes. What a good idea." And what a good man you are, she thought, afire with love for him.

"Kendal may not think so, if the scoundrel makes off with the silver."

"Sir?" The boy stamped his foot. "The cove what you left me with 'as gone to sleepin'. You got work fer me or no?"

"This is a holiday, Jemmy. Have yourself a nap or visit with the horses or raid the pantry. Just stay out of trouble. And if you want work, tell anyone who comes home in the next few hours that my wife and I are not to be disturbed. Understood?"

"Yessir." Jemmy vanished in the direction of the kitchen.

"Thank you yet again, Alex," she said as he carried her along the passageway. "Jemmy is a wonderful gift. The best gift ever."

He kicked open the door to his room and set her on her feet beside the bed. "Don't speak too soon," he said, reaching around her to undo her apron and tug it away. "I mean to give you a great many things." He sat her down and dropped to one knee to pull off her shoes. "I can afford it, since I'll be spending your money."

His hands reached under her skirts, sliding up her legs to where her stockings were tied. He took a deliciously long time removing the ribbons. "You have only to ask, Diana. Whatever you want, I will try to provide."

He had said the same words, she remembered, or words much like them, the night they were married. And he had kept to his promise, withholding only himself. Until today. Until now.

The scent of the rose she was still holding melted into the touch of his hands and the soft urgency of his voice as he made her new promises. And then she was naked in his arms, gone wild with desire for him, and he gave her the best gift of all.

Chapter 20

Diana was sitting precisely where he'd left her, cross-legged at the center of the bed, still wearing her dressing gown. Her disordered hair tumbled around her pale face and slumped shoulders.

Alex closed the door behind him, regarding her with concern. "Are you not feeling well?"

"You may say that I am ill, if you wish, although that is not the case." She raised her chin and regarded him steadily. "I'm not going with you, Alex."

"The devil you say!" His hand went to the hilt of his sword. "Dress yourself, madam."

She raised a brow. "Will you slice me to flinders if I refuse?"

"A reflex only," he said, dropping the offending hand to his side. "You took me aback. I cannot credit that you mean to dishonor your word."

"When you asked, I told you that I would come with you. And so I did, as far as London. We never specified that I was to attend the wedding."

"It was understood! What in blazes did you *think* I meant?"

"Oh, precisely that. And I hoped that I could. But I gave no explicit promise, and now I find myself unable to accompany you."

She looked markedly determined, he thought, but also despondent. Even ashamed. The scar was vivid on her cheek, as if she'd been rubbing at it.

"Then we'll neither of us go," he said, shrugging. "I didn't want to in the first place."

"But you must!" Her eyes pleaded with him. "When you meet with your friends, you will find that they have never given the slightest thought to what has obsessed you for so many years. They will deal with you as they always have, Alex, and hold you in the same esteem."

"So you have always said. Well, I am willing to take your word on it. No need to put it to the test." He stripped off his gloves. "And since we now have the day free, would you care to go sightseeing?"

She scrambled off the bed and charged at him like all seven of the Furies come together in one fierce young woman. He would have backed up, but his back was already to the door.

"You are going to that wedding!" she informed him, poking at his chest. "How am I to learn to be brave if *you* are not? This time I have failed you, and doubtless I shall fail you again, but one day you will be proud of me. I *will* do better. And think on it, Alex." She poked him again. "If I am with you, your friends will be excruciatingly polite. They will be so busy wondering why your wife is veiled that you'll learn nothing from them. And you'll be so busy worrying about me that we'll *all* be distracted. You will come away with nothing. Our long trip will have been wasted."

"Nonsense." He slipped away from her and unbuckled his sword belt, reflecting on the four long days alone in a comfortable carriage and the four long nights in the best rooms at the finest posthouses. They had not made up for all the celibate months of their marriage, but they'd had a considerable go at it. "Would you prefer that we had not taken this journey, madam?"

She ignored the question, although color rose in her face. "What's more, this day belongs entirely to the bride. She cannot wish a stranger in a veiled bonnet drawing attention from her."

"You are rationalizing, Diana. These are wretched excuses for your own faintheartedness."

"Undeniably. And I am ashamed of myself, although what I have said is nonetheless true. You won't be able to deal with your friends as you ought if I am with you."

"You refine too much on what you imagine will occur. Wear a damned veil if you must, but come with me. I will most certainly not go without you."

She met him eye for eye. "So it has come to a battle. Which

of us is the greater coward? Well, sir, I claim the prize. Hands down, I win. You will be at the wedding because you have the courage I lack. And because I cannot bear to show my face and am too proud to wear the veiled bonnet, I shall wait for you here at the hotel. So there you have it."

For all her defiance, her chin quivered. Tears had stolen into her eyes. He knew her well enough now to sense her hurt, although she was such a brave little thing that it never failed to astonish him when she let that damnable scar vanquish her.

It had done so this morning, precisely when he had meant to lean on her for support. He *needed* her with him. But she knew that. If she was sending him on his way alone, her need must be greater than his. And if he refused to go without her, he would only add to her hurt. To her guilt, because she trembled with guilt and sorrow for letting him down.

He would throw himself in front of a bullet before hurting Diana.

Taking her in his arms, he brushed a kiss against her scarred cheek. "You win indeed," he said. "I'll go. So long as you are here for me to come back to, I could face down the Imperial Guard."

He retrieved his sword and gloves, smiling at her over his shoulder. "But don't be surprised if I reappear within the hour, scampering for cover under your skirts."

"I very much doubt that you will," she said, returning his smile. "But you are always welcome under my skirts."

Alex held to that delicious thought while the carriage took him through the crowded London streets to St. George's, Hanover Square. The driver, calling back that the main thoroughfares were clogged, chose a circuitous route through backstreets, but they were soon stalled in a crowded intersection.

Alex stuck his head out the window. "How close are we?"

"You'll do better walking," the driver advised him. "Go two streets ahead and turn left. Can't miss it."

If the others were mired in traffic as well, perhaps he would arrive in time for the wedding after all. Alex jumped from the carriage, feeling conspicuous in scarlet regimentals with a ceremonial sword dangling from his hip. He noticed that passersby were careful to keep out of his way.

When he turned onto George Street, he saw Max Sevaric standing between two of the enormous portico columns, scanning the street with one hand held to his forehead as a shield against the bright morning sun. Behind him, clustered under the pediment, were four men. He could not make out their faces, but Alex recognized two uniforms of the 52nd—Sevaric's regiment—and an officer of the Coldstream Guards.

There was no mistaking the bridegroom. Major Lord Jordan Blair shamelessly confessed to buying colors in the 10th Hussars because he would look so well with a fur-edged overjacket slung across his shoulder.

Jordie had always put him in mind of Kit—outspoken, outrageous, and with enough self-confidence to boil water. Alex had been drawn into his circle of friends at the Officers' Mess, where Jordie held court like a princeling. He didn't admit just anyone, and Alex—a taciturn loner until he was inexplicably singled out—had felt flattered to be included in such company.

Now he had to face them again, these men he so respected, wearing the shame of his failures. There was no use hoping they didn't know. Soldiers gossiped as freely as women, and word quickly spread when a man had distinguished himself—or done otherwise.

He ordered his feet to move forward, and saw the moment when Sevaric spotted him on the pavement. And he kept moving, because he had committed himself. At worst, they would turn their backs to him. More likely they would be distantly polite. He didn't dare hope for the best.

But in a rush, all five men swept down the stairs and surrounded him, grabbing for his hand and clapping him on the back.

Stunned, he shook their hands and said their names in a gruff voice. "Blair. Trent. Sevaric. Corbett. Pageter."

"Bad enough that m'bride appears to have deserted me," Jordie said with a theatrical groan. "I was just thinking that if I had to spend tonight drowning my sorrows, I'd be wondering why the blazes you didn't show up either. Don't tell that to Emma, by the way. She'd rather I'd have been thinking about her. If she comes, of course, and if you ever meet her."

"We are drawing a crowd," Trent pointed out with his usual calm.

Sure enough, passersby were gathering around them, attracted—Alex reckoned—by all the swords and medals and regimental lace.

Sevaric walked beside him up the stairs and into the vestibule. "Blair is fit to be tied, so pay him no mind. He hasn't spoken a word of sense since we got here."

"I heard that," Jordie said, grasping Alex's arm. "Sevaric wouldn't know sense if it bit him on the arse. So where the devil have you been, Valliant? Last I heard, you were off to South America. Well, not quite last. Met up with your brother, which you know or you wouldn't have got m'message, and he said there were rumors you'd come home. Must be true, for here you are."

Sevaric gave Alex an I-told-you-so look.

"I was nearly two years in South America," Alex said stiffly. "The American War did not suit me. When it was done, I—"

"When it was *lost*, you mean." Jordie shook his head. "Tell you what, old man. You had the worst of it there. Take no offense, but I never could see the point dispatching good English soldiers across the Atlantic to fight for no reason. In your place, I'd have sold out."

"Not if your regiment had to go on without you."

"Right." Jordie grinned. "I'd have stayed with them and hated every minute of it. Bloody politicians ought to be taken out and shot, that's what. At least you'll be giving us some new stories to talk about at the club. We've rehashed Waterloo into the ground."

"I wish I'd been there," Alex said darkly.

"We could have used you. On the other hand, we managed to win without you, even if it was only by the skin of our teeth." He glanced over his shoulder. "Hah! What's this?"

A hackney had pulled to the curb directly in front of the church.

"Your bride must have arrived," Alex said. "Aren't you going down to meet her?"

Jordie turned back to him with a frown. "Can't be Emma.

She's coming in my carriage with Dori Sevaric and Allegra Trent. Unless she's jilted me and they've all gone shopping."

Alex watched over Jordie's shoulder as someone opened the hackney door and lowered the steps. For a considerable time, no one emerged. Finally a gloved hand wrapped itself around the panel and a foot came down on the top step. He saw honey-gold skirts, and then the crowd gathered around the hackney and blocked his view.

Of a sudden, they all went quiet.

Heart pounding, he shoved Jordie aside and went to the top of the stairs.

Diana, her auburn hair spilling over her shoulders, was standing helplessly on the pavement, surrounded by curious onlookers. She had used the two Spanish combs he'd given her to hold her hair back from her face. Her scar blazed in the morning sunlight.

With an oath, Alex cut through the crowd like a sword and seized her hand, bowing over it to brush a kiss on her wrist. "You came," he said, his voice breaking. "My brave, brave girl."

She gave him a tremulous smile. "I'm terrified, you know. My legs are shaking like reeds in the wind. But how did it go with you, Alex?"

"Just as you said, of course." He was so proud of her he thought his heart would shatter, just when she'd made it whole again. "Come meet the troops."

She took his arm, and he led her up the stairs to where his friends were waiting. "My wife, gentlemen. Diana Valliant."

Jordie was the first to make his bow. "Welcome, madam. I am honored to meet the only lady gracious enough to attend my wedding. Not excluding my would-be bride, I hasten to add, who appears to have dropped from the face of the earth."

"She'll not fail you," Diana assured him, clinging to Alex's arm as he introduced the men in turn. One by one they bowed, speaking words of welcome, absorbing her into their circle as if she'd always been among them.

Her eyes glowed with pleasure when Nick Trent trotted out a miniature of his son for her to examine. Max Sevaric advised her not to believe a word Dori told her about him. Jordie Blair promised to let her know what her husband had *really* been up to on the Peninsula. Before a few minutes had passed, she had loosed her death grip on Alex's arm and was laughing at one of Jordie's absurd stories.

Alex was the only one to notice that the carriage had arrived. "If you can tear yourself away from *my* wife, Blair, yours is waiting for you on the pavement."

"The devil you say!" His face splitting in a grin, he rushed down the stairs and caught her up and spun her round and round.

Trent and Sevaric followed, dodging the bride and groom to claim their own wives, and soon the bridal party was sweeping down the wide aisle toward the altar where the minister was waiting with an impatient look on his face.

Alex held Diana back from the others, taking refuge in the shadow of a marble column to kiss her thoroughly. Rather breathless when he was done, he brushed a tendril of hair behind her ear. She smiled up at him, her eyes shining like golden stars.

"Shall we wed each other again in our hearts?" he asked softly. "Say the words along with Jordie and Emma, say them to each other?"

"Please, yes. Let's do. I wasn't really attending last time, you know. I hadn't even decided to marry you." A single tear streaked down her scarred cheek. "But oh, Alex, I am so very glad that I did."

"Come then," he said, leading her down the aisle. "Let us take the vows once more. And this time, my soul, we will speak them with love."

ON SALE NOW

MIDNIGHT RIDER
By Diana Palmer
The *New York Times* bestselling author of
The Long, Tall Texan series

To Bernadette Barron, Eduardo Cortes is the enemy. A noble count with a sprawling ranch in the grand state of Texas, Cortes challenges her with dark, penetrating eyes that seem to pierce her very soul. For theirs is a marriage of convenience—he needs a rich wife to save his land; she needs a titled husband. But can't he see the burning truth: that she loves him?

It is a secret Bernadette vows to keep until desire turns their marriage bargain into a passionate battle of wills. For it is love's fiery initiation that will make Bernadette aware of her own capacity for pleasure, and it is the sheer force of her own love that will give her newfound strength to battle against the odds to claim a man she will not be denied. . . .